I0678022

BEAST

OR

MAN?

BEAST

OR

MAN?

by

Sean M'Guire

RAMBLE HOUSE

©1930 by Sean M'Guire
Introduction © 2009 by John Pelan
This edition © 2009 by Ramble House

ISBN 13: 978-1-60543-274-8

ISBN 10: 1-60543-274-1

Published: 2009 by Ramble House
Preparation: John Pelan and Fender Tucker
Cover Art: Gavin L. O'Keefe

DANCING TUATARA PRESS #1

Sean M'Guire and the Lost Race Novel

The lost-race novel was in its time a robust genre. The Stuart Tietler collection boasted over 2,500 items and the actual total of books on the theme is probably closer to 3,000. Noted author and scholar Jessica Salmonson has catalogued and provided brief synopses to over 1000 titles at violetbooks.com. The genre received its greatest boosts from Sir H. Rider Haggard with his wonderful adventure novels of Allan Quatermain. In Haggard's time, the source of the Nile had yet to be found, the interior of South America was an enigma and the possibility that dinosaurs still roamed the jungles as per The Lost World of Sir Arthur Conan Doyle seemed a distinct possibility. The North and South Poles were as of yet unexplored, and the idea of gateways to the interior of the Earth and subterranean cities peopled by the descendants of Atlantis or Lemuria seemed quite plausible.

The genre slowly began to die, not by lack of reader interest, but by the hands of cartographers and explorers. While it was said "there is always something new out of Africa", by the early 1900s it was apparent that these new things would be unlikely to include fabulous cities of gold or descendants of Alexander the Great living in the African interior. By the time that Sean M'Guire authored his two exceptional novels, *Spider Island* and *Beast or Man?*, the lost-race genre as known by Haggard and his scores of imitators was mostly a thing of the past. Thanks to the efforts of an American author, who took his cues from no less an author than Rudyard Kipling, a new twist on the theme had become popular, that of the human raised in savage environs by anything from tigers to gorillas to the missing links of the Tarzan novels.

In Sean M'Guire's *Beast or Man?* we have a novel that is of interest for several reasons. The book starts as relatively prosaic tale of African adventure and goes on to touch on some very serious themes such as conservation and the inherent wrongness of man's willy-nilly invasion of the forestlands and the banality of trapping intelligent creatures for no greater purpose than to serve as menagerie exhibits. These concerns alone are sufficient to raise this book head and shoulders above most of M'Guire's contemporaries, who were much more likely to support such concepts as "manifest destiny" and the inherent supremacy of the European.

There were scores of pallid imitations of Haggard and Burroughs, generally books that at best served as weak pastiches of the originals, (Otis Adelbert Kline, Roy Rockwood, etc.) captured all that was bad in either author's style, or were just outright racist trash with the noble white man easily triumphing over the "evil" schemes of the savage black men. (The fact that said "evil" schemes" generally involved resistance to the "noble white man" helping himself to ivory, gold, diamonds, or anything else that happened to catch his fancy was downplayed by the authors.) By the 1930s, anyone expecting anything of greater substance from this genre was most likely in for a disappointment . . .

M'Guire's novel was a breath of fresh air, as was his earlier *Spider Island*. That both books saw only marginal commercial success is a sad statement regarding the readers of the day that were likely far more comfortable with the racist trash of Edgar Rice Burroughs than with adventure stories that actually called upon the reader to think about serious moral and ethical issues. If I'm making this book sound like a dull philosophical tract, please excuse me, it is anything but. Both of M'Guire's novels are in the vein of H. Rider Haggard (putting them several notches above Burroughs from the get-go); however, both are far deeper than anything Haggard attempted, though both operate easily enough as pure pulp adventures.

Wherein lie the differences? M'Guire is not at all afraid to show that there are right bastards both black and white. His noble characters are also flawed . . . Dick Fearless reflects on the banality of his life as a big-game hunter and the titular character's hands are red with the blood of innocents; (there was certainly a good deal of provocation for his actions, but whether the response is disproportionate or not is a question for the reader to reflect on.) As well defined characters as exist in fantastic fiction, the cast of characters presented by M'Guire are all memorable. We readers may guess from the start that the act of training and organizing gorillas to defend their homeland is foredoomed to failure, but M'Guire is a skilled enough author to keep us turning the pages. We may also suspect that the fate of the missionaries that sets the events in motion will not be pleasant, but I was caught by surprise by the sheer horror of the torture scene that would not have been at all out of place in an issue of *Terror Tales* or *Dime Mystery*.

The first quarter of the book is a tale of tragedy set in Africa, with no elements that would have been out of place in the American pulps such as *Argosy* or the general fiction magazines of the

UK such as *McClure's* or *Cassell's*. The novel switches gears abruptly in Chapter Six with the introduction of a new cast of characters and veers into the realm of the fantastic with a highly intelligent and organized troop of club-wielding gorillas doing their level best to drive away the humans (both black and white) that are encroaching on their territory.

What makes M'Guire's novel unique is that the archetypical character of the human boy raised by apes is mostly an off-stage figure and it his progeny, the half-man, half-gorilla who becomes the central character of the book and who is the subject of the titular query.

On one level Sean M'Guire has authored a "page-turner" which combines adventure, mystery, and the fantastic; on another level, he poses some serious questions about what it means to be human and that nobility is not merely the province of the more advanced species.

Sadly, M'Guire was not a prolific author; I've been unable to find any short fiction under his by-line and a careful search of the most comprehensive bibliographies shows only this book and his earlier lost-race novel, *Spider Island*, (which, if anything is even more firmly in the realm of the fantastic with the lost-race being webfooted amphibians). We hope to bring you a new edition of *Spider Island* in the very near future, and the search for other works by M'Guire will continue . . . Assuming that these two novels are his only contributions to the realm of fantastic fiction, Sean M'Guire still deserves to be remembered alongside his more famous contemporaries such as Talbot Mundy, Ganpat, and Mark Channing.

John Pelan
Midnight House — 2009

BEAST

OR

MAN?

CHAPTER I

MARTIN HILLIER-MISSIONARY

FOR WELL OVER AN HOUR Martin Hillier had been sitting in the office of the Landeshauptman, the German Commissioner, of Kamerun, and all the efforts of that worthy official had failed to turn him from his purpose. Hillier was a good and very earnest man in a way, a brilliant preacher and absolutely fearless. There is no doubt that had he remained in his own country he would have risen to a high position in his chosen walk in life, for he had everything in his favour—brilliance, influential friends, energy and a certain amount of money. But he chose to forgo all the advantages that might have been his and devote his life to missionary work in the west of Africa.

However much one may feel that there is no adage more truthful than the one which insists that charity should begin at home, however desirable it may seem to the layman that his own house should be cleansed before the houses of other people are gratuitously interfered with, nobody could do anything but admire the zeal and self-denial of a man who was prepared to do so much in the cause of what he believed to be right as Hillier was. But unfortunately he was not satisfied to take the whole burden of his self-sacrifice on his own shoulders.

Twelve months before migrating to Africa he had married a young girl, the daughter of very well-to-do parents, who had been used all her life to the enjoyment of every luxury and, although his mind had been fully made up before ever he had gone so far as to propose to her, he had made no mention of his intentions. Without suggesting that she had married for any other reason than affection for her husband, it is safe to assert that her parents, if not the girl herself, had seen in the alliance a good match for their only daughter and the promise of a comfortable home and an assured position in county society within a few years. Their astonishment and, indeed, their rage may be imagined when, immediately after the honeymoon, their son-in-law had resigned the excellent living to which he had been appointed only twelve months before, booked two passages for Dualla, and vanished with their only girl.

It was all done so unexpectedly, as far as they were concerned, and in such a hurry that they were too flabbergasted to make more than a half-hearted protest, and almost before they realised what had happened a white pocket handkerchief waving from the deck of a rapidly receding steamboat was all that was visible of the daughter they were never to see again. Some weeks later she and her husband had landed on the Gold Coast where Hillier had, to use his own expression, "laboured" for a year and somehow she had managed to survive the terrors of that unaccustomed climate. At the end of that time he had received a "call" which had taken him to Dualla, and his wife and baby had gone with him, in spite of the protests of the doctors and to the great indignation of what few white women there were, for the child was so young that Mrs. Hillier was not in a fit state to be moved even under favourable conditions. But nothing must stand in the way of this fanatic's work and he was not sufficiently unselfish to see that that work could have gone on just as well while his wife was in the comparative comfort of a fairly big station. Where he went she too must go he insisted, not caring a row of pins whether she wanted to or not, not considering for a moment whether it might not be the signing of her death warrant.

It was owing to this heartless obstinacy of Hillier's that so much of the Commissioner's time had been taken up on the evening on which our story opens—an evening of October in the year 1880. It was bad enough in all conscience to bring a delicate woman, not yet recovered from the birth of her first child, to such a place as Dualla was in the days of which I write, but what he proposed to do now was nothing short of murder. It was no less than to take his wife and child right into the very heart of the Kamerun, to places where the foot of a white man, or at any rate of a missionary, had never trod, and there to set up a station of his own.

Ever since the time of Alfred Saker, who died in 1840 after thirty-six years' work amongst the natives of the Cameroons—as it was then—the price paid in lives by missionaries to the west coast of Africa has been appalling. In the first ten years of the Wesleyan Missionary Society's work on the Gold Coast eight of its members died—three out of the first four after a sojourn of less than eight months—without a church being established or a single convert baptised. At the celebration in 1897 of the North German

(Bremen) Society's Jubilee of its work in New Guinea it was announced that, out of a total of a hundred and fifty-seven workers sent out, fifty-six were driven home by ill health and sixty-four (besides children) laid in an untimely grave. In the little burial ground of Christianborg, near Accra, are tombstones recording the deaths of six missionaries between February 18th and May 22nd, 1896, and the list is almost endless.

These few instances are mentioned as showing the dangers which attended life on the west coast and in the interior they must of necessity be greatly increased. They had not all occurred when Hillier went to Dualla, so they could not all be brought up in argument against what he said he intended to do; and even if that had been possible there can be no doubt that it would not have made any difference. Once he had made up his mind to do a thing Hillier did it if it was humanly possible at whatever cost to himself or anybody else. The Landeshauptmann was a youngish man and new to his job; but he knew well enough that if once Mrs. Hillier disappeared into the primeval forest on her way to the interior she would never be seen again, and he used every argument short of physical persuasion to induce her husband to listen to reason. But he might as well have saved his breath.

"It is my duty to show the light to those poor, ignorant savages," Hillier insisted, "and who am I to refuse to do the bidding of my God? It is equally the duty of every woman to follow the man to whom she is bound by the sacred ties of holy matrimony. Would you have my wife fail in what is hers to do? I should be proud to give my life in so noble a cause. She, too, would be proud; and if it be God's will that I and my wife and child perish in His service, so be it. A crown of glory will await us there above. We shall be numbered amongst the elect. What greater reward could be wished for by man, woman or child?"

"I do wish you would talk sense for a minute and listen to cold, common reason," persisted the Commissioner, who was a man eminently straightforward in his speech and his dealings and altogether unused to the flowers of rhetoric. "Your crowns of glory may be all very fine in their way and I do not wish to say anything derogatory about them. But problematical golden diadems are not going to save Mrs. Hillier and her baby from sickness, danger, endless discomfort and probably pain. Jiggers are one of the least of the things to be considered and they are bad enough, as I know from experience, for a man, and must be ten times as unpleasant for a tender-skinned woman and worse still for an infant child.

They will probably suffer from hunger and certainly from thirst. There will be no drugs or conveniences in case of the inevitable sickness. If you feel you must go on this crazy expedition, go by all means, and the best of luck go with you. But you cannot possibly take your wife and child."

"We start, all of us, tomorrow morning," was the only answer which Hillier would vouchsafe.

The Commissioner made one last effort to dissuade the fanatic from his purpose, for he had no legal right to stop him.

"In the name of the God whom you serve," he adjured, "think again. You preach charity. Be charitable to your wife and child. You preach love. Show your wife and child that you love them. You preach duty. Your duty is to watch over the welfare of your wife and child. I sympathise with you to some extent because every man suffers from madness in one form or another. But for God's sake remember that if they go they will never come back. Don't be so damned selfish, man, and keep thinking only of yourself and the reward that you certainly expect to get or you would not be so pigheaded and idiotic. There are other people in the world besides you and the lives of two of them at any rate, Mrs. Hillier and her baby, are far more valuable. As a Government official I can promise you no help when you find yourself in the trouble that you inevitably will find yourself in. If you take those two poor, defenceless creatures with you into the interior your name will stink for ever throughout West Africa and beyond as the deliberate murderer of your helpless wife and child. Now what about it?"

The Commissioner had lost his temper badly but Hillier remained unruffled and unmoved.

"It pleases you to be foul-mouthed and blasphemous," he said, as he rose to his feet. "We start to-morrow."

"Then get out and be damned to you for the dirty, selfish, unchristian swine that you are," was the parting shot of the now thoroughly-enraged Landeshauptmann as the door closed behind his visitor. "I only hope you come back so that I may have the hanging of you, you murdering woman killer."

And there is no least doubt that he meant every word of it.

When Hillier had gone the Commissioner sat and thought. He had been to see Mrs. Hillier on her arrival, partly in accordance with his usual custom as the leading official of Dualla and more particularly because they had mutual friends, as he had been informed by letter, on the Gold Coast. He had found a frail, pretty little woman in her very early twenties and had taken an immediate liking to her. It was clear that she was suffering severely both from the climate and the after-effects of her son's birth, and he was very sorry for her indeed. Hillier he had disliked from the first, chiefly because of his utter and unconcealed selfishness. An invitation to a meal at the Commissioner's house, which would have made some little break in her monotonous life, was refused because it might interfere with the hour Hillier sometimes devoted to writing. An offer to conduct her round the few sights of the neighbourhood was turned down with scant courtesy and a broad hint that no man was to be trusted alone with a woman except, of course, Hillier himself. A few little gifts of fruit and literature were returned with a note, in her hand writing but obviously dictated by her husband, saying that she had sufficient for her needs and including no word of thanks.

Hillier was a good man, as I have said—according to his lights. But he allowed no smallest pleasure to be enjoyed by his wife, he forbade her any intercourse, except in his presence, with another human being, male or female, and he seemed to go out of his way to make her life as uncomfortable and miserable as he conveniently could without putting himself out in any way. That, at any rate, was how the young German official saw it, and how it would have struck any ordinary observer. And now, he reflected, the curtain was to be rung up on the last scene of all, the final chapter of what had once been such a happy life was on the point of being written. And he could do nothing.

He sat for a long time on the verandah outside his office pondering over the situation before he rose and went over to his writing-table and even then it was the best part of an hour later that he called a boy, satisfied at last with the letter which he had written and rewritten half a dozen times. The final draft was terse and to the point the language in which it was couched stiltedly official. It announced in the approved phraseology of his Department that Martin Hillier proposed to start at once with his wife and infant child for some destination in the interior unknown even to himself; that he, as Commissioner, had done all he could lawfully do to dissuade him, but without success; and that he had warned him that he could neither officially recognise the expedition nor, in the event of complications arising, take any official action. This letter he sealed and enclosed with a number of reports and returns in a large envelope addressed to the office of a very important personage in his own country. Then he had the one daily drink which he allowed himself and went to bed.

He was a light sleeper and a rustle on the verandah a short time, as it seemed, after he had closed his mosquito curtains roused him in a moment. He glanced at his watch in a moonbeam, saw to his surprise that it was after midnight, and jumped silently from his bed. It was the work of a moment to shuffle into his slippers and grab the loaded rifle which always stood handy and in a very few seconds he was peering cautiously out into the darkness. A flutter of something white at the far end of the verandah caught his eye immediately, and with rifle raised he challenged it.

"Don't shoot me! Oh, please don't shoot me!" came to him in a soft voice which hardly rose above a whisper. "It is me. Mrs. Hillier. I wanted to talk to you and there was no other way."

"Mrs. Hillier! What on earth are you doing out alone at this time of night? Where is your husband?"

"I am not alone. I have got baby with me. And I want to talk to you. I told you so. That is why I came. My husband is asleep. Or at least he was asleep when I started. May I come in?"

The short, disconnected sentences were proof of the nervous condition in which the woman was, as well as the way in which she clung for support to the verandah rail. The Commissioner, who had laid down his rifle as soon as he had recognised his unexpected visitor, took her gently by the arm and led her into the office. He pulled up a chair for her, then excused himself and hurried off to get into a few clothes more suitable for the reception of ladies than the silk pyjamas which he was wearing at the moment. On his return he found her more composed and asked at once what he could have the pleasure of doing for her.

"It is about my baby," she replied. "Martin, as you know, has made up his mind that we shall both go with him to-morrow, and I dread it. Not for myself—I do not care one little bit what becomes of me—but for my boy. It is not right that he should be dragged through these awful forests, exposed to all those dreadful dangers. It would kill him I know. It will kill me too but that does not matter. And you can save him for me. I have brought him to you and I want you to keep him; to hide him until we are gone and then send him away. He is very good. He won't be much trouble to you and it is only for such a short time. You will take him for me, won't you? You will save my baby?"

She held out the child towards him as she spoke and dropped on her knees with the tears streaming down her face. Was ever man placed in so horrible a position, the Landeshauptmann thought to himself? What on earth was he to do? How could he, a bachelor with only men in his household and no white woman within hundreds of miles undertake the care of an infant child even for a few days? What official steps would be taken if he agreed to this mad proposal and was found out—as he most certainly must be? He had his career to think of and he was just beginning to get on. But he was a man with a heart and he soon realised that he had the child and the woman to think of as well, the mother who was ready and eager to part with her only son forever for that son's sake. And it was the child and the woman who won.

"I will do what you ask," he said at last, and held out his arms to take the baby from her.

She made no fuss but gave it to him with a smile of gratitude for, though her tears had ceased to fall as soon as he had given his assent, she was for the moment incapable of speech. For long minutes they stood, he holding the child in unaccustomed but gentle arms, she gazing down into her son's face. Then she slipped a little ivory crucifix on a thin gold chain round the baby's neck.

"He shall wear that always," she whispered, "and perhaps, some day, you will let him know how it was placed there. I must go. Good-bye and God bless you always."

One last, long kiss she gave her first-born, then turned with tearless eyes towards the door. But she had lingered too long. It was too late.

"I find you in good company though the hour is somewhat advanced," she heard in a voice choked with suppressed rage. "I congratulate you, Mr. Commissioner, on your conquest. My precautions in not allowing my wife out with you were evidently necessary but, I regret to see, not wholly successful. Come, Mabel. It is late and we have an early start before us."

Without a word she took back her child and prepared to follow him. But the Commissioner's temper was up again, and small wonder.

"You filthy swine," he shouted. "You dare to make such insinuations against your own wife, against a woman who has stuck to you through all your hare-brained foolery ever since you inveigled her into marriage under false pretences? You shall not take her with you now if I have to put you in irons and ruin my career by doing it. I am not going to stand idly by and see murder done under my very nose. Get out of my way, you foul beast. I am going to have you put under arrest here and now."

"But certainly, Mr. Commissioner. I am the last person in the world to obstruct you in the execution of what you doubtless consider to be your duty," smiled Hillier, and stood aside to let him pass. But before he reached the door, while his back was turned to the missionary, the butt of a heavy crop fell with stunning force on the back of his skull, and he fell senseless. The Landeshauptmann had received a coward's blow on the head which would have been enough to kill most men and for the time he knew no more of what went on in his office.

The Commissioner was a young man, as has been said. He was also a strong man who all his life had made a point of keeping himself in first-class condition. Further he was blessed with one of those exceptionally hard skulls which are more common amongst the Teutons than in most countries. It was many a long hour before he recovered his senses, but he did so at last and found himself lying on his bed with a splitting headache, while a native servant bent solicitously over him. For a time his muddled brain refuse to function properly and he could remember nothing. He felt sick and ill and his head buzzed in an aggravating manner. But bit by bit his thoughts grew more connected and main incidents came back to him. With an effort he pulled himself together sufficiently to question the servant and learned that he had been found lying in a pool of blood on the floor of his office and that they had put him to bed and tended him as well as their limited knowledge would permit. There being no European doctor within reach they had called in an old native who boasted that he knew something about first aid and had assured them that there were no bones broken. It was he who had put some sort of healing ointment on the wound and bound up the Commissioner's head.

However meagre the old man's knowledge may have been the concoction he had applied seemed to be effective, as also did a very unpleasant-looking draught which he had prescribed and which the patient, rather than argue about it in his weak state, had risked taking. Not long after he had regained consciousness he fell into a deep, refreshing sleep that lasted for some hours, and when he woke once more his head was fairly clear and most of the pain had gone, though he still felt uncomfortably weak.

"How long have I been asleep?" he asked; and when he was told that his last sleep had lasted for nine hours and his first—that is, his unconsciousness—for two days and three nights, he realised what a vicious blow he had received.

The whole episode had returned clearly to him now—the visit from Mrs. Hillier, his impulsive promise to take the child, the untimely arrival of the missionary—and he remembered that it was when he was on his way to make arrangements for the last named to be put under arrest that he had been attacked. He determined to carry out that intention now, whatever the ultimate harm to him self and his career that might result, and gave instructions accordingly, only to be informed that the whole party had left for the interior even before he had been found unconscious in his office.

He held his still-aching head in his hands and wondered what he was to do now. They were a good three days' journey ahead of him and might be almost anywhere by this time. It was useless for him to follow them even if he could leave his post, which was impossible. Hillier had won, then, after all, he reflected angrily, and that poor woman and her little boy must surely die. Their going had simplified matters extraordinarily as far as he himself was concerned, had made things easy for him in a way. But he could not get the thought of those two innocent martyrs to a man's selfish pig-headed-ness out of his mind and in his rage he bit his nails until they bled. But he was helpless; he could do nothing.

"God grant that they die soon," he prayed, "and be spared the horrors which they must other wise know. I would give years of my life for five minutes' fair fight with that man Hillier."

Two days later he was able, with the help of a servant, to get out of bed and sit in his office. He was weak and pale and bandages still swathed his head but, much to his surprise, the ministrations of the native doctor had proved effective and he was on the high road to complete recovery. On his desk lay a baby's sock which, he surmised, must have dropped to the floor on the night Mrs. Hillier's visit and been put there by his servant. For a long time he sat with it in his hand, thinking. Then, with a sigh, he locked it carefully away in a drawer.

There, for a time, we may leave the man who had been willing to risk his whole career for the sake of a baby child he had never seen until the night on which he was struck down from behind by its father. Or was it, perhaps, not for the sake of the child but of the woman? He had met her only two or three times, it is true, had never even touched her hand, having always greeted her with the courtly bow characteristic of the German gentleman. But love is a funny thing—a strange disease, I had almost written—and may come unbidden without a moment's warning.

Thus it was that a mad missionary, a devoted mother and an innocent babe left the shelter of Dualla and disappeared into the primeval forest on their way to the unknown.

CHAPTER II

THROUGH THE FOREST

IT WAS GETTING ON for two o'clock when Hillier and his wife left the Commissioner's house and they were due to start on their first day's journey at half-past four. This meant that there could be no rest that night for the weary woman, but Mabel Hillier was past feeling. The coming of this last blow just when she had believed that her plans to save her child were going to be success-ful had completely stunned her and she did whatever she had to do mechanically, without thought or feeling. All hope had left her now. The fighting spirit which had nerved her to pay her midnight visit to the Commissioner, to creep silently from the side of her sleeping husband, was broken. The mother love which animated her, and which doubtless animates even the lowest creatures at some time, remained as strong as ever and she would have gladly given her life for her child if the occasion arose; but she no longer schemed for it as had been her wont. She was like a dead woman endowed with the power of movement; a woman with a broken heart and an atrophied brain.

If Hillier noticed the change in his wife he gave no sign of do-ing so. He went about superintending the final preparations for departure without speaking a word to her unless it was to give some crisp order. He was in his element and the men jumped to obey his slightest wish. They were obviously afraid of him but it was equally clear that they did not love him. Any experienced man would have seen at once from the looks that were thrown every now and again in his direction that there was trouble to come, and that soon. Men may be ruled by fear but they will not submit to such a rule any longer than they can help and it does not offer the same inducement to work well that respect does. However care-fully Hillier might watch over his carriers plenty of opportunities for desertion were sure to arise and his chances of getting men to re place any who chose to run away were problematical.

Under his guidance the final preparations were completed well up to time and on the stroke of half-past four the long cavalcade filed slowly out of the village and disappeared into the depths of the forest. As they passed the Commissioner's house Mabel Hillier hesitated and clutched her baby more closely to her. For a moment it looked as though she contemplated breaking away and rushing up the verandah steps in one last, despairing effort to claim protection for her child, but a painful grip on her arm and a harsh command from her husband seemed to cow her and she tramped wearily on, neither did she so much as glance back at the house afterwards.

Through the long aisles of the forest they journeyed for hour after hour, the black men with their burdens balanced on their heads, the woman clasping her child, Hillier, silent and scowling, at her side with his rifle in his hand. At times the path was easy for considerable distances, at others great rotting tree-trunks barred their road, tangled with climbing plants. Sometimes a way had to be made round these but more often it was possible to clamber over them, though not without great exertion and much danger of falling, which wearied the already weary woman to such an extent that it was only her indomitable spirit and the harsh commands of her husband which kept her mechanically tramping on. Time after time there were streams to be crossed, rushing torrents which raced past at a terrifying speed, and these were the greatest trial of all. It was generally by means of a convenient fallen trunk that the passage was made and more often than not these were a few inches under water and slippery to a degree. The natives crossed them in pairs, one with his hand on the shoulder of another and neither taking a step until his companion had got a firm footing. They were used to negotiating such sunken bridges, but to Mabel Hillier they were a dreadful ordeal. Time after time she was within an ace of falling into the water and her arm was soon black and blue where her husband had gripped it. It was not for herself that she feared, though the experience was enough to frighten any woman, but the thought of what would happen to her baby if she were to fall filled her with a constant terror which did not leave her even in her dreams.

Day after wearying day they travelled on through the endless forest. The monotony, had she been in a condition to appreciate it, would have become unbearable; but Mabel Hillier appreciated nothing. She walked in a dream, never looking to right or left, never speaking, never smiling even at her baby. Only once did she wake from her lethargy and that was when one of the carriers, an elderly man who was quite unfit for the work, collapsed from sheer exhaustion and fell in his tracks. The sight roused the maternal instinct inherent in every woman and in defiance of Hillier's commands she knelt and bathed his head with water from a nearby rivulet, then bound it up with a strip torn from her skirt and wetted in the stream. By the time he was fit to pick up his load and continue the journey the rest of the cavalcade was far on the road, for Hillier, when she had refused to obey him, had deliberately left her and marched on.

"We have another five miles to go and I dislike writing up my diary by artificial light," he had told her. "If my notes are to be completed by an hour before nightfall I have no time to spare while you waste your sympathies on this unregenerate heathen. If you choose to disobey me you must take the consequences"; and without another word or a backward glance he had left her, and it was long after nightfall before she rejoined him.

Once since leaving Dualla they had heard the far distant trumpeting of an elephant, and on another occasion passed a spot where a herd of those great beasts had crossed the track, crashed a tunnel through the dense undergrowth and, later, returned again to the path and followed it for some distance. Once an okapi, the shyest of all the forest animals, the connecting link between zebra and giraffe and at that time unknown to science, crossed their road, and twice they caught glimpses of ngati, the fierce buffaloes or bush cows. These sights came at intervals of days, and it was not the big animals that the travellers had most to fear or which most troubled them. It was the great tree-trunks which had to be scrambled under, over or round; the rivers to be crossed; the rocky valleys to be negotiated. It was the everlasting attacks of the mosquitoes, the sweat flies with their irritating bite, the jiggers which burrowed into their feet and laid their eggs there. These were the things that made life a misery for the woman, and it was small wonder that she grew daily thinner and weaker, that her baby seemed to be heavier each time she picked it up.

At long intervals, sometimes not more than twice in a week, they would come to a native village, a collection of square huts with an open sort of market-place in the centre of which there invariably grew a great tree used for look-out purposes. The natives were friendly, although few if any of them had seen a white face before and it was possible to buy eggs and milk. They would even set aside a hut for the use of the travellers but, after two attempts to sleep in these, they preferred their tent for, though the human inhabitants had vacated them, there were other less considerate and eminently nocturnal creatures which refused to do so.

Mabel Hillier welcomed the eggs and milk for the sake of the child, but otherwise she loathed the villages. The people were so indescribably filthy. A walk of half a mile to the nearest stream entailed far too great an exertion to be undertaken by any of the men, and not unnaturally their wives objected to their using any of the big jars of water they had carried up so laboriously for such an unnecessary thing as washing. The nearest approach to an effort at cleanliness that she ever saw was when a woman filled her capacious cheeks with the fluid and squirted it over her loudly-protesting children.

As might be expected under such unsanitary conditions disease was rampant and much of it horrible to see. Cases of elephantiasis and other complaints borne by different kinds of mosquitoes were to be seen in every village. Hillier said quite openly that his business was to cure souls and although he had considerable medical knowledge, he refused to make any attempt to relieve the bodily suffering that confronted him on every side. But his wife did what she could, especially for an affection of the eyes from which a good half of the people suffered, and these kindly ministrations helped not a little to lighten her own load.

And so the dreary, changeless days dragged on until one evening they arrived at a village of some size, where Hillier announced his intention of remaining permanently. The carriers threw down their loads, as was the custom, in the shade of the look-out tree, and pitched Hillier's tent—a feat which never failed to arouse the most intense wonder and admiration in the minds of the natives, who thought it marvelous that a man should be able to carry about a house, wind-proof, sun proof and water-proof, on his back—while he went off to interview the *sarikin gari* or village chief. A week later a hut had been built for him, and in spite of his overbearing manner he was getting on well with the natives.

Patience was far from being Hillier's strong point but he had sufficient sense to see that he could only attain the end he had in view by going to work slowly. His inclination was to start by throwing down the idols and burning them in front of those who worshipped them as Cortes and his followers did the gods of the people of Montezuma. Instead of this he set up a cross in the market-place and held daily meetings in its shadow, which were more or less well attended, thanks to the innate curiosity of his hearers.

They were much like children in some ways and the simple Bible stories he told appealed to them. It must be regretfully admitted, however, that it was as stories only that they appealed. They looked up to Hillier as an entertainer of great merit, as a man with a vivid imagination and the laudable gift of being able to express his thoughts in an interesting way. But when it came to expecting them to believe that what he told them was true, that the events he recounted had actually occurred, it was quite a different matter. They were content to listen to his tales for hours on end, but the idea of them being true only sent them into fits of childish laughter.

Hillier raged inwardly, but outwardly he only smiled in return. He was satisfied with the progress he was making and, thanks to the gift of a very old and rusty musket, which made a great deal of noise but was absolutely harmless except to the man who was handling it, he had already obtained a considerable hold over the *sarikin gari*. This hold he intended, and contrived, to strengthen day by day and he foresaw a not far-distant time when his word would be law in the village and himself the founder and head of the most successful mission station ever established on the whole continent of Africa.

All this time Mabel Hillier was ministering patiently and tenderly to the many afflicted inhabitants of the village. By some miraculous means she had escaped the various fevers and other ills that beset her on every side and her baby throve in a wonderful manner. Her little stock of medicines was painfully inadequate for the work there was to be done, but she made use of it unsparingly and with skill. Bit by bit she wormed her way into the affections of the native women and in quite a short time was able to persuade them to make some attempt to keep themselves and their homes and children more or less clean—far cleaner, at any rate, than they had ever been kept before.

The beneficial results of this innovation made themselves felt almost immediately—very much sooner than might have been expected. Fevers of various kinds still persisted, it is true, but there was a marked diminution in the eye trouble and the people realised by degrees that it was to their comparative cleanliness that this was due. At first the women had been shy of her, as timid as deer. None of them had ever seen a white face before, so their cautiousness was in large measure understandable. They seemed to have an idea that all white people had anthropophagous tendencies and this disgusted them for, although they could not be altogether exonerated from the charge of cannibalism themselves, it was only as a rite after a tribal battle or on very special and rare occasions that they would eat the flesh of their fellow men. When they saw Hillier and his wife sit down to a meal of fruit and eggs and milk, the very food they were accustomed to eat themselves, it never failed to cause obvious astonishment and relief, though bottled food they looked upon as something mysterious and not to be tasted by them.

But their curiosity was greater than their timidity and though, for a long time, they would run if any attempt was made to approach them too closely they gained confidence in the course of a few days and were soon so persistent in their attentions to Mabel Hillier as to become an embarrassment. There could be no doubt, however, of the very real affection they bore her, and this affection might have stood her in good stead but for an untoward event over which the natives had no more control than the whites and which shall be recounted at the proper time.

Abu, the old man whose head she had bathed, was her devoted slave and never far from her side. He alone of the carriers had remained in the village, all the others having claimed their money and taken their departure the very morning after their arrival. What Mabel Hillier would have done without him it is difficult to say, for he fetched and carried for her, did her washing, nursed the baby, who adored him when she was busy, and made himself useful in a thousand ways from morning to night. Nothing was too much trouble for him and he asked for no greater reward than a smile from his mistress.

From Hillier she seldom heard a word. Since the night before they had left Dualla he had never once opened his mouth to her unnecessarily, and his longest speech had been the one he made when she had insisted, against his will, in staying to tend Abu. It was only at meal times and at night or when she attended his services, which he forced her to do however tired or ill she might feel, that she saw anything of him except at a distance. Much of his time he spent in the hut of the head-man of the village, to whom he talked for interminable hours, not always on matters of religion. His primary aim was to get complete control over that individual, and he was rapidly getting it. How he was doing so is a matter which does not concern this story.

The women loved Mabel Hillier, then, and the people generally tolerated her husband, neither from affection nor fear, but because he amused them and whiled away the hours with his stories. There was one man, however, who had conceived a great hatred for him. He was young, considered handsome by the ladies of his tribe, of remarkable strength and progressive in his ideas. Also he was the acknowledged leader of the men of his own generation. His ideas of progression, however did not coincide with Hillier's. The missionary had sensed the antagonism of this youth and knew that he was not a man to be considered lightly. He had far more power with the young men of the village, the men who would count if there was trouble, than Hillier cared to acknowledge even to himself and he had spent many hours scheming how best to get rid of him. In the end he consulted the *sarikin gari*, and the story he told him, I regret to say, was not true.

This young man, whose name was Kofi, was, as I have intimated, considered handsome by the village maidens, and well he knew it. Added to the charm of his good looks were the glamour of his strength and his prowess in games and he did not hesitate to make use of the opportunities that admiration for him put in his way. In fact he was an incorrigible flirt and not an evening passed on which he might not be seen going from or returning to the village attended by some dusky damsel. It was on this weakness of Kofi's that Hillier seized and he elaborated upon it shamelessly. He told the head-man that he had by chance come upon Kofi and that worthy individual's daughter, who incidentally was no better than she ought to have been, in a secluded glade in the forest just outside the village, and the things he accused them of are not for the printed page. As a matter of fact Hillier had not come across them at all, though he had admittedly seen the two walking together, but the sariki of course believed every word he was told and raged and swore accordingly.

This was exactly what Hillier wanted and he followed up his advantage eagerly, fanning the fires of the old man's righteous anger. There was only one thing to be done, he insisted, when he considered that he had worked him up to the required pitch, and that was to expel Kofi from the village with ignominy. The head-man agreed with him but pointed out that he was unable to do this on his own responsibility. It would be necessary to call a meeting of the elders, as it were, but he had no doubt that they would fall in with his wishes, and with this Hillier had perforce to be content, though he would have infinitely preferred to have seen immediate action taken.

Neither of them saw a dark form slip silently away from the shadow of the hut as they emerged or it may be that Hillier would not have been so satisfied with his evening's work. It so happened that the *sarikin gari*'s daughter was truly in love with the all-conquering Kofi and, like her lover, disliked the missionary cordially. It was at his instigation that she had lain listening outside the thin walls of her father's hut with the intention of learning what it was he and Hillier had such long conversations about; but it was only by the merest luck that she had happened to overhear that particular conversation. She hurried hotfoot to the dwelling of Kofi and told him every word she had heard. He was not the kind of man to submit meekly to having lies told about him and hurried in his turn to the huts of his friends, one after the other. He spent no more than a minute in each, then returned to his interrupted slumbers; but an hour before dawn an observant man might have seen two score young men slip singly and unostentatiously away from the village and disappear into the forest. Kofi and his followers were going to hold a council of war.

One of this youth's progressive ideas concerned the marriage laws of his people. At the present time it was not permissible for anybody to marry a member of their own Village and Kofi had set his heart on marrying the head-man's daughter. Whether this was purely a case of love may be doubted, for there is some reason to believe that by so doing he hoped to step automatically into his father-in-law's shoes when he died and this would suit his book admirably. But before such a marriage could be recognised those laws must be altered.

The custom as things were was for a would-be bridegroom to set out decked in all the finery which passed for fashion in that land and smeared from head to foot with a red pigment made from the bark of a tree, for any neighbouring village. Arrived there, if he saw a damsel who met with his approval, he would squat down and watch her at whatever task she was engaged upon and, after a time, a few words would be exchanged. The gallant swain, love-sick would hardly be an appropriate adjective, might then tell the girl that he was satisfied with her and hurry off to break the news to his prospective father-in-law, to whom he would present as earnest-money goods to the value of about half a sovereign.

On the day fixed for the wedding the bride would leave her home at nightfall and her arrival at the village of the bridegroom be announced by a loud shout. His friends would then cover her head with a piece of cloth and conduct her in state to her new home, while the local priest climbed a tree and in a stentorian voice called down curses upon anyone who should ravish, seduce or in any way harm her. Later wedding gifts would be presented and the final installment of the agreed price paid to the lady's father. These ideas were altogether too old fashioned for young Kofi's liking and he meant to have them altered.

It was over quite another matter, however, that he had called his early morning council of war, namely to scheme the downfall of his enemy; but it did not take long, for he had his plan cut and dried and all he had to do was to explain to his companions the part that each was to play. He knew from experience that the council of the elders would be called for the following afternoon or evening and, though it was not customary for any but those elders to speak, that the entire population of the village would be there and listening to every word that was said. Kofi would be given an opportunity to defend himself, as also would the girl, while Hillier would be called upon to state at length all that he averred he had seen occur and charge the culprits therewith.

This time-honoured method of procedure, strangely reminiscent of our own courts of law, had been witnessed many times by each of Kofi's little band, and all that was necessary was for him to tell them what position to take up at the assembly and what to do when he gave the agreed signal. He explained this briefly but lucidly, and to make sure that there should be no hitch in his arrangements had a sort of dress rehearsal, arranging his men as they should be at the critical moment if they took their right places, and giving the signal which was to call them to action. Satisfied with their performance the council disbanded and all had returned unseen to the village long before the self-satisfied Hillier had awakened from his slumbers.

That morning passed much as other mornings had done, but there was a feeling of suppressed excitement in the air. The news that a council of the elders was to be called in the evening had early got about and they were sufficiently uncommon to raise the greatest interest. It was known, too, what the case was that was to be tried, though this was contrary to the rules, and the elders were much puzzled as to how the news had leaked out. Hillier's morning service was not so well attended as usual and those who came to it were fidgety and inattentive. The missionary himself found it difficult to fix his thoughts on what he was supposed to be doing and his address lacked conviction and was shorter than was generally the case. Perhaps he regretted having concocted the story he had told the head-man and dreaded having to tell it again before the whole village. But it was essential, he reflected, that Kofi should be removed and he comforted himself with the thought that in removing him, even by the means he had adopted, he was furthering his work.

So he pulled himself together and, as the great drum boomed out its summons to the meeting, walked firmly to his place at the side of the *sarikin gari*.

CHAPTER III

THE TRIAL OF MARTIN HILLIER

IN A ROW under the shade of the great look-out tree sat the twelve elders of the village and, slightly in front of them, the *sarikin gari* while, ranged in two-thirds of a circle before them, the remaining inhabitants squatted expectantly. In the forefront of the ring the young men of Kofi's band were scattered unostentatiously, each with his spear in his hand. On the head-man's left were his daughter and Kofi himself, the accused parties, and on his right the camp-stool brought from Hillier's tent for his use. All this the missionary noted as he strode across the market-place to the seat reserved for him, and he judged that the only people absent from the meeting were his wife and Abu, and, of course, his baby son. All the native children of however tender an age were there and sat wide-eyed, awed by the magnitude of the concourse and the sense of suppressed excitement which prevailed. Even the aged and infirm had been carried out to take part in the important proceedings that were pending.

With Hillier's arrival the meeting formally opened. The headman, without rising from his seat on the ground, as befitted the dignity of the presiding magistrate, gave a very brief recapitulation of the story that he had heard from the lips of the missionary and at the same time paid him a tribute for his public-spirited action in coming forward. He explained, untruthfully, that it was not because the chastity of his own daughter was in question that he had summoned the council, but because he had learned from Hillier that it was his duty, as the official father of them all, to watch over the morals of the village as a whole. He explained, instigated by the promise of certain gifts from the accuser "if justice was done," that the way in which Kofi was wont to carry on with the opposite sex was notorious, that the daughters of none of them were safe from his wiles, and that the sooner the village dispensed with his presence the better it would be for everybody except, perhaps, from their point of view, the girls themselves. When the murmurs of approval, which were largely conventional, had subsided and he had enjoyed to the full the effect of his address, he turned to Hillier and called upon him to state his case and repeat his story.

The accuser felt extremely uncomfortable and he looked it, although his perturbation of mind may have escaped the notice of his audience. To give the man his due, he was unused to telling untruths and it went against the grain with him to do so now. But he had put his hand to the plough and his inherent obstinacy would not permit of his turning back even if it had been safe for him to do so. Again he tried, not altogether successfully, to comfort himself with the thought that any means which he might see fit to adopt were legitimate if they would further his work and help lead to the saving of souls in the long run. He went so far as to try to make himself believe that by bringing about the expulsion and disgrace, possibly the death, of Kofi he would be doing that young man a good turn inasmuch as he would thus become a martyr, in a sense, to the propagation of the gospel and receive his reward in the life to come. Then he rose to his feet.

Hillier was not a man to let opportunities slip by and he seized eagerly upon the one that was offered to him now of addressing the entire population of the village. He stressed what he had often told them before, that he had come thousands of miles from his own country with no thought of gain, simply and solely to help them to lead a better, a happier, and a more comfortable life. He impressed upon them that all men were brothers, that the white were no better than the black, and he made much of what his wife had done to ease, if not to cure, their complaints, while omitting to mention that she had done it against his will.

And then he explained how he had hated telling the head-man the story that he was called upon to tell them all now, but that it was the duty of everyone of them, however disagreeable it might be, to do all in his power to suppress and punish sin and unseemly conduct, though there was nothing more reprehensible than to bear false witness—which was exactly what he was going to do. After that he told how he had, unwillingly and by chance, stumbled upon Kofi and the girl in a secluded glade of the forest, and his tone was sad and apologetic when he recounted what he had seen there. He elaborated upon the sariki's insistence that the daughters of not one of them were safe while Kofi remained in the village and begged the elders to remember that by expelling him the good they would do their loved ones would far exceed the well-merited injury they would inflict upon one man.

Hillier was a powerful speaker and his words carried conviction. There were not a few who disliked Kofi for the power that he undeniably held over the younger generation, and when he rose in his turn the trend of public opinion was decidedly and unconcealedly against him, for the accuser's address had been received with murmurs of approval, while the equivalent of hisses greeted the defendant on more than one side. He paid no outward attention to these but swaggered forward and stood, tall, straight and handsome, before his judges and prepared to defend himself.

According to custom Kofi alone of that large company, as the accused man, was unarmed, all the other men present carrying spears. He folded his arms across his great chest, looked haughtily round the entire company with slow and deliberate glance, and then began such a speech as had never been heard in the village or indeed in the whole country side. He began by calling his accuser a liar to his face and that the shot told was evident from the red flush which spread over Hillier's countenance. He admitted freely that he had walked in the woods on the evening in question with the head-man's daughter, that he had often done so before, and that he had every intention of doing so again as many times as he wished. Whether from feeling or thanks to histrionic ability his voice grew soft and tender as he told, straightforwardly and unashamed, of the love which they bore one another, and rolled out sonorously when he swore by his gods that he would marry her in the face of all the laws which forbade such a union.

Could there be love, he asked, between a man and a strange maid whom he had bought like a chattel? A momentary animal passion perhaps, but certainly not love. And was it not the children of a real love who became the finest men and women?

"Look at me," he cried, and he was well worth looking at as he stood there in the pride of his youth and strength. "Who is there amongst you who can boast so fine a body as I can boast? Who has such perfect limbs? Who such strength? Which of you can compete with me in the fight, or the hunt, or the race? Is there one of you who can cast a spear so far, or two together who can throw me to the ground? You do not answer. You know there is none. And why is this? I will tell you. It is because my father lived for many years in a village that was not his own, where he learned to know and love my mother. It is because my father married his heart's desire, and she hers. It was because I was born of a woman who adored the man who sired me, and sired by a man who worshipped his mate. That is why I am the man that I am. That is why not one of you is my equal.

"Would you have children who shall grow up to be like me, my brothers? Then wed the woman of your choice instead of leaving your home to buy an unknown, unloved stranger. In no other way can your wish be granted. Refuse to be governed by our effete marriage laws. Strike out for yourselves. Choose for your mates women whom you know and love and you will become the ancestors of a race which shall rule the world. I have spoken."

Kofi resumed his seat on the ground in a dead silence. The probability is that everybody was too flabbergasted at his speech to give any indication of approval or disapproval. Or it may have been that lacking Kofi's fearlessness, they dared not do so. The expressions on the faces of the elders were a study. The head-man sat with his mouth wide open literally gasping at the effrontery of anyone who dared to say what the accused had said. As a speech it was a masterpiece. As an appeal it was magnificent. But as a defence it was not calculated to improve the chances of the accused with his judges and Hillier knew instinctively that the result would be what he had so earnestly hoped for.

The members of the bench, when the head-man's daughter had said her little say, which was only an echo of Kofi's sentiments and fell very flat after his impassioned appeal, rose and gathered in a group at a short distance from the squatting circle. For no more than three minutes they conferred together before resuming their seats, the head-man alone remaining on his feet to deliver the sentence of the court. It was unanimous and to the effect that the accused should be immediately stripped of all he possessed, severely beaten, and driven from the village with sticks and stones, never to return.

A long-drawn moan, whether of approval or sympathy, came from the squatting circle of onlookers and it was this moment that Kofi chose to give his signal. At a double call, like the hoot of an owl, two score young men sprang, spear in hand, from their places and rushed upon the startled elders. With his bare hands their leader seized the throat of the head-man and gripped it in a grip of steel. Even before the blade of a spear entered his body his eyes seemed to be shooting out of his head and he died without a struggle or a sound. The twelve elders suffered a like fate at the hands of twelve of the attacking party; two, one on either side, held Hillier, who had been too astonished to move; the remaining six-and-twenty stood in a line covering the killers, their weapons poised, ready to resist a counter attack if any were attempted. Kofi had rehearsed his men well and they had followed his instructions to the letter.

There was a counter attack but it was a very halfhearted affair and soon Kofi's two score of followers were more than doubled. A few men were wounded, though none of them severely, on either side, but in little more than five minutes after the first rush the coup was a complete success. The head-man and the elders were dead, Hillier and about a dozen others who had been so foolish as to attempt resistance were prisoners, and Kofi had taken over the reins of government by the unanimous vote of his supporters. Never had a revolution succeeded in quicker time.

The first care of the new sariki was to see to the appointment of elders to take the place of those who had so suddenly and unexpectedly vacated the office and, instead of choosing them himself, he greatly strengthened his position and enhanced his popularity by leaving the selection to the vote of all the male members of the community who had reached the age of puberty. As soon as this was settled he was formally married to the lady of his choice and, as her father was in no fit condition to receive payment for her, being very untidily dead, he gave her some trifling present for herself.

By now night was drawing in but Kofi insisted on having things all shipshape as far as possible before calling it a day so, while a number of men removed the bodies of the slain and made some attempt at tidying up, he and his elders sat in judgment on the prisoners. The fate of the natives was soon sealed; they were to be reserved for the Feast of Death which, it was decreed, would be held in a few weeks' time. Hillier's case was more difficult and eventually the court decided to adjourn until the following day. The prisoners were confined, natives and white man together, in one hut under a strong guard, Kofi disappeared with his bride into the dwelling until lately occupied by his deceased father-in-law, and peace settled down over the village.

It will be necessary now to go back a little way. At the first sound of strife Mabel Hillier, followed by the faithful Abu, had hurried from her hut and arrived at the scene of the conflict in time to see her husband struggling in the grip of two natives, but too late, mercifully, to witness the death of the elders. In spite of the way in which he had treated her for months past she would have gone to the side of the father of her child, but was prevented from doing so by the women who forced her, as gently as they could, to remain on the outskirts of the excited crowd. It was not until the rising was an accomplished fact that the bride-to-be happened to catch sight of her and came to the rescue. By her she was led before Kofi, who received her with every mark of respect but informed her that, much to his regret, it would be necessary for her to consider herself a prisoner for the time being. She should have absolute freedom of movement within the confines of the village and Abu should continue to wait on her. The only thing forbidden her, in fact, was to go outside the boundaries or visit the prison house where her husband would be confined, a regrettable necessity caused by certain actions for which he must stand his trial.

Mabel Hillier realised that concessions were being made to her and was grateful. She was naturally worried but she did not know the full tale of all that had happened, so her worry was not extreme. She tried hard to feel miserable about her husband, to pity him in his captivity, but he had utterly killed the love she had once borne him and, though she had kept telling herself for weeks that she did not hate him, there can be no doubt that in actual fact she did. For herself and her baby she had no fear. In a way she was glad of the coming of the little revolution. There was a chance that it would be the cause of their return to a more civilised environment, and hope beat high in her breast at the thought that there was still a chance for her boy. She was ready to bless Kofi for the part he had played, and so thinking she fell asleep.

At an early hour next morning the elders, with the new sariki in front of them, took their seats in the shade of the look-out tree. Two minutes later Hillier, an armed native on either side of him, was marched across the market-place to take his trial. He was halted and made to stand, still under guard, in front of his judges, and Kofi, after deliberately eyeing him up and down for some moments, gave the opening address.

"It is customary," he said, "for the sariki to explain to the elders and the people the reason for which a council is called and the charge preferred against the accused. When he has spoken the accuser states his case and the defendant replies, after which the elders consult together before delivering their verdict. We, the new rulers of this village, approve of that time-honoured method of procedure, but in your case the greater part of it will be unnecessary. Your own lips have condemned you. Your own tongue has decided what your punishment shall be. Your own words have sealed your fate. Listen now to my words.

"But last night, standing to accuse me, you told the people that there was no sin greater than to bear false witness. Is it not so, my brothers?"

"It is so," came in a dull, unanimous rumble from the attentive circle.

"But last night, standing to accuse me, you bore false witness against me and against my woman," Kofi continued. "You yourself committed the sin than which there is none greater. Is it not so my brothers?"

Again came that low, menacing rumble of assent.

"What have you to say in your defence? I would be just."

The head-man addressed himself directly to Hillier now, and Hillier knew that, whatever he might answer, his fate was sealed. With all his faults he was a brave man and he faced the crisis as only a brave man could. With head thrown back and folded arms he looked his accuser unflinchingly in the eye and spoke, clearly and with no tremor in his voice, no sign of the fear he must most surely have felt.

"It is true, Kofi," he said. "I bore false witness against you and against your woman and that is a sin for which I must suffer. I did it because I believed that in so doing I would bring peace and happiness to this people. You are a spiller of blood, Kofi, a debaucher, a seducer of women, a foul growth upon the face of the earth. You are evil, evil through and through and no rest can come to this village while you live. Kill me if you will but listen to my last words. Before the moon has twice reached her full a great curse shall fall upon this village. The huts shall be destroyed, the people shall be slain and scattered, you shall be cast down from your high estate and the rest of your days shall be spent in sorrow and affliction. I have spoken."

"It is enough," Kofi broke in. "You have borne false witness and, by your own showing, to bear false witness is as great a sin as murder. Therefore it is the punishment for murder that you shall suffer. Is it not so, my brothers?"

And for the third time came the low rumble of assent, though not so heartily now, perhaps because of fear of Hillier's words.

At a nod from the head-man the prisoner was led away and the crowd dispersed while preparations were made. Kofi, perhaps with a kindly desire to save her unnecessary pain, had ordered some alterations in the arrangements he had made with regard to Mabel Hillier, and when she attempted to leave her hut she found an armed guard at the door who refused to let her pass. An hour later the head-man himself came to see her and assured her that this enforced detention would last for only a few hours, though the reason for it he refused to divulge. He had come primarily to ask whether she would attend to the hurts of those of his men who had been wounded on the previous day and, when she assented, said that they should be brought one at a time to her hut. A few minutes after his departure the first of them arrived, and for many hours thereafter she was washing and binding spear cuts and treating them with antiseptic, so that the time passed quickly and her curiosity had not many opportunities of obtruding.

Meanwhile all had been made ready for the punishment to be inflicted upon Hillier, and two hours before sundown he was again led out into the market-place. He found the crowd in much the same position as he had last seen it, except that the circle was larger, and a dead silence prevailed. As he entered the living ring a long knife was thrust through both his cheeks, which prevented him from speaking, and a rope flung round his neck by which he was dragged, half suffocated, before Kofi and the elders. For a minute he stood there then at a sign from the head-man, his guards began to lead him slowly round and round the silent circle.

Death he had expected and was ready for, but the thought of torture had never once entered his head. How long would it be before they killed him, he wondered; or were they not going to kill him at all, only maim him and, when their blood lust was satisfied, turn him out into the forest and leave him to the mercy of the wild beasts? He had been stripped of his clothing before being led from the prisoners' hut and was as naked as at the moment when he was born and this, somehow, worried him more than anything, trivial though the matter was in comparison with his sufferings. A thousand thoughts chased each other through his aching head. What were his wife and baby doing now? Did she know that her husband was being tortured, killed by inches, within calling distance of her hut? How cool the pool used to be under the willow trees at his old home in Kent. What were the names of the first couple that he had joined together in holy matrimony? It was stupid of him not to be able to remember that.

And so his thoughts rambled aimlessly on while he remained oblivious to what was actually happening to him and about him until he was brought back to realities by a sharp pain in the calf of his leg. It was caused by the point of a spear and was only the forerunner of many a score of wounds that he was to receive before the sun sank behind the encircling trees. For well over an hour his guards led him slowly round and round the circle while the people, men, women and even little children, prodded at him with spears and knives. At first the wounds which he received were slight, almost tentative, and infrequent; but as the minutes passed his tormentors seemed to pluck up courage, or perhaps the sight of the red blood on his white skin made them less able to control themselves. Twice he stumbled and almost fell from weakness and loss of blood, but on each occasion he was halted while some fiery liquid was forced between his teeth, which had the effect of restoring him to complete consciousness.

It still wanted nearly half an hour to sundown when he was stopped for the second time before Kofi and the elders. There was hardly a square inch of skin on his body that had not been cut and from head to foot he was smothered in blood. A native with a great sword in his hand stepped out of the ranks and the tortured man heaved a sigh of thanksgiving. This was the end, he thought, the merciful end. But he was wrong. Instead of putting him out of his misery the swordsman used his weapon to hack one of his arms, held out by a guard, rudely from his body, and he was bidden to dance. He shook his head in refusal, but it was no good. Burning brands were brought and thrust under his remaining arm, between his legs, pressed against his bleeding breast and back until the smell of scorched flesh rose on the evening air—and he danced.

From the moment he had entered the circle not a sound had been heard from the crowd of men and women but the panting of the victim and his occasional hardly-suppressed groans. For close on two hours he had suffered, but consciousness refused to leave him. How much longer must this martyrdom go on, he wondered, and prayed anew for a speedy release. And this time his prayer was answered.

The sun had dropped behind the trees for some minutes when for the third time he was halted before Kofi and the elders. He was thrown roughly to his knees and, as the great drum boomed out the signal announcing the close of another day—the first sound that he had heard since he was led from the hut, the last that he was to hear in this world— his executioner stepped into the circle and dragged the knife from through his cheeks.

"Into Thy hands," came in a hoarse whisper from between parched lips: then the executioner drew back his arm, there was a flash of light on bright steel, and the broad blade of a spear buried itself deep in quivering flesh.

Martin Hillier had gone to face his God.

CHAPTER IV

THE FEAST OF DEATH

THE RESTRICTIONS put upon the movements of Mabel Hillier did not extend to those of Abu. He was allowed to go where and when he would and enjoyed the same liberty as he had done ever since his arrival in the village. He seldom left the side of his mistress, unless it was at her bidding, especially when, as now, she was in trouble, but on the afternoon of Hillier's death his curiosity had overcome every other feeling, even his affection for the woman who had been kind to him, and he had made his way to the market-place to find out what was going on.

He reached it only just in time to witness the final act of the tragedy and, though he hated Hillier with all his heart and soul, he was filled with horror and trepidation, How was he going to break the news to his mistress, was the question which flashed unbidden into his mind, and how would she take it? For the dead man he had no pity. He had got no more than he deserved, he considered, and there was nothing that Abu himself would have enjoyed more than an opportunity to assist at the execution and bear his share in inflicting some of the many wounds which had been given and received.

But the woman was quite a different matter. No harm that he had been able to prevent had ever come near her, no sort of worry or trouble that he had been able to take upon himself. His great aim had always been to save her from hurt, and now it was he who must hurt her by telling her of Hillier's death—for he felt that if the news were brought to her by anybody else it would not be broken so gently as he himself would break it. He spent as long as he dared thinking things over before he re-entered the hut and when he did so had decided on his plan of action. The tortures that had been inflicted on her husband must be hidden from her at any cost and he would only tell her the bare fact that he was no more—had been killed for some offence, real or fancied, against the laws of the natives. He thought, by omitting all details, to soften the blow and had great hopes that, thanks to the pain and indignities she had suffered at her husband's hands, the mere announcement of his death would not come as a great shock to her.

She received the news bravely and it may be that she was not altogether unprepared for it. She shed no tears, did not even turn pale, and when Kofi bowed at the door of her hut, as he did half an hour later, she was able to receive him collectedly. Before he had time to speak she told him that she had heard of her husband's death, adding that she bore him no ill-will—for she knew how important it was for her to keep in his good books, to make a friend of him, if ever she hoped to get safely away to Dualla. She even went so far as to congratulate him on his election as head-man of the village and flattered him by expressing her conviction that it would prove to be for the great and lasting good of the community. Finally she pleaded that she was often lonely and begged him to come to see her from time to time when his public duties would permit.

When he left her in the end it was, as she had intended, in the belief that, like many before her, she had fallen victim to his charms and he began to dream dreams. His power in the village was already absolute, but with a white wife that power would spread over other villages. There were ways and means open to a man in his position of getting rid of his newly-married bride—accidents would happen—and then there would be nothing to prevent him and Mabel Hillier from getting wed according to the rites of his own religion. For the moment that was impossible, as the tribe was strictly monogamous, but it could be arranged without difficulty.

It was with such thoughts as these chasing each other through his head that he entered his hut and the presence of his wife, and she was quick to notice some subtle change in his manner towards her. It has been said that that lady was no better than she ought to be and there is a strong possibility that she feared something might have come to his ears which she was anxious to hide. But as time passed and he said no word about any of her numerous indiscretions her fears subsided and at long last left her altogether. She resolved, however, to be careful in the future.

Next day Mabel Hillier received another visit from Kofi, and she thought the time was ripe to suggest that he should send her and her child with a sufficient escort to Dualla. In return she promised him a rich reward and the friendship of the Commissioner, but even this did not tempt him. He had become infatuated with her delicate fairness, her golden hair and slim build—so different from the opulent charms of the dusky damsels of his own race—and had fully made up his mind to have her for his own. Without telling her this outright he hinted broadly that life in the village would be very pleasant for her and that she would enjoy much power as the wife of the handsomest man in the countryside.

As for her leaving the village, of course she should do so if she wished, but not just yet. He could not spare the men to accompany her for the moment, and besides it was only fair to her that she should be given the opportunity of considering what he had mentioned. Therefore her departure would be postponed for a week or two at any rate and in the meantime she would be at liberty to go where she would within the confines of the village. She consented to this arrangement with a brave and disarming smile and he left her fairly confident that she would marry him of her own free will and absolutely certain that she would become his wife eventually whether she liked it or not.

To be allowed to roam where she would within the confines of the village, Mabel Hillier realised, was tantamount to being a prisoner, and with quick intuition she divined Kofi's real intentions. She was sure that he would never allow her to leave of his own free will and the only thing that remained, therefore, was to force him to let her go. The great question was how this could be done and there was but one answer to it. Somehow or other news of her plight must be brought to the Commissioner, and the man to carry the message was undoubtedly Abu. Having travelled the road already he knew it better than the natives, who seldom went far from their own village, and was therefore the most suitable messenger even if he had not been the only man within reach whom she could trust. For long hours she debated whether she should entrust her baby to his care, but eventually decided against it. She trusted her faithful old servant implicitly, but the child was still only a few months old, the road was long and dangerous, Abu was not strong and he would be unable to provide her baby with the food and care necessary to its existence.

At last she called the old man into the hut and told him what she wanted him to do, but for a long time he refused flatly to leave her. It was only when, with infinite trouble, she had succeeded in persuading him that in no other way could he save her from a life of misery and shame, that in the end he unwillingly consented to undertake the journey. On a tiny scrap of paper torn from the edge of a page of her diary she wrote her little message. It was only a few words, for Abu had nowhere to hide a note and she dreaded lest it might be found and its meaning somehow come to be understood.

"Martin murdered. Prisoner. Help. Mabel Hillier."

That was all she wrote and the bit of paper was so small that it could easily be hidden in the mouth and swallowed as a last resource if the necessity arose. She gave it to the faithful old man, clasped his hand in both of hers with a prayer for his success and blessings on his head, and a moment later he had disappeared silently into the darkness of the night.

For a time the woman stood at the door of the hut staring into nothingness. She had extinguished the light before letting Abu out, for fear that his departure might be noticed and prevented, and much depended upon his getting a good start. He was the only hope she had left. After a time she reentered the hut and flung herself, fully dressed as she was, on her bed. What would happen when Abu's absence was discovered, as it must be in the morning, she dreaded to think, but she relied on the affection which the women had for her to save her to some extent.

She began to try to calculate how long it would be before she might reasonably expect her message to be answered. Her husband and his heavily-laden cavalcade had travelled very slowly and the route they had followed had not been a direct one. He had had no definite objective from the start and his road had been chosen more or less at random, though always leading farther and farther into the interior. Also they had travelled for only a few hours each day and their tent had always been pitched a full hour before nightfall. Abu, with nothing to carry but a little flour and nothing to turn him from a direct course, might be expected to complete the journey in well under half the time it had taken them and the return was sure to be made by forced marches. So far she had got in her calculations when fatigue overcame her and she fell asleep.

With no servant to rouse her she woke late in the morning and the sun was already high in the heavens when she stepped out of her hut. While she had been making her toilet she had determined to take the bull by the horns and, as our American cousins say, to put up a bluff. With this end in view she went straight to Kofi's dwelling and demanded whether he had given instructions for Abu to wait on her no more, as she had not seen him that morning.

The head-man immediately sent men to search for him and in the meantime detailed two girls to attend to her wants, and Mabel Hillier returned to her hut more than satisfied with the success of her ruse. Not unnaturally all efforts to find the recalcitrant Abu were fruitless and Kofi came to see her later in the day full of apologies for his absence. There could be no doubt, he said, that he had been taken by some wild beast or drowned in the stream, and he feared that any further search would be mere waste of time. With this Mabel Hillier hastened to agree and begged that he would take no more trouble to find him.

The days and weeks slipped slowly by with nothing to break the monotony for her but the visits of the head-man. Though he never failed to remind her each time he came to the hut of the manifold advantages that would be hers if, at a later date, she were to marry him, he did not exactly press his suit. This was for two reasons; firstly, because he did not dare to do so until he had got rid of his wife, and he was not sufficiently tired of her to do that yet; and, secondly, because he was afraid that if he was to worry her too much she might mention the matter in the presence of some of the women and his intentions thus become known, which might well lead to considerable unpleasantness.

In his vanity Kofi still entertained the belief that Mabel Hillier would come to him in the long run of her own free will, and to further this desirable end he did her many little kindnesses. The two girls whom he had detailed to wait upon her did their work well and cheerfully and he had not only allowed her to bury the body of her husband in a spot just outside the village and set up a rude cross over it, but even permitted her to visit the grave dally, though not alone. For this concession she was grateful, but it would have been perfectly safe to let her go alone, because the thought of escape never so much as entered her head.

She thought sometimes of her husband's prophecy and wondered if there was any likelihood of its coming true.

"Before the moon has twice reached her full a great curse shall fall upon this village. The huts shall be destroyed, the people shall be slain and scattered, you yourself shall be cast down from your high estate and the rest of your days shall be spent in sorrow and affliction."

Mabel Hillier was disinclined to believe it but she could not help speculating, and it passed the time to do so. If it was to come true it must mean that Kofi would resist the Commissioner and his men when they arrived, as she felt sure they would do. She hoped he would foresee the possibility of this and bring a sufficient force. Day by day her hopes rose ever higher, for she felt that the time of her deliverance was drawing near, that soon she would be safe at

Dualla and all her worries over. Already the moon had once reached its full, within the week it would have done so again, and in spite of her unwillingness to believe the prophecy she subconsciously relied upon it to some extent.

And then came the day set aside for the celebration of the Feast of Death.

That morning for the first time the two serving girls failed to attend to their duties with their usual cheerfulness. That air of suppressed excitement which had been noticeable on the day of Hillier's death and during the first council of the elders, was again in evidence. The inhabitants of the village stood or squatted about in groups as though not knowing what to do with themselves. There was an unwonted silence. Even the dogs omitted to bark and the children to cry or play in the dust.

What the proceedings were which attended the celebration of the Feast of Death Mabel Hillier did not know exactly, but she had gathered from the whisperings of her servant girls that they included the execution of the men who had been taken prisoner during Kofi's successful rising and determined to keep closely to her hut from the moment there was any sign of their beginning.

She visited the grave of her husband early and had returned from that daily duty long before the great drum boomed out the mid-day hour. Barely had the last sound rolled away before the prisoners were led from the hut in which they had been confined each with a rope round his neck, and dragged into the centre of the circle which had been formed. As twice before Kofi and the elders, the head-man slightly in front, squatted in the shade of the look out tree with the entire population of the village before them. The same deathly silence reigned as during the torturing of Hillier and there was the same strained, eager expression on the faces of the onlookers. Blood was to be shed and the thought of it appealed in some strange way to their appetites.

Presently the drum was beaten again, two heavy blows. "Death, death," they seemed to say, and death was what they foretold. One of the waiting prisoners was dragged roughly from amongst his companions and forced to his knees in front of Kofi and the elders. For what must have seemed an eternity to the doomed man they sat staring at him, then, at a sign from the *sarikin gari*, two natives detached themselves from the silent crowd and ranged themselves one on either side of the prisoner. The first carried a great, wide-mouthed bowl, the other a heavy sword.

At a second sign from Kofi the drum boomed out again, three notes this time and, after a short interval, a fourth; and it was during that interval that the deed was done. As the third note trembled away into silence the man with the sword stepped forward, his hands rose high above his head and the heavy, two-handed weapon flashed down on the neck of his victim, while the second man hurried forward to catch the streaming blood in his bowl. It was as the severed head fell to the ground that the fourth note was sounded.

The steaming bowl of blood was handed to Kofi, who walked with it reeking in his hands to a hut in which were laid the remains of his ancestors. There he washed their bones and skulls, then poured what was left upon the ground, after which he returned to his place in the shade of the look-out tree, took his seat, and again the drum boomed out its dread message—"Death, death."

And so the celebration of the Feast of Death went on. All day long the drum beat out its terrible message—"death, death-kill, kill, kill-dead." All day long the victims were led to the slaughter, the bones of Kofi's ancestors were washed in blood, and the sun had gone to rest behind the encircling trees before the last of the prisoners, who had been forced to watch all his companions die, was flung to his knees in front of the elders.

The drum-beats Mabel Hillier was compelled to hear and she guessed more or less at their meaning. In her ignorance she thanked God that her husband had suffered no such long-drawn agony as, she felt sure, these men must be suffering. She knew that as a rule the death penalty was not inflicted swiftly and mercifully, that torture was its frequent accompaniment in that part of the world. Surely these people would be punished for their sins, would be made to suffer as they had made others suffer. She prayed that Hillier's prophecy might come true, that the houses might be destroyed, the people slain and scattered, and Kofi himself cast down from his high estate and made to spend the rest of his days in sorrow and affliction. And so praying she fell asleep.

It was within a week of the full moon, the second since the rising in the village, and the country was bathed in a light almost as bright as day. In the dead of night, when no soul stirred and every member of that little community was sunk in sleep, worn out by the excitements of the day, dark, silent figures might have been seen creeping slowly up to the huts and their unsuspecting inhabitants. Over a hundred strong, they were as numerous as the villagers and more so. Inch by inch they made their way across the deserted market-place, in the centre of which stood one of their number, taller than his companions, who directed them by signs in which direction they were to go. Not a sound broke the stillness but the signs were understood and obeyed implicitly and soon every hut was surrounded.

Then, and not till then, was the voice of the commander of the raiders heard. A double hoot he gave, like the call of an owl— almost the same signal as had been given by Kofi before the murder of the elders—and immediately caution was thrown aside and his followers attacked. Some dashed in through the doors of the huts, but the vast majority did not wait to do this. With superhuman strength they tore them to pieces and trampled them under foot. They strangled the villagers, still half asleep as they were from the excitements of the day and the effects of copious draughts of palm wine, with their bare hands or dashed their brains out with heavy clubs. They spoke no word, made no sound and their ferocity was bestial. In five minutes the village, lately so peaceful in the silver moonlight, was a shambles.

Hardly any resistance was put up against the midnight raiders. The people had been taken so utterly by surprise that no resistance had been possible. Peace reigned throughout the land and they had known of no reason why guards should be posted, and taken no precautions. Kofi had seized a spear and been ready to put up some sort of a fight, but before he could use it a club had descended with stunning force on the back of his head through a hole torn in the hut and he had known no more. The rising that he himself had engineered had been completely successful, but no more so than the attack which had now been delivered against him.

His wife was dead with her throat torn out before she had more than opened her eyes. It was a somewhat peculiar thing that the majority of the victims were killed in that way—more even than were brained by the heavy clubs. They were no respecters of persons, those bloody raiders. Men, women and children all suffered the same fate, a swift and merciless death, and there was no attempt made to take any prisoners. Kill, kill, kill, was the one thought which seemed to animate the attackers until they believed that no single soul was left alive, and it was only then that they began to collect all the food they could find and any little trifles which happened to appeal to them.

The leader of the raid had taken no part in the slaughter. He remained in the centre of the square giving silent directions until he was told that the last of the villagers was dead. Then he moved across to where one of the bowls which had been used to catch the blood of the men executed on the previous day still lay beneath the look-out tree and picked it up. That was the only thing he took away with him from the village.

Mabel Hillier had been sleeping soundly when that double hoot, the signal for the attack, had been given. She wakened to see a dark form outlined in the moonlight which shone through her open door and for a moment believed that Abu had returned ahead of the Commissioner and risked his life to comfort her with the news that deliverance was at hand. But soon she realised that whoever it was who stood there watching her was far too broad and massive for Abu, and the horrible thought flashed through her mind that it was Kofi who had come for her, that his inflamed passions would no longer be denied.

It would be waste of breath to scream, she thought, for he was all-powerful and, even if her cries brought anybody to her help, he would easily be able to invent some excuse and assert his right to visit his prisoner at any hour of the day or night which might seem convenient. Ever since the death of her husband she had carried, concealed on her person, a little phial of deadly poison, taken from the medicine chest, which she meant to make use of as a last resource. She held it ready in her hand now but would not take it until the last possible moment because of her child. She could not make up her mind to kill her own son, although she had often thought of it, and dreaded what might happen to him when she was gone.

She was still hesitating, wondering what it was best for her to do, praying for guidance, when the shadow left the doorway and advanced towards her bed in a stooping attitude. Her nerves could stand the strain no longer. One wild shriek she gave, a shriek of utter terror, and as her scream broke the silence the figure of her enemy sprang. Long fingers of unbelievable strength encircled her neck and for a second she struggled helplessly. Then her throat was torn out and she knew no more. She had gone to join her husband in another world.

And then her murderer did a curious thing; for her baby boy, instead of being ruthlessly slaughtered as every other child in the village had been, was picked up and carried tenderly out of the hut. A moment later a double hoot, like the hoot of an owl, was heard for the second time that night and the attackers began to stream away from the village. The screams of Mabel Hillier's child grew faint and ever fainter as he was carried further into the forest, until at last they ceased altogether and silence descended on that scene of blood. The prophecy of the missionary had been in great part fulfilled.

CHAPTER V

THE GRAVES IN THE FOREST

WHEN ABU LEFT the hut of his mistress with her note for the Commissioner he slipped as silently as a shadow past the sleeping dwellings and so out into the darkness of the forest. Once he thought his flight was going to be discovered, for a dog began to bark at him loudly and persistently and for a time his heart stood still; but at a volley of harsh curses from its master in a nearby hut it slunk away and its barkings turned to low, menacing growls. That was the only fright Abu got before the shelter of the forest was reached and he felt that, for the time being at any rate, he was safe from detection or pursuit.

The darkness was intense and he had great difficulty in finding his way, even along the well-worn track which he was following. Also he was considerably frightened, not only at the possibility of encountering some marauding beast of the forest intent on securing a meal but also of the less tangible, though equally deadly, spirits which he devoutly believed roamed the woods at night. The only way he could retain sufficient courage to go on was by reminding himself continually that it was all for the sake of the mistress whom he loved and that if only he could win through to Dualla it would be him, Abu, who had saved her and her child.

After he had been travelling for some hours the moon rose and a certain amount of light filtered through the trees, which made the going easier; but even then it was far from simple. The great fallen trunks which barred the way every here and there were bad enough in the day-time; at night they were a thousand times more difficult to negotiate. The rushing streams with their natural sunken bridges were a terror in the broad light of day; in the darkness they were a very real danger. But Abu struggled bravely on and by the time dawn was beginning to break had put a longish distance between himself and the village.

But he did not rest. Without a break almost, with no more to sustain him than an occasional mouthful from his scanty stock of coarse flour, he journeyed on throughout the day, and he had travelled for nearly twenty hours on end before it was borne in upon him that sleep could no longer be denied, that if he did not rest for a few hours he would overstrain himself and his object never be accomplished.

With this thought in his mind he looked carefully about him for a suitable tree, scrambled up it with extraordinary agility for a man of his age, and settled himself down in the fork formed by two big limbs. For safety's sake he unwound his loin cloth and bound it firmly round himself and one of the branches, then he composed himself gratefully to sleep, secure in the thought that he would not tumble from the tree, and that the chances of his falling victim to any wild animal were minimised.

The night passed uneventfully and Abu slid down from his airy perch, stiff but refreshed by sleep, at an early hour. There was no sign of any pursuit and very soon he was on his way once more. All that day and until an hour after dark he hurried on, then chose a fork in another tree for his second night's rest. And so it went on, day after day—long hours of feverish traveling, alternating with nights of broken sleep amongst the branches—until late one evening a weary and emaciated figure staggered painfully up the steps of the verandah and fell senseless at the feet of the astonished Commissioner.

The Landeshauptmann called a servant, then stooped and, lifting the unconscious figure in his arms, laid Abu on a long wicker chair. A stiff glass of spirits soon had the effect of opening his eyes but, though it was plain to see that he was desperately anxious to communicate some news, not one word would the Commissioner listen to until his unexpected visitor had been fed and looked after. As soon as he was stronger he was led back to the verandah and allowed to present his scrap of paper, sadly crumpled and so dreadfully dirty as to be almost indecipherable.

The Landeshauptmann smoothed it out as well as he was able and with great difficulty succeeded in reading the few words scrawled on it.

"Martin murdered. Prisoner. Help. Mabel Hillier."

He repeated the words aloud, then looked up and began to question the man, who had remained standing In front of him.

"Your name?" he demanded in his terse official manner.

"Abu is my name."

"You have brought this message from Mrs. Hillier?"

"I have brought the message. I have travelled or many days."

"Sit; and tell me all you know."

Abu sank gratefully down on the floor of the verandah, for he was very tired, and told all he knew, helped by an occasional question interpolated by the Commissioner. He spoke briefly of their journey to the village, though making much of Mabel Hillier's care of him. He told of Kofi's rising, of the murder of the elders, of the trial and death of the missionary, of the woman's fear of what the fate might be that was in store for her— a fate worse perhaps than death itself. He spoke of how he had at last consented, much against his will owing to his reluctance to leave his mistress, to be the bearer of her message, and told in a few words the story of his return to Dualla, making light of the dangers he had faced, the fatigues he had undergone, and the hardships he had borne. He finished by imploring the Commissioner, on his knees, to hasten to the rescue of Mabel Hillier, offering himself as guide.

The Landeshauptmann was in a quandary. It came to him with startling suddenness that Mabel Hillier meant a great deal to him—more, in fact, than anything else in the world—and he was vastly surprised. It had never occurred to him before that he was in love with her, but now he knew it. What on earth was he to do? She was at the mercy of a dirty, unscrupulous native miles away from the nearest white man. He must do something, but by now his letter telling how he had refused to undertake any official responsibility if Hillier insisted on dragging his wife with him into the interior was in the hands of his chief. It was impossible for him to go to this far-distant, unknown village. It was impossible for him to leave his post, even for a day—and such a trip would entail many days journeying. Trouble was brewing in more than one place and he must be on the spot to direct things or the smouldering fires would inevitably break out into flame. And then it was that he thought of Treverrick.

Treverrick, as may be guessed, was a Cornishman. He was also a mighty elephant hunter, and two days before the sudden and unexpected appearance of Abu, a letter had reached Dualla announcing his immediate arrival there. He and the Commissioner were old friends and the latter knew that he could rely upon him to help him out of his difficulty. He should arrive some time next day and must be persuaded to start out at once to the rescue of Mabel Hillier. Nobody knew more about the country, he had a large company of men in his service—almost a little army—and the promise of any out-of-the-way kind of excitement was sure to appeal to him.

So well did the Landeshauptmann know his friend, and so sure of him was he, that he considered himself justified in telling Abu that a great hunter and warrior would arrive at Dualla on the following day and that within thirty-six hours he should start on his return journey in the capacity of guide to the rescuers of his mistress. In the meantime he must possess his soul in patience and rest himself in order to gather strength for the task before him.

As things turned out his confidence in Treverrick was not misplaced. Just before the Commissioner sat down to his mid-day meal the Cornishman hove in sight at the head of his men. The two friends greeted each other warmly and sat down to eat together but, though they had not met for some years and had much to say to each other the matter of Mabel Hillier's deliverance was the only subject to be broached. The story was told at length, from the time of the arrival of the missionary at Dualla to the sudden appearance of Abu, and no item was omitted. The promise of excitement alone would have been sufficient to make Treverrick eager to undertake the long journey, and added to this there was not only the compelling duty of going to the help of a woman in distress but he sensed that it was something more than an ordinary interest which animated his friend in the case of this particular woman, although such a possibility had not been deliberately suggested by either of them.

The elephant hunter had a great and abiding affection for the Commissioner and welcomed the opportunity of helping him. He was able to guess the agony of mind that his friend must be suffering, tied down to his post as he was, unable to go to the assistance of the woman he loved. He thanked whatever powers had decreed that he should arrive at Dualla at so opportune a moment, and the look of gratitude which he received when he announced his intention of starting for the interior on the following morning was in itself ample reward for what he had undertaken.

And so it came about that for the second time in a few weeks a long cavalcade might have been seen winding its slow way out of Dualla at half-past four in the morning and disappearing into the depths of the primeval forest.

Of Treverrick's journey it will be unnecessary to say anything. Everyone of his party was an experienced traveller and they travelled light, so that good progress was made from the start, though never good enough to satisfy the impatient Abu, who did not fail to complain every time a halt was called. Forced marches were the order of the day and, as Mabel Hillier had calculated, the journey was completed in considerably less than half the time occupied when she had done it with her husband. One evening Abu announced that they had arrived to within two hours' march of the village and Treverrick accordingly ordered a halt considerably earlier than was his custom. Nobody was more anxious than he to get there, but he considered it unwise to do so by night. There can be no doubt that he was absolutely right in taking the precautions that he did, though, if only he had pressed on, the rest of this story might never have had to be written.

The march was resumed an hour before daylight, but before they started Treverrick addressed his men. He insisted upon absolute silence being maintained after the first hour's journey and instructed the leaders, whom he had selected specially for that position, to go warily and report any sign of natives. He told them why they had come on this long march and promised that if Mabel Hillier was rescued they would be in high favour with the Commissioner as well as with himself. He also told them that they should receive double payment.

More and more cautiously they advanced as the village was approached, but never a sign of a native did they see. This worried Treverrick and he began to fear that a trap had been set for him, that the villagers had got to know of his arrival and were lying in ambush, and he gave orders to go more carefully than ever. At last Abu suggested that he should go on ahead to see if he could find out anything, and this the elephant hunter agreed to. A halt was called and the old native slipped silently away while Treverrick sat on a fallen log to wait with what patience he could command.

Well within the hour Abu returned and told his tale. He had crept up to the edge of the clearing in which the Village stood, he said, and seen what we already know of. The huts had been torn down and no living thing moved, where so short a time before all had been bustle, but a few dogs. For some little time Abu had lain watching, then, without quitting the shelter of the forest, he had returned to make his report.

Treverrick decided that the village must have been deserted for some reason and pressed on. In spite of what Abu had told him the sight which greeted his eyes when he emerged into the clearing half an hour later came as a shock. Never was there such a scene of confusion. Not a hut was left standing, not a living soul was there to be seen. He walked across the market-place to what had been the largest building and it was only when he reached it that he received some vague intimation of what had occurred. An arm, well-shaped and obviously a woman's, protruded from the remains of the hut. He called some men to pull the timbers aside and soon they were able to drag out the body of Kofi's bride, and the sight of her ripped-out throat turned Treverrick sick.

"Search amongst the ruins of the other huts," he ordered, and as he spoke saw a movement almost at his feet. "No," he corrected, "move the rest of this one first."

It took only a few moments to do as he said and presently Kofi was lying on the ground in front of him. He was alive and half conscious, but if Treverrick had not been quick he would have looked his last upon the light in that moment for, with a snarl of rage, Abu leapt at him with knife raised high. But he found his arm held in a grip of steel and Kofi's life was saved.

"Who is this man? Why do you wish to kill him?" Treverrick demanded.

"He is Kofi, the murderer; Kofi, the persecutor of my mistress; Kofi, the seducer of women."

"Do not be a fool then. Let him live. There is a fate in store for him far worse, if I am not greatly mistaken than death at your hands. Be patient."

It was not long before Kofi had come to his senses sufficiently to understand what was going on. The blow from the club on the back of the head which had stunned him had been a severe one, but his skull was remarkably thick, and it is possible that the force of the blow, delivered as it was through a hole torn in the side of the hut, may have been slightly broken by some obstruction in the opening. A rapid examination by Treverrick satisfied him that there was no fracture and as the man had already recovered his full senses, he proceeded to question him forthwith.

"Tell me exactly what has happened here." he ordered.

But Kofi could tell him practically nothing. He had been fast asleep, he said, when somebody had entered his hut. Who it was or what village the man belonged to he had been unable to see in the darkness, but he knew instinctively that he was an enemy. He had sprung to his feet and seized his spear, but before he had an opportunity of using it something had hit him on the back of the head, and the next thing he remembered was being pulled out of the ruins of his hut a few minutes ago.

Treverrick had no alternative but to believe this story, unsatisfactory though it was, so he set two men to guard the prisoner, whom he intended to take back to the coast with him to answer for the murder of the missionary, and went off to see what else had been discovered. His men had been working hard and the ruins of all but one or two of the huts had been searched. Dead bodies in plenty they had found, of men, women and children all plenty they had found, of men, women and children all of them either strangled, brained, or with their throats torn out, but no sign of any living being. Kofi was the only human creature who had escaped with his life.

Soon after Treverrick joined the workers they uncovered the remains of Mabel Hillier and he knew for certain that what he had been fearing for sometime was only too true, that he had come too late to save her. They searched high and low for some trace of the child but in vain. It must be somewhere, the white man argued to himself, and to make absolutely certain that it should not be over-looked he ordered the remnants of the huts to be carried piece by piece into the centre of the market-place and burned.

Evening was fast approaching by the time this task was accomplished but no sign of the baby had been found and Treverrick was forced at last to give up all hope of finding any. His last care before camping that night, which he did at a little distance from what remained of the village, was to bury Mabel Hillier at the side of her husband, for to carry her body all the way to the coast coffinless would have been an impossibility. That last rite performed he sat down at the door of his tent, as was his invariable custom, and entered up the events of the day in his diary.

There was nothing further to be done but, before starting on the return journey, Treverrick sent out men in every direction to see if they could pick up any trace of the raiders. It was Abu who made the only discovery of note. Caught in a thorny bush he had found the greater part of a baby's garment, which he brought to the white man with the tears streaming down his face. Treverrick put it carefully away and that was the only relic which he brought back with him from his unsuccessful expedition.

The journey back to Dualla was uneventful and in course of time the Commissioner and his friend sat down once more together for their mid-day meal on the verandah. Treverrick had arrived only an hour before and had had the unpleasant job of telling the Landeshauptmann all that had occurred. He had been prepared for the news by a letter which the elephant-hunter had sent on ahead of him by a fast runner, which made the task rather less hard than it would otherwise have been, but both men were much relieved when the tale had been told. By the time their meal was ready the Commissioner had quite recovered himself to all outward appearances and was ready to talk about the raid.

"I cannot understand who can have done it," he was saying. "There are one or two tribes who are dissatisfied and from whom I have rather been expecting trouble, but none of them live in that direction. As far as I know, and I am kept extremely well informed, none of the people anywhere near the country you have just visited have made any complaints and perfect harmony exists between the various villages. Only last week one of my best men returned from a long trip round that part and he assured me that all was quiet. It is quite incomprehensible."

"I know nothing about the state of feeling existing between your people," Treverrick rejoined, "but there are other things connected with this business that have puzzled me for days. I have some good trackers amongst my men, some of the finest in the whole continent, but not one sign of the marauders could they find once the forest was reached and the tracks in the village itself were too confused to be of any use. And then again, look at the way these people were killed. I personally examined every body found and not one of them had been speared. A few had apparently been strangled, considerably more than half had had their throats torn out—a thing which, in a long and varied experience of this God-forsaken country, I have never seen before and trust I may never see again—and the rest had been brained. As far as I could judge no women had been carried off and no bodies either, unless it was bodies of the attackers, and you know as well as I do that cannibalism is pretty general after such a show as that and that they were more likely to leave the corpses of their friends behind them than those of their enemies. As you say, it is quite incomprehensible."

All that afternoon and until far into the night they talked the matter over, striving to find some solution of the mystery. Treverrick had his trackers up one after the other and cross-questioned them, but all to no purpose. They were as puzzled as he was himself. Abu was no better and Kofi stuck firmly to the tale he had told in the first instance. Try as they would they could find no explanation and eventually turned in without having got any nearer to the truth than they were when they started.

On the following day the Commissioner had much to do. It was necessary for him to write a long and detailed report of all that had happened for the information of the chiefs of his Department and he did not find it easy. The more he thought of the death of Mabel Hillier the more fully he realised how much she had come to mean to him, even though he had done no more than speak to her a few times. As far as doing his duty as Commissioner was concerned his conscience was clear, thanks to the timely arrival and help of Treverrick, but that failed to ease the ache of his heart. Chiefs of

Departments, too, were unreasonable beings who expected their underlings to find some explanation for everything that might occur in the districts under their immediate charge, and he had an uncomfortable feeling that they would not be satisfied with his failure to find a solution to the mystery of the raid. It was quite possible that they would order him to go and make further inquiries on the spot and he comforted himself with the thought that if they did, it would at least give him an opportunity of visiting Mabel Hillier's grave.

It took him all that day and part of the next to finish his report to his satisfaction and then it was time for him to turn his attention to Kofi. It may be remembered that the Commissioner was a hot-tempered individual and nothing would have given him more satisfaction than to shoot the man off hand. But he was eminently just and the native, who was by now quite recovered, was given every opportunity to defend himself.

The court sat publicly in the open air outside the house of the Landeshauptmann. He, as chief magistrate, sat in a cane chair on the verandah and a large crowd of natives were grouped in a semi-circle in front of him. The case proved to be a very simple one. Abu told what he had seen and heard prior to his starting on his lonely journey to Dualla. Mabel Hillier's message announcing the murder of her husband and her own detention was read and explained. The assassination of the elders was recounted at length. And then it was Kofi's turn.

As once before he stood, unarmed, straight and fearless. As once before he answered his accusers proudly and without a tremor in his voice. And he admitted the truth of every word they said. Hillier had died, he said, as he deserved to die in punishment for a sin than which he himself had said there was no greater. He, Kofi, had kept the woman a prisoner and had intended to marry her, but never had he done her any injury. Who had attacked the village or where the child was he did not know.

"I have lost everything," he concluded. "I, who was a sariki and dreamed great dreams, am a prisoner. Do with me what you will. I have spoken."

The Commissioner could do no other than feel for the man after he had stated the case in the way he did. But no considerations of sympathy must be allowed to obtrude where his duty was concerned. Kofi had taken life as, according to his lights, he had the right to do, not for the sake of committing murder. He had done no injury to the woman. Therefore, unless a higher court reversed the

Commissioner's decision, he should not die, but for the rest of his days he should be a prisoner of the white men and work at their bidding.

And so the last part of the missionary's prophecy was fulfilled, for Kofi was cast down from his high estate and the rest of his days were spent in sorrow and affliction.

CHAPTER VI

JOHN PASSINGER—MILLIONAIRE

MABEL HILLIER had been the only daughter of a yeoman named Humberlayne. Her elder brother, William, was killed in the hunting field some years before her unfortunate wedding. The younger, Francis, married the daughter of a clergyman, who bore him one son, also named Francis, and these were the only Humberlaynes in existence. In due course a notice appeared in The Times and a few other papers announcing little more than the bare fact that the Reverend Martin Hillier and his wife, Mabel, had been killed by natives while engaged on missionary work out in West Africa, and one journal, which may have been short of copy, went so far as to give a short sketch of his life—from which it appeared that he was far too good for this world and that heaven was the only suitable residence for a creature so perfect in every way as was the Reverend Martin Hillier.

Unfortunately the general public is not vastly interested in missionaries—the form of the horses entered for one of the classics which was due to be run shortly after the news of Hillier's death reached London was considered of far greater importance by the ordinary man in the street—and it is doubtful whether a dozen persons beyond those immediately interested troubled to read the obituary. The Commissioner, as he had anticipated might be the case, received orders to go to the scene of the murder, but he found out nothing and in due course returned to his native land, where he eventually married a buxom German lady, became the father of a numerous family and, before he quitted this world of sin, rose to a high position in his chosen career. Treverrick went out elephant hunting once too often and died a very untidy though probably painless death beneath the knees of a wounded tusker. What became of Abu is not known. He left Dualla one fine day without warning and was never heard of again. Kofi worked as a convict for thirty years and eventually fell victim to a shark when trying, unsuccessfully, to save a drunken sailor from drowning. Many things can happen in half a century, many changes may take place, and half a century passes between the hour of Mabel Hillier's death and the time at which our story is resumed. Not one of those who were prominent in the first part of it is left alive.

John Passinger was a millionaire. That was no fault of his, for he had never done a stroke of work of any kind that he did not thoroughly enjoy. His father had started life as a boot-black and had somehow or other managed to save up enough money to buy his own box and the utensils necessary to the carrying on of his trade. By the time he was seventeen he had half a dozen boys working for him, and throughout his long life he never once looked back. He invented some special kind of blacking which was no better than any other kind, starved himself to advertise it, and before he was fifty had made his million two or three times over, thanks to Passinger's Perfect Polish. He had married the only daughter of an impoverished baronet, sat in Parliament as the representative of the East End constituency in which he had first seen the light of day, and, much to the annoyance of his wife refused a knighthood. She bore him two children—Marjorie, who was successful in entrapping a duke when she was still in her teens, and John.

Marjorie was never a favourite with her father although she was his firstborn. He was essentially an honest man—outside his business at any rate—and there were certain things against which he set his face very firmly. He had married much above his station, it is true, but he had done so primarily because he was deeply in love with the lady who became his wife and believed, at the time, that his affection was returned. Before she was twenty his only daughter had married a duke, with an unenviable past, over fifty years older than herself, and openly boasted that she had done so for the sake of his title and for no other reason. Old Passinger, disgusted though he was, made no attempt to stop the wedding and gave her a very handsome settlement but he never spoke to her again, and, when he died, left her not one single penny. It is more than probable that he would have treated his wife, who was largely instrumental in engineering the match, in precisely the same way, as far as his will was concerned, had she not been so accommodating as to save him the trouble by predeceasing him.

The case of his son, John, was quite different. John was as honest as his father and, though he was no worker in the generally accepted sense and could not be persuaded to take any interest in the business, he was far from being a waster. At the University he had not shone as a scholar, but neither had he disgraced himself, and his tutors had regarded him as a conscientious plodder. In the field of athletics he had made a great name and carried off a double blue, which pleased his father infinitely more than if he had won the Newdigate or been Senior Wrangler. He was a fine shot with both gun and rifle—an unusual combination—and a fearless horseman. Old Passinger worshipped him and his allowance was enormous; but John did not throw it away. He was generous to a degree, entertained his friends lavishly, and was always ready and eager to help a lame dog over a stile. But he did not give diamond bracelets to engaging ladies who were walking advertisements for tooth-paste, and though he never bought any thing that was not of the best and never stinted himself in any way, he could not be accused of extravagance for a man of his wealth and made a point of seeing that he got full value for his money.

In appearance John Passinger missed being striking without being commonplace. He was no wavy-haired Apollo, but he had a fine, open countenance, very bright blue eyes set wide apart, and rather crisp brown hair which he kept cut unbecomingly short. In height he was well under the six feet and looked less than he actually was owing to the great breadth of his shoulders. A very fair idea of his character may be gained from the fact that children and dogs adored him.

It was to this young man, then, that old Passinger bequeathed every penny he possessed when his time came. He left him, in addition to his millions, a huge house in Berkshire, another in London, a castle in Scotland, a whole fleet of motorcars, and the very last word in yachts. That would have been enough, surely, for most men, but John wanted something more exciting. He was not satisfied to sit on a shooting-stool with a couple of loaders behind him and slaughter pheasants however high they might come, and the same applied to driven partridges and grouse. It gave him no pleasure to be led within range of a stag by a stalker without, probably, catching so much as a glimpse of it until the moment came for him to press the trigger. He had twice gone for long trips in search of big game, which may have spoiled him for the kind of sport to be found in England, and had been thrilled and, incidentally, killed specimens of everything that he wanted to kill; but even that had palled after a time. He longed for something new, yearned to do some thing that nobody else had done.

Not long before the death of his father he had conceived the idea of setting up a private menagerie on a huge scale and had made a commencement by laying out a considerable tract of ground in the most up-to-date manner and purchasing a few animals. But his great ambition was to do his own trapping, and this he had been unable to think of seriously owing to his unwillingness to leave his father, who for some years had been in a very weak state of health. Now that the old man had passed away there was nothing to keep him in England, and he intended to start on a lengthy expedition as soon as decency would permit and so fulfill the desire which was rapidly becoming an obsession with him.

The chief things he had to decide were what animals he was going in search of and where to look for them. At first, as was perhaps natural, he thought of lions, but soon decided that they were too "common". Then he dallied with the thought of rhinoceros, of snakes, of giraffes, and a dozen others. One day a friend whom he had taken into his confidence suggested chimpanzees, and it was that which gave him the great idea and finally decided him. He would go after gorillas.

So rare were gorillas in captivity that Passinger had never seen one. To be absolutely truthful, although he knew from pictures what the general appearance of the creature was, that was all he actually did know. He had some vague idea that they were about eight feet high and roamed the forests of Borneo, and it was not until he read books about them that he learned how far from the truth he was. The first thing the books taught him was that even the largest gorilla seldom exceeded five and a half feet in height and that they were found in West Africa. Having learned so much his next care was to find out how best to set about the work of getting to the most suitable part of that country, how to obtain the necessary permit to trap wild animals there, and how to secure the services of an experienced man to accompany him—for he was far too sensible to imagine for one moment that there would be any use in his going out alone or to expect to be successful in trapping gorillas or anything else without the assistance of somebody who knew something about it.

In this last he was remarkably lucky. He had a friend who was one of the curators of a famous natural history museum to which he had presented a large collection of duplicate heads of animals shot by himself, which had been considered of sufficient importance to become known far and wide as the Passinger Collection. To this friend, whom he had come to know as a result of that presentation, John Passinger had hurried hot-foot and he came nobly to the rescue. It so happened that a short time before an acquaintance of his, a man whom he had first met in the house of a famous taxidermist, had returned home from a trip through the very country in which Passinger was interested. He had been sent out by a German Zoological Society in a fruitless endeavour to trap an okapi and had spent two years in the interior.

This man, Passinger's friend assured him, was one of the best trappers of big game that the world had ever known. He had been engaged at different times by practically every large circus proprietor and half the best-known Zoological Societies to collect for them, and the curator believed that it was he who had caught and shipped two gorillas over to Hamburg some years before, though about this he was not altogether sure. The important thing was that he was disengaged and there was no doubt he would consent to go out with John Passinger if he wanted him.

Nothing could have suited our friend better and within ten minutes of hearing these particulars he had dragged the protesting curator away from his stuffed beasts, bundled him into his car, and was driving considerably faster than the regulations permitted to the address of the trapper whose name, he had learned, was Dick Fearless—a remarkably appropriate cognomen, as Passinger was to discover before he was many months older.

They found the man whom they sought sitting in a deep armchair with his feet on the mantelpiece and a huge calabash pipe in his mouth. He rose as they entered and greeted his visitors with a friendly smile. He was an almost alarmingly big man, not less than six feet in height and broad in proportion, with a shock of unruly red hair and a huge beard of the same colour. His eyes, like Passinger's, were of a strikingly bright blue, and there was a twinkle in them which told of a well developed sense of humour. Nonetheless it was plain to see that they might well become hard and menacing if the occasion arose and that Fearless was not a man to be trifled with.

He slapped the curator, who was rather a weedy individual, with such heartiness on the back that it was some moments before he could recover sufficient breath to introduce his friend. When at last he did manage to do so the trapper's eyes lit up with pleasure and he extended a large and hairy hand.

"Passinger?" he said. "Surely not the John Passinger who scored that last magnificent winning try in the Varsity match three years ago?" and, on being informed that he was indeed that individual: "By Jove, I am proud to meet you, sir. That was the finest bit of work I have seen since MacGregor dodged the whole field in the ninety-nine International after nearly braining me with his great foot when I tried to tackle him low."

"Are you Fearless, the three-quarter then? Dreadnought Fearless, as we boys used to call you?"

And so two famous Rugby players met and for nearly an hour the little curator was forgotten. It was a thirst induced by incessant talking that at last brought them back to the present, away from the football fields of years gone by. Fearless walked across to the sideboard and it was while he was busy with a syphon of soda that the little man ventured to remind Passinger of the reason for his visit. After that they came to business and it was not long before all was settled to the entire satisfaction of everybody concerned.

By then it was getting late, so the two footballers went off to dine and spend the evening in company while the curator, the cause of their coming together, who had hastily and emphatically refused an invitation to join them, hurried away to his modest abode, thankful to escape from the company of two men who, as far as he could judge, were never really happy unless they were pitting their wits against the ferocious beasts of the forest or rolling each other in the mud on a football field.

Passinger found the next few weeks very strenuous. He would never have believed how much there was to arrange, and although Fearless took the vast majority of the work off his shoulders and provided lists of everything that it would be necessary for them to take with them, he found his time very fully occupied. It was only then that he realised wholly what a terrible muddle he must inevitably have made of things but for the assistance and experience of the trapper. The more he saw of him the more he liked him, and his liking was returned. Both men frequently blessed the powers which had decreed that they should cross each others paths.

There was one factor in the life of John Passinger which has not yet been mentioned—to wit, the inevitable girl. As has already been said, those ladies who were, or hoped to be, in the public eye had no attractions for him. The well-rehearsed flashings of their pearly teeth, the long-practised play of their beautifully made-up eyes, left him cold. Neither was he intrigued by the equally sophisticated, if less obvious, enticements of the girls of a better class whom designing mothers delighted to leave him alone with in cosy boudoirs or cleverly-shaded conservatories. He never entered a drawing-room, never graced an at-home or a ball with his presence, if he could possibly avoid it. He infinitely preferred the clean air of the country to the vitiated atmosphere of town, and spent as much time in it as he could.

But it cannot be expected that a young man in his early twenties can have travelled even so far along the road of life without having conceived something more than a mere platonic friendship for some girl. It would not have been natural, and John Passinger was essentially natural. Two years before he met Fearless he had been hunting in Leicestershire and had one day been able to render some assistance to a girl who had taken a rather nasty toss. She was not hurt, luckily, beyond a few bruises and considerable shock, but Passinger had had to gallop over three fields before he had succeeded in catching her horse, and, by the time he had brought it back, to think of catching up with hounds again was out of the question.

"I have spoiled your run for you," were her first words. "I shall never forgive myself."

"My worthy steed and I have both had quite enough of it," he had replied, "and it is always a pleasure, when the opportunity arises, to help a lady in distress. Are you sure that you are quite all right?"

She set his mind at rest on that point by placing her foot in his hand and springing lightly into the saddle.

"I am always falling off," she smiled. "I am getting quite used to it. That is the worst of having to ride such old crocks."

The short winter day was drawing to a close, so they turned their horses' heads for home, having found that the little hotel at which Passinger was stopping was close to her father's house, and were soon chatting like old friends. In an hour they had arrived at the village and the girl made as though to bid her companion good-bye, but he insisted on seeing her to her door, and she raised no objection. It was opened by a tall, pleasant-faced, elderly man in a suit of rough tweeds which had seen much service.

"Hallo, Mary, my dear," he greeted the girl. "Had another tumble? You'll be breaking your neck one of these days."

"Yes; I suppose I shall," she replied with a laugh "but not to-day. Goodness knows what time I should have got home if this gentleman had not given up his run to catch my recalcitrant steed. You must thank him nicely for me and give him a drink."

"My thanks he has already. The drink is only a matter of a very few moments. Perhaps you would be kind enough to introduce us, you ill-behaved baggage."

"Can't do it, Daddy. You must do your own introducing. No

names have been mentioned since we met."

The introductions were soon effected and a minute later John Passinger was following the Reverend Francis Humberlayne into his study while his daughter disappeared to change her muddy clothes. He did not stay for more than a few minutes, but when he left it was with a promise to come to dinner on the following night and spend a quiet evening.

The acquaintance thus formed soon developed into friendship, and, in due time, into love. No word of their feelings had passed the lips of either of them but the girl was sure in her heart that John Passinger loved her and equally sure that he would speak in his own good time. She was quite content to wait and carry out her simple duties at her father's vicarage until that time should come, and she had a strong suspicion when she read of the death of old man Passinger in the paper that it would not be long delayed.

Mary Humberlayne's lover had not failed to keep her informed of his plans but it was not until a week before he was due to sail for the West Coast that he could find time to journey up to the little Leicestershire village to see her. It was a beautiful afternoon in early autumn when he arrived and was met at the station by the girl herself in the little governess cart which was the only conveyance her father could afford. They drove through the first dusk of evening up the little avenue which led to the old vicarage and found that the vicar had not yet returned from a visit to a sick parishioner; so they wandered out beneath the lime trees in the garden.

There is some subtle charm about a country garden, and especially about a vicarage garden, that cannot be explained. On the evening when John and Mary found themselves alone there that charm was at its strongest. For a long time they paced up and down without a word being spoken, then sank onto a rustic seat. Somehow or other her hand slipped into his, naturally, without either of them having suggested it. And still no word was spoken. But there was a whole world of love and trust in her eyes as they gazed into his and they both knew that there was nobody else who could take the place of either of them.

"Must you go after your horrid gorillas?" she asked at last.

"It is not exactly that I must go, sweetheart," he answered her, "but it is just as well that I should. I shall be quite safe with Fearless. There will be nothing for you to worry about. You know it would hardly do for us to get married so soon after my father's death, and I am sure neither you nor your father would wish it.

What I suggest is that we should keep our engagement to ourselves—by the way, I suppose we are engaged?" he interrupted himself to ask and was hastily and very pleasantly reassured—"that we should keep our engagement to ourselves, then, and tell nobody but your father. When I get back to the coast again, which should be in less than twelve months' time, you could be there to meet me and then we could be married and come home to England together. How does that plan strike you?"

"I am quite content to do whatever you think best, dear," she agreed as she kissed him. "Look; here comes father at last."

"Bother him," muttered John. "I don't mean that exactly but I wish he had given us another half hour. We have only been here for about ten minutes."

Mary glanced at her wristwatch and jumped from the seat.

"We have been here for exactly two hours and a quarter and it is long past supper time. Come along at once and tell father."

The news these two young people had to break to the Reverend Francis Humberlayne did not come as a surprise to that gentleman. He had seen it coming for a long time, as anybody who was not stone blind must have done, and was pleased. He dreaded the thought of losing his daughter, for she had been his right hand for years, but he had heard nothing but good of his prospective son-in-law and her comfort must come before his own. Passinger's millions did not worry him much but he realised the value of money and all the good, as well as harm, that it could do and felt that it was in worthy hands.

So everything was arranged just as John had suggested in the garden, even to Mary's going out to Africa to be married.

"It is strange that you should be going out there," her father said as they sat over breakfast on the following morning just before John left to catch his train. "I can remember my mother telling me of a great-aunt of yours who went to the same country soon after her wedding. Her name was Mabel Hillier, and she and her husband, who was a missionary, and their baby boy were all killed by natives. Things have changed very much since those days," he added hastily, fearing that he had said a rather foolish thing, "and there is no chance of such a tragedy occurring now."

An hour later John Passinger was sitting in the corner of a first-class smoking carriage on his way to London. A week later he was lounging in a deck chair by the side of Dick Fearless on a steamer bound for the west coast of Africa.

The great adventure had started.

CHAPTER VII

THE NEW COMMISSIONER

To THE ACTIVE MAN a long sea voyage becomes painfully monotonous, and both Passinger and Fearless were essentially active. They did their so-many times round the deck religiously every morning and manage thereby to keep themselves in some sort of condition, but It was a poor amount of exercise for men who were accustomed to spend the greater part of their days engaged in some sort of sport—shooting, riding, racquets, football or whatnot. Deck quoits thrilled them but little more than shove-halfpenny would have done and they looked forward eagerly to the day when they would be able to stretch their legs on terra firma once more and get some real man's exercise, if it was only a sharp walk up hill and down dale.

Neither of them were great lovers of the printed page, but Passinger read the more of the two. The boat on which they were boasted a considerable and fairly representative library, and he managed to wade through several volumes dealing with the country he was to spend the following months in before the time came for them to land. The spoken word, however, was far more attractive to him and he delighted to sit and listen while his companion told tales of his experiences while trapping wild animals. He would lounge for hours in a folding chair or tramp up and down the deck without saying a word more than was necessary to keep the ball of anecdotes rolling and he learned a lot. Fearless was a good talker when he could be got to talk, which was only to those by whose friendship he set much store, and he had a happy knack of going into details and explaining at length the why and wherefore of things without breaking the thread of his story or becoming a bore. He gave minute explanations, assisted by many neat plans and diagrams, of how he proposed to set about catching the gorillas, and at the end of a fortnight Passinger felt that his own presence on the trip would be more of a help than a hindrance to the trapper—as he had feared—for he had got a good working idea of the traps that it was proposed to use and the method of employing them.

The little curator who had been responsible for introducing the two men to each other was wrong in his belief that it was by Fearless that two gorillas had been brought to Hamburg some years previously. The gorilla was one of the few animals that Fearless had never trapped or attempted to trap; but he had been in their country and knew as much about them and their habits as most people. He had no doubt in his own mind that he would be able to catch them all right and asserted that he could already have done so more than once if he had thought it worth his while. But he had never been commissioned to procure one of the animals and the chances of getting one alive to Europe or America were so remote that he had not considered the risk worth the necessary expenditure himself. Several attempts had been made and great sums of money had been spent but hardly any of the animals had survived long enough to reach a foreign shore, and the few that had done so had lived on for only a very short time.

The reason generally given for this was the gorilla's extreme delicacy, in spite of its enormous strength, but Fearless had a quite different theory to account for it. His contention was that they had a far greater share of what we are pleased to call human intelligence than is generally supposed, and that it was that, rather than any organic weakness, which was mainly responsible for their deaths when they were taken to a strange country. He went so far as to express his belief that even if the temperature, humidity and atmospheric conditions were exactly the same in the new surroundings to which they were carried as in their native land they would die just the same. Homesickness, he said, was the main factor. Every death might be accounted for by that strange malady commonly known as a broken heart. Certain feelings were as fully developed in gorillas as in man—feelings of pain and feelings of affection; so, according to Fearless, was memory; but they lacked the human power of resigning themselves with stoicism if not with cheerfulness to the inevitable and of putting out of their minds things which they might wish to forget by turning their thoughts into other channels.

"Take a very young gorilla, for instance," he had said one day, "not necessarily a baby but one of an age equivalent to that of a young human child. It is trapped and taken from its parents by strange creatures who must look very terrible to it, it is surrounded constantly by weird, hairless animals, which there can be no possible doubt it fears instinctively, it is deafened by unaccustomed sounds, terrified by unaccustomed smells, and it behaves exactly as a human child would do under similar conditions. It pines for its playmates; it yearns for the familiar forest trees and the platform of sticks amongst the branches that was its home; it longs with a longing that is insupportable for the comfort of its mother's breast and the soothing protection of her encircling arm. And so it dies—of a broken heart. I am not going to deny that in a case like that the natural delicateness of all young creatures may be a contributory cause, but first and foremost it is sorrow which kills it and sorrow, I take it, is the chief feature of heart-break.

"Now take the case of a full-grown female. The strange sights and sounds, the unfamiliar scents, may be less alarming to her than to the younger animal, but her feelings will be quite as bad. She may have young of her own that she knows she will never see again, or a mate whom she loves, or even brothers and sisters—for I am firmly convinced that love amongst these creatures is as great as it is with us. And the same thing applies to the adult male. He will be wondering how his loved ones are getting on without him there to protect and care for them; wondering, perhaps, if his mate will be bothered much by the attentions of some hated rival or, on the other hand, suffering them appreciatively. In either case he will be worrying and, as I have already insisted, he has not the human power of occupying his mind with other things and so forgetting for a time, he has not the human power of resigning himself to his fate. I have spent my life trapping live animals because it is my living and I have no cause to complain. But candidly, Passinger, I loathe it sometimes and myself for doing it."

John Passinger made no reply. He was more than half convinced that his friend's theory was correct and he did not feel altogether comfortable. But the dinner bell reminded him of a very healthy appetite and he had soon forgotten gorillas and their troubles, for the time being at any rate.

At last the morning dawned on which they reached their port of disembarkation and their long voyage was over. Dualla, for it was there that they landed, had changed greatly since the morning on which Hillier and his wife and child had disappeared for the last time into the forest. It had spread enormously, the houses were bigger and better, and the post of Commissioner had become vastly more important.

The successor of the Landeshauptmann who had loved Mabel Hillier was a very different individual in every way. He was filled with a terrific sense of his own importance, he bullied the men under him unmercifully, and he did not confine himself to a single drink after sundown as his predecessor of fifty years before had done.

It was to this overbearing and swollen-headed person that Passinger had perforce to go to present his credentials and have his permit endorsed, and he made the visit as uncomfortable as he could. It was with the greatest possible difficulty that the Englishman refrained from hitting him, hard and with satisfaction, and so creating further trouble for himself. As it was there was a somewhat stormy scene.

"I will not endorse your permit," the German declared. "It is not in order."

"What is the matter with it?"

"It is not in order. That is sufficient."

"I understood that you were endeavouring to explain that it was not in order, but I do not accept your statement that that is a sufficient answer to my perfectly civil and very reasonable question. You will oblige me by telling me in what way it is not in order."

The Commissioner went purple with rage.

"It is not my duty to waste my time explaining things to every wandering, impertinent English man who chooses to visit my town and force himself into my presence. You will leave your permit here and when I see fit it shall be forwarded to the proper quarter for inspection. Go!"

But John Passinger made no move to go. Instead he fumbled in his note-case and produced two papers, one of which he handed to the Landeshauptmann.

"Read that," he said. "It may interest you." The official snatched it from his hand and read. It was an order, signed by a very high German statesman and addressed to the Commissioner, instructing him to afford every assistance to the bearer.

"This should have been given to me before," he stormed. "It regularises your permit to some extent. I will endorse it when I have examined it more carefully and it shall be returned to you in the course of a few days. Now go. I am busy."

But still John Passinger made no move to obey. "And now read this," he said, handing him the other paper. "You should find it even more interesting still."

Again the document was snatched from the Englishman's hand with a muttered curse and the Commissioner began to read. As he grasped the import of what he held in his hand he grew more purple than ever, then as white as a sheet and large drops of perspiration stood out on his brow. The letter he was reading was signed by the same hand as the order and it began "Dear John". It went on to say that complaints had been received concerning the behaviour of the Commissioner of Dualla to both the natives and people visiting the country and begged Passinger to let the writer know exactly how he was received and what was his considered opinion of the Landeshauptmann. He asked him not to do this until he had made all the inquiries he could without divulging his reasons for making them and wound up with expressions of affectionate regard and apologies for giving him so much trouble.

The Commissioner's face was a study and he was so taken aback that for a time he was unable to speak. Before he had recovered himself sufficiently to do so Passinger had forestalled him.

"Suppose you were to sign that permit," he suggested. "I have a lot to see to and I dislike the atmosphere of your office."

It was signed immediately, in silence, and then the Englishman resumed—and it must be admitted that he was enjoying himself.

"I have already formed my opinion of you, Mr. Commissioner, and I have no least doubt that it will be endorsed by the inquiries which I have every intention of making. It is possible that you may be able to soften somewhat the report which I consider it my bounden duty to make before I leave Dualla. That will be in two days' time. In the meanwhile I will send round to you a list of things which I wish to have done or know. I am inclined to think that on the way they are done your future will largely depend."

Then, without another word being spoken, he walked out of the office and betook himself to the house of the head of the Mission Station which had sprung up within the last, comparatively, few years and was now in a flourishing condition.

The Reverend Henry Rogers was an excellent fellow in every sense of the word. He was a good shot, a fine preacher, a keen naturalist, and a man of that broad-mindedness which is found not uncommonly amongst sporting country parsons but seldom amongst other members of the cloth. John Passinger had been at the same University as himself, which may perhaps have accounted in some measure for the warmth of the reception accorded to Fearless and him, though the hospitality of the missionary was notorious. He chuckled with delight over the way in which the Commissioner had been treated by his visitor and opined that it would do him a great deal of good but at the same time warned the two men that they had a very vindictive and, he feared, unscrupulous character to deal with and begged them to be careful. It was quite likely, he said, that the Landeshauptmann would try to get his revenge and, if so, he would probably not be too particular how he got it.

With regard to the main object of their journey he was able to be of great assistance. The fauna of the country had, after his missionary work, been his constant study and delight ever since he had arrived in that part of the world, and he had been able to collect a vast mass of notes and material. Birds and butterflies were what he went in for chiefly and he had very fine collections of both. He explained that he had been tempted to specialise more or less in these because of their greater accessibility, their smaller size and the comparative simplicity of both studying and preserving them. But he had by no means confined himself to the study of those two branches of natural science. Nothing in that line came amiss to him and he had made careful notes of anything of interest which came to his ears. He had been able by degrees to raise a certain amount of enthusiasm amongst the natives and make them understand that things which seemed quite ordinary to them and not worthy of mention might be considered of the greatest importance by white men who had not the opportunity of seeing them.

The result of this was that tales and legends of every kind were brought to him, which he had arranged as well as he could, doing his best to separate the true from the false, the likely from the impossible, and he was now able to tell with a certain amount of exactness the district in which any animal might be expected to be found. With obvious pride he brought out a large, leather bound, hand-written volume and laid it on the table round which the three men had been seated. Then he turned to a neatly-made index and looked up Gorilla.

A great deal of the matter which he had written down with such care was of no value to his visitors; in fact the majority of it only bore out what was already well known to science. Much of the remainder was devoted to tales and legends of the animals, and more particularly of the "bachelors", as they were called, exceptionally large and fierce specimens which were never seen other than alone. But there were one or two things upon which Fearless seized with avidity, and foremost amongst these was a rough sketch-map showing as nearly as possible where gorillas were to be met with and, more important still, whether in large or small numbers.

One circle with a radius of, perhaps, a hundred miles was marked as being particularly thickly populated by the animals and it was for there the trapper decided at once, that they must make. Rogers readily gave his consent to a request that it might be permitted to make a copy or tracing of the map and soon afterwards the two men returned to their quarters carrying the precious volume with them. The tracing was made in duplicate before they turned in for the night, as well as a copy of anything Fearless thought might be useful to them and, for safety, the trapper slept with the book under his pillow.

There was much to be done on the following day and it passed all too quickly. Their first visitor was a man recommended by the missionary as trust worthy, strong, sober, and a suitable person to be appointed head-boy over their carriers. There after there was a constant stream of applicants for jobs. Some of them were sent by the Commissioner, who was thoroughly frightened and doing his utmost now to make a good impression; some came at the instigation of Rogers; some found their way there on their own initiative or drawn by curiosity. And they were of all stages of fitness and unfitness for the various jobs they sought. A gentleman who announced that his name was Sam and demanded the post of cook, had spent some years on a steam-boat and knew a few words of English, though most of them were unintelligible and the rest quite unprintable. His assurance that he was "a . . . good cook and could make a palatable dish out of any . . . thing they . . . well liked to give him" was accepted with reserve but, as there were no other applicants for the job, he got it.

Before dusk the last of the long procession had been interviewed and engaged or otherwise and the weary men felt justified in taking an hour's rest. But they were not destined to be left in peace. Barely had they settled down before a messenger arrived with an invitation to dine from the Commissioner. Apart from the fact that he knew this would mean a drunken orgy and, probably, the introduction of native women into the proceedings, Passinger had no intention of becoming friendly, even outwardly, with that gentleman and sent back a curt refusal. Half an hour later the Commissioner himself arrived, begging them to reconsider their decision; but his longing glances at a bottle of whiskey which stood on the table were ignored and he was sent about his business, thirsty as ever and with the same answer as before.

Only another twenty minutes had passed before Henry Rogers appeared, full of apologies for disturbing them but with some additional facts about gorillas, which he had overlooked on the ditional facts about gorillas, which he had overlooked on the previous night and thought might be useful, and a pressing invitation to eat their evening meal at the Mission house. In spite of their weariness the missionary was welcomed and his invitation gladly accepted, but by the time he had left them it was too late to think of resting any more. They had comfortable time to spruce themselves up a bit before strolling slowly across to their host's dwelling, and that was about all.

As they sat talking on the verandah after supper Passinger bethought him of what his prospective father-in-law had said at the breakfast table on the morning he had left the little Leicestershire village where the only girl in the world was waiting for news of him. It was just possible, he thought, that the missionary might know the story and be able to amplify the somewhat meagre statement of Mr. Humberlayne.

"Yes, indeed, I can tell you all about it," he said when the question was put to him. "This mission, the Hillier Mission, is named after the husband of the lady about whom you are inquiring. Humberlayne was a contemporary of mine at Keble and I know his family well and all about them, though I have been out of touch with him for years now. Mrs. Hillier's name before she was married was Mabel Humberlayne and she had two brothers, one of whom was christened Francis and the other, I think, William. William, if that was his name, was killed in the hunting field. Francis married and became the father of one son, who was also christened Francis, and is our mutual friend. As you know, he followed in the footsteps of his maternal grandfather and entered the Church. There you have the relationship explained in detail.

"Martin Hillier, who married our Francis Humberlayne's aunt, was an extraordinarily good man. Soon after his wedding he gave up everything to come out here and his wife insisted on accompanying him. Not only that but she refused, when he went into the interior, to allow him to go alone, insisting that her place was at his side. The good that he did was wonderful, and he had made enormous strides towards the christianising of his chosen locality when an unexpected rising, which would never have occurred had the Commissioner of those days been a capable man, undid all his work. He died striving to protect his wife and child, and so much did the natives think of them, in spite of the fact that they murdered them, that they buried them side by side and set up the symbol of the cross which they knew they worshipped over their graves.

"What nobody was ever able to find out, however, was what became of their child, who was at that time only a few months old; but that all happened fifty years ago and if it was not killed something would very surely have been heard of it by now. It is curious that you should be so specially interested in that story, because the scene of the murder was the village you found marked on my map last night in the middle of the best gorilla country and suggested as your headquarters. You should certainly find the graves if you go there because I have heard that somebody caused the wooden crosses of the natives to be replaced by stone ones soon after they were found."

"You say that nothing was ever heard of the child. Is there any possibility of its having escaped with its life, been brought up by the savages, and turned native?"

"Not the very slightest I should say or some rumours of it must most surely have got about. When the government expedition was sent to the village to inquire into the murders immediately on news of them being received, they found that it had been attacked and utterly overwhelmed. There was no living soul left to tell the tale of what had happened and so the perpetrators of the crime were never brought to justice, never punished for their great sin in this world. Neither, as far as I know, was it ever discovered who it was who had slaughtered the inhabitants. For many years the village was deserted, but about a decade ago some wanderers who passed that way took a fancy to the spot and rebuilt it. It is of some size now, I believe, but that you will find out for yourselves soon I have no doubt."

"A very sad story, Mr. Rogers," said Fearless.

"A very sad story indeed," the missionary agreed. "It is terrible to think that a man who devoted his whole life to the care of his fellow creatures, who went about amongst the savages risking every sort of disease as well as other dangers to heal their bodies no less than their souls whose one great delight was to serve others and, above all, his beloved wife, should be thus ruthlessly cut off in the very prime of his life. Never was there a better man born than Martin Hillier, whose name we immortalise in our Mission. And if only his wife had listened to the prayers of her devoted husband and not insisted on accompanying him, she and her son might have been alive now to carry on the great work which he began."

It is thus that the passage of years covers up and transforms the weaknesses and wickedness of some while at the same time it brings into prominence those of others. Hillier was glorified; his wife was condemned; the man who truly loved her was despised. And so the pages that we call History are written.

CHAPTER VIII

NGANDA

TWO DAYS LATER they started. The Commissioner had done all that had been required of him and Passinger had to admit that he had done it well. On the evening before his departure he went to see him and explained that he had written two letters to the high German official who was his friend. One of these, which merely stated that the Landeshauptmann had been very helpful when once he knew who it was who required his assistance, would go by the next mail; the other, giving a full account of his first interview and a resume of what he had learned as the result of discreet inquiries, was in the hands of Mr. Rogers, who would keep it until the return of Fearless and himself to Dualla, unless anything happened to him for which the Commissioner might be held even remotely responsible. In this way he hoped to protect himself against any underhanded attempts at revenge by the official for the manner in which he had been treated and at the same time ensure his continued assistance if it should be required.

Dawn was only just beginning to break when they set out on their long journey but, early though the hour was, the missionary was there to see them off. Passinger, who felt that he simply must talk to somebody about it, had told him the arrangements that he and Mary Humberlayne had made for their marriage and expressed a hope that Henry Rogers might officiate at it. There was more than a possibility, too, that his fiancée's father might come out with her and he thought that the clergyman would be glad to know that there was a likelihood of his seeing his old friend again. Then the last good-byes were spoken, cumbersome-looking loads were picked up and balanced on woolly heads, and the march commenced.

The road to Nganda, as the village where Hillier and his wife had been killed was now called, was much the same as it had been fifty years before and would be, in all probability, for twice fifty years to come. The same rushing torrents with their natural bridges had to be crossed, similar massive tree-trunks lay across the path, and the same slimy marshes must be passed through. If Nganda had been on a main route or even on what might perhaps be called a secondary track and visited at all regularly, some sort of attempt might possibly have been made to improve the conditions of travelling. But as there was nothing to attract anybody to within many miles of it and only natives, and they but occasionally, passed that way, there was neither inducement nor necessity to bother about the state of the road.

As it was quite without incident it will be unnecessary to say anything about the journey. The only noteworthy item was provided by Sam, the black cook, who had declared that he could make a palatable dish out of any . . . thing". It so happened that Christmas Day fell during the week before they reached Nganda, and the travellers had brought with them a plum pudding, thoughtfully presented to them by Rogers, who had received two or three from friends in England. This was handed to Sam with instructions to boil it and Fearless and Passinger sat down that evening in the expectation of celebrating the anniversary, in one respect at least, as people were doing in more civilised localities. Fish caught in a wicker trap would not have been at all bad if Sam had not omitted to clean it properly, and some sort of jungle-fowl made an excellent, if somewhat tough and underdone, substitute for turkey. But it was the plum pudding, of course, which was to be the piece de resistance, and the two exiles looked forward to it eagerly.

At last Sam arrived bearing triumphantly above his head a large bowl, which he set before them with the flourish of a born *maitre d'hôtel*. Never, surely, was there seen such an unappetising mess as it contained. A sloppy, brown, greasy sort of thick soup, on the top of which floated unpleasant looking lumps of fat, was what the two men saw when they looked eagerly into the bowl, and they stared at Sam and then at each other in dismay.

"What on earth has your little ray of sunshine been doing?" Fearless demanded when he had recovered somewhat from his surprise.

"Imprimis, he is no more mine than yours—not so much, in fact, because it was you who engaged him; secondly, I can see no resemblance to a ray of sunshine about him unless it is that permanent idiotic grin which one would think was painted onto his black face; and thirdly, if you want to know what he has been doing ask him yourself: how do you expect me to know?"

"Plum pudden," Sam broke in at this juncture with a flash of white teeth.

"Plum pudding be blowed," Fearless retorted. "What on earth have you been doing to it?"

"Boil um," grinned back the unabashed cook, "same as master told um."

"Do you mean to tell me you have been such an ass as to boil our one and only plum pudding after taking the cloth off it?" demanded Passinger.

"Master no tell um boil cloth," Sam replied as though it was all a huge joke, and there was no gainsaying the fact that he spoke the truth.

And so it came about that the exiles had to go without their Christmas pudding; but it was not wasted, for every scrap of it was consumed with apparent gusto by Sam and his particular friends. Neither had the unboiled cloth finished its days of usefulness, though the rest of them were spent encircling the middle portion of an extremely dirty West African.

They reached Nganda at sundown three days later. The village was hardly as large as they had been led to expect from what the missionary had told them, but there were a number of huts and some fifty natives came out to greet them. The great look-out tree under which the elders had sat still stood, and beneath its shade the carriers dumped down their burdens. A very few minutes after their arrival the *sarikin gari*, who had scuttled into his hut at their approach, emerged clad in a very worn strip of velvet and an ancient felt hat, and advanced to greet them. He was an elderly man, extraordinarily ugly, and huge rolls of fat made progress a matter of some difficulty for him; but there was about him, none the less, an air of quiet dignity which did not escape the notice of his visitors and his reception of them was both courtly and cordial.

Fearless and Passinger were very favourably impressed by this little local potentate and foresaw the possibility of making of him a useful friend and ally. Subsequent experiences proved them right in their estimate and from the very first he put himself out to serve them in whatever way he could. That same evening he himself led them to the little clearing in the centre of which were the graves of Mabel Hillier and her husband, and it was with strange feelings that Passinger looked upon the last resting place of the great-aunt of his bride-to-be and realised how long a distance separated her from her own country.

The inscriptions on the stones which, as Rogers had heard, had replaced the original wooden crosses, puzzled him. The missionary had distinctly said that Hillier had died defending his wife and child, from which it was only reasonable to conclude that she had been killed at almost the same time as he had. But the dates on the stones, although the year was the same on each, were many weeks apart, the death of the woman being recorded as much later than that of the man.

And there was another thing which was even more puzzling. The gravestone of the man had on it. "Martin Hillier" and the date. Above the date on the woman's was inscribed "In ever loving memory of Mabel". Why Mabel, Passinger wondered? Why not Mabel Hillier? He did not know, he probably never would know, of the love the Commissioner of that time bore her, so how would he guess that this was his way of calling her just once by her Christian name—a thing which he had never done while she lived.

It was not a matter of any consequence, Passinger concluded as he turned back towards the village. She was buried and lay, he imagined, at the side of the man who adored her and whom, presumably, she adored. That was surely what she would have wished and if the inscription above her head happened to seem a strange one to him, it could at least do her no harm.

The greater part of the next two days was spent in making arrangements for a prolonged stay in Nganda, disposing of their belongings where they would be sheltered from the tropical rains and as safe as possible from the attacks of insects, and questioning the *sarikin gari*, who rejoiced in the name of Msuta, concerning gorillas.

The news Msuta gave them was rather surprising to Fearless, and at first he was disinclined to believe it. Gorillas are more or less sedentary, inasmuch as they are not in the habit of travelling far from the spot they have chosen for their home; but, according to the sariki, they were sometimes very numerous in the neighbourhood of his village, while at others no sign of one might be seen for months on end. There had been times, he insisted, when reports had been brought to him of fifty or sixty being seen together, an unheard of thing in the experience of Fearless, and on these occasions he was careful to have sentries set all round the village at night for fear of attack.

No such attack had ever been delivered, and as far as he knew none of his people had ever suffered death at the hands of these "men of the woods". They were careful not to interfere with them in any way and Msuta, together with all his people, believed that the gorillas appreciated this, and left them alone in return. He had an idea, though what put it into his head he was unable to say, that the inhabitants of Nganda many years before he had come there had not taken this precaution, and there was a belief, very generally held by his people, that it was by gorillas that the village had been destroyed half a century ago.

His hunters had spoken of a few single animals observed recently and it was noteworthy that it was always after some had been seen alone that there was a large influx. Therefore a number might be expected in the neighbourhood soon, and already Msuta had given instructions for certain parts of the forest to be regularly patrolled so that ample warning might be given of their arrival.

It was plain that the trappers had chosen the right centre for their operations—if they were lucky; and they had been extremely lucky up to now. Their journey from the coast had been accomplished without more than usual difficulty, they had suffered no casualties from sickness or any other cause, and they had been well received at the village they had fixed upon for their headquarters. But there was bound to be a fly in the ointment somewhere, and the fly in this case was the very strong objection the villagers had to the gorillas being interfered with. They were absolutely convinced that if anything was done to annoy the "old men of the woods" in any way they would wreak a terrible vengeance on the people of Nganda, and very naturally they did not like the idea, and protested volubly with Msuta at their head.

For days Fearless argued in vain and it began to look as though they would have to go elsewhere if they were to do any good. The difficulty was got over in the end by Passinger giving the sariki a gun at once and promising that he would send him a dozen more and a supply of ammunition as soon as he got back to the coast. He did not stop to consider what the government might have to say about this arrangement if ever they were to hear of it, and it probably would not have worried him very much if he had. The great thing was to enlist the sympathies and co-operation of the natives. It would have been all right if they had been uninterested, passive spectators, but to have them actively hostile would be fatal to success.

Even before this arrangement had been effected Fearless had set men to start on the making of the traps that he proposed to set. They were constructed of strong bamboo bound with tough creepers, and he had them built in sections which could be carried without difficulty or overmuch labour to wherever it was decided to set them up. He had arranged for six of them to be made, and by a coincidence they were finished on the very night that news was brought to the village of a number of gorillas having been seen in the neighbourhood.

On the following day Fearless had his rather strange-looking contraptions carried to that part of the forest where the animals had been observed, and superintended the setting of them up. He himself saw to the springs which were an essential part of the traps, and when he and Passinger returned to the village late in the evening after a long and hard day's work they were as confident as they well could be that within a week they would have captured their first gorilla.

The time of waiting, for Fearless had decreed that the traps should not be visited for a week, was very trying, especially to Passinger, in spite of the fact that there was much to do and plenty to occupy their minds. Other parts of the forest were visited daily and the ground reconnoitered. Sections of further traps were made so that there might always be some in reserve. Three solid cages of strong stakes were constructed in readiness for any gorillas which might be captured, and nothing that could possibly be needed was overlooked.

On the appointed day, exactly a week after the traps had been set, a strong party of men, headed by Fearless and Passinger, started out from the village at an early hour. The latter could not conceal his excitement and impatience and bombarded his companion with an endless stream of questions the answers to which he hardly troubled to wait for. Fearless too, was excited, but he was better able to conceal his feelings. He had been trapping for so many years and had so many thrilling experiences that the present one did not affect him as much as it might have done; but at the same time gorillas were new game to him and the excitement of Passinger was infectious.

He was very hopeful that the traps would be found to contain at least one of the animals and he would not have been at all surprised to find more. So confident was he, indeed, that he had sent out men to gather a stock of the leaves of a vine to which gorillas were known to be especially partial. But he was destined to be disappointed. The first trap that they came to was sprung but empty and so were the second and third and all the rest. Round each of them were the tracks of the "old men of the woods", which showed that they had been there, and right inside the last one of all were some droppings not more than two or three days old. This looked to Passinger like a deliberate insult and he was almost cross about it until the humorous side struck him.

Fearless was bitterly disappointed but by no means despairing. He was one of the most patient men that ever lived and, if he had had many successes, he had had just as many failures. Patience is the one quality above all others necessary in a man who wishes to catch wild beasts. He may have to set his snares, or whatever they may be, a score of times before he is successful. In the case of the former many a cunning animal has been known to roll on them and so spring them without being caught. The fact that all six of his gorilla traps were sprung did not make Fearless despondent, but he was sadly puzzled to know how it had been done. A more careful inspection showed that the last they had visited was not the only one which had been actually entered, for footprints were found in no fewer than three of the others. After thinking the matter over carefully he decided to reset them where they now stood and this time to leave them unvisited for only two days. He was not altogether sanguine that the gorillas would approach them again, but having had no previous experience of the animals he could not be certain.

When they returned two days later it was to find that they had had no better luck. Four of the traps were sprung and in all of them were fresh tracks of gorillas. The other two had apparently done their work successfully and two of the creatures had been trapped; but unfortunately they had not been built strongly enough to stand up against the huge muscles of the imprisoned brutes and had been torn to pieces. There was considerable evidence that the gorillas had not been satisfied by merely escaping for they had smashed up every length of bamboo until not a piece more than twelve inches long remained.

Fearless was less disappointed over this second failure than he had been over the first. He knew at least that his traps were right in theory and was confident that all that was necessary now was to make them stronger. He had all the sections carried back to the village and set about the work of strengthening them at once. Many of the bamboos were replaced by thicker ones and the bindings were doubled. When the work had been completed, three days later, they were taken back to the same spot and set once more. But exactly the same thing happened again. They were still not strong enough.

The only thing to do was to make fresh traps altogether, and they were put in hand immediately. It took over a week to make them and this succession of delays began to get sadly on the men's nerves. It was not so bad for Passinger because he could always get away for a bit of shooting, but Fearless was not satisfied unless he superintended every bit of the work, and consequently he was tied to the village. But they were completed at last and for the fourth time traps were set in the same place. It had become clear that the week that had been allowed to intervene between the setting of the first lot and the visiting of them was an unnecessarily long time, and therefore they set out to see what luck had come their way after only forty-eight hours had elapsed.

As before, five of the traps were sprung, but the sixth and last contained an adult male gorilla. It was not a particularly big specimen, but it stood over five feet in height and the breadth of its chest was enormous. Its rage when its captors came in sight was terrible to behold. It tore at the bars of its prison and shook them until there was imminent danger of the whole structure being over-turned. It roared with fury until the woods echoed and reechoed again and again. It beat its black, hairless chest with its fists, making a booming noise like the beating of a big drum, and its grimaces were quite horrible.

Passinger was in the seventh heaven of delight and Fearless was no less pleased, though he was not so demonstrative about it. He felt that he had justified his engagement and earned his pay and this pleased him even more than the fact that he had pitted his wits successfully against the gorilla. He set to work at once on the long, difficult and somewhat hazardous task of getting the creature back to the strong cage that awaited it in the village. Long poles were thrust, not without difficulty, through holes made for that purpose and the whole trap was carried on the shoulders of over a score of men. When a short distance had been covered the heavy and un-wieldy burden was set down and the bearers relieved by others. After another short distance these were replaced by the original party, and so on.

Arrived at the village one end of the trap was put close up against the opening in one of the cages and secured there. Fearless himself lived up to his name by undertaking the dangerous job of climbing onto the top of the cage in order to lift the door of the trap, which an ingenious arrangement permitted him to free. The bars of both trap and cage were set fairly close together, but there was always a chance, and by no means a remote one, that the en-raged creature might find some weak spot or succeed in forcing two of the bamboos, strong though they were, sufficiently far apart to thrust its hand through; and if this should happen, anybody unlucky enough to get gripped by it was likely to have a very un-comfortable time.

At last the door was raised to its fullest extent and the way into the cage was clear. All that was necessary now was for the gorilla to pass from one prison into the other one, and as soon as it did so the cage door would be dropped and all danger of the animal's escape done away with. Or so, at least, Fearless fondly hoped and believed. Unfortunately the prisoner refused flatly to change its quarters. It seemed to have developed a sudden affection for the trap and to prefer it infinitely to the cage in spite of the fact that the latter was abundantly furnished with soft bedding and that vine leaves of the most succulent kind were spread temptingly within it.

Every device that Fearless could think of he tried, to get the creature to move, but in vain. He did not dare to use force because, although the trap had proved strong enough so far, he was none too sure that it would stand much more, especially since the re-moval of the door was bound to weaken it to some extent. Pass-inger also tried his hand but was no more successful than his com-panion and began to fear that the task was a hopeless one. The pa-tience of Fearless was extraordinary. For hour after hour he re-mained at the side of the trap, cajoling, coaxing, even pleading. At long last he decided to leave it for a few minutes and the two men walked across to their hut for a cup of coffee. And when they re-turned, less than a quarter of an hour later, the deed was done. As soon as they had turned their backs, as soon as, through sheer wea-riness, they had given up trying to persuade the brute for a time, it had walked quietly into the cage and settled down under the bed-ding provided.

It was the work of a few moments to get the door in place, and secured, and as the last strong bolt slipped into its socket Fearless heaved a sigh of relief.

"Thank heaven for that," he grunted. "Now we shall be able to go to bed without any fear of this gentleman escaping. He is far stronger than I think he is if he can manage to break out of that."

"Yes; It would certainly take a bit of doing," Passinger con-curred. "By Jove, I am tired."

"So am I. Let's go and eat and then turn in. This chap will be all right and in a day or two I hope we shall have another one to keep him company—a female for preference."

Half an hour later the two men were sleeping soundly.

CHAPTER IX

THE RESCUE

I T HAS BEEN MENTIONED in a previous chapter that, as soon as gorillas were reported in the neighbourhood in any numbers, Msuta was in the habit of posting sentries round the village at night to guard against attack, although no such attack had ever been delivered or even threatened. Up to now they had only been seen singly since the arrival of Passinger and his party, and then not very often, so the *sarikin gari* had not considered it necessary to take any unusual precautions.

The night which followed the capture of the gorilla was much like that on which Mabel Hillier had been killed. The moon was nearly at its full and the light it shed was bright enough to read by. Close to the look-out tree might be seen the three cages, in one of which the gorilla was imprisoned, and within a few yards of them the figures of two men who had been instructed to keep watch over the captive and report immediately to Fearless, at whatever time of the night, if it became violent or made any determined effort to escape. They, not unwisely, concluded that any exhibition of rage on the creature's part would be attended with sufficient noise to rouse them if they were to fall asleep, and to sleep they promptly went.

Had they carried out their duties conscientiously and as they were expected to do—had they remained awake, in fact—they might have seen, about midnight, a number of dark forms creeping cautiously, inch by inch, across the market-place and converging on the cages. Not a sound was to be heard, but one figure, taller than the rest, stood in the centre of the open space and seemed to direct them by signs. At long last two of those forms had approached close to the sleeping sentries, were within reach of them. A double call, like the hoot of an owl, was given by the central figure and immediately these two leapt upon the unconscious men. There was no fight, no sound, for before they were awake their throats had been torn out and they had gone to another world where sleep is not supposed to be a necessity. Then the leader walked across to the middle cage, the occupant of which had stood, leaning on its knuckles, silently watching all that was going on, and began to fumble with the bolts.

For a long time they resisted his somewhat clumsy efforts, but at last first one and then another shot back and soon the door swung open. Without undue haste the captive walked out, free once more, and then, as silently as they had come, the dusky forms crept back across the market-place and disappeared into the darkness. The leader was the last to go and when his shadow had faded into the surrounding gloom there was nothing to tell of that midnight visit but the open door of the empty cage and the blood-stained corpses of the two watchers who had slept at their post.

A woman on her way to fetch water from the stream as dawn was breaking was the first to discover the tragedy. She promptly dropped the big bowl she was carrying and ran screaming through the village, with the result that in less than a minute every hut was discharging its occupants. Fearless, rifle in hand, was amongst the first to appear, closely followed by Passinger. They had been fast asleep when the woman screamed and were at first under the impression that the village had been attacked by some hostile tribe. But they saw that everybody was running towards the cages and the trapper feared at once that something must have happened to his precious gorilla.

His fears, as we know, were well founded, and when he saw the empty cage with its wide-open door he was furious. At that time he had not seen the gory bodies of the two men and he caught hold of Msuta by his woolly hair and would certainly have thrashed him soundly before all his people had not Passinger intervened when, with obvious reluctance he let him go. Fearless was absolutely convinced—and said so in no measured terms—that Msuta had either released the animal or connived at its release. How else could the bolts have been drawn, he demanded? It was quite impossible for the gorilla to have drawn them itself because they were well out of its reach. The door must have been opened by some outside agency and therefore by one of the villagers. He did not think of the ungrateful reception that anybody who dared to give the gorilla an opportunity of getting at him was likely to enjoy, but Passinger, who was less ready to jump to conclusions, did.

"Send all the people back to their huts, Msuta," he commanded. "I want to see if we can find any tracks of whoever has done this."

In a very few minutes the market-place was deserted except for Fearless, Passinger and the thoroughly frightened Msuta, though inquisitive heads poked out from every doorway. But the order had been given too late. The whole population of the village had been trampling in the dust of the market-place and effectually obliterated whatever tracks might once have been there. It was clearly no good wasting time over the immediate neighbourhood of the cages so they began at once to search farther afield, gradually working away from them, and at last there came a call from Passinger.

"The gorilla passed this way," he shouted. "I have found a footprint"; and then, after an interval so short that Fearless had not had the time to join him, "Here are a lot more and, as I live, some of them are pointing towards the village instead of away from it."

Examination confirmed what Passinger had said and led to the discovery of many more footprints, both going and coming.

"This is extraordinary," Fearless exclaimed. "If I am not very much mistaken over a score of gorillas must have passed this way last night. Can it be possible that they came deliberately to free the one we caught? That might account for the way the two men were killed. It must have required enormous strength to tear their throats out in that way and I very much doubt whether any human being could have done it. Next time I catch a gorilla I will have padlocks put on the door of its cage and sleep with the keys under my pillow. I am not going to be made a fool of like this twice and have all my work for nothing."

Fearless, it must be regretfully admitted, was in a towering rage—and when he was in a rage people were generally very glad to keep out of his way. At such times he was an alarming figure. His great beard seemed to bristle, his shock of red hair to stand on end, and he stamped up and down like a son of Anak gone mad, shaking his fists above his head. It must be admitted that in the present instance there was some excuse for him. It was more than annoying to have travelled thousands of miles by land and sea, spent weeks in making his preparations, overcome a succession of difficulties and attained his object, only to have the prize snatched from him when he thought it was safely his. If he had realised it, and he may have done so to some extent, Msuta had had a very narrow escape. Fearless in a temper lost control of himself altogether; neither, as a rule, could anybody else control him, and if, for some unexplainable reason, he had not happened to listen to Passinger, there is no possible doubt that he would have done old Msuta some injury, if no worse.

The morning was fast passing before the two men returned to the hut which they had had built for them. They had reluctantly been compelled to come to the conclusion that there was nothing to be done—and they foresaw complications. The villagers had said, and believed implicitly, that if any injury was done to the "old men of the woods" they would exact a terrible revenge. It was true that not one of the inhabitants had been injured, for both the dead men had been in Passinger's service and come with him from Dualla, but there was a strong probability that they would look upon this raid in the light of a warning. If gorillas would do that sort of thing to two men they were quite likely to do it to others, and the villagers did not credit them with sufficient intelligence to differentiate between the people of Nganda and the men employed by Passinger. They would probably dislike the idea of having their throats torn out intensely, and who could blame them?

A gun was a great treasure to a native and he prized it above almost anything, in spite of the fact that he could do far greater execution at far less risk to himself with the more familiar spear of his forefathers. Msuta thought the world of the somewhat ancient weapon that had been presented to him, but he thought more of his life. As for the promise of others—what were promises after all? The people of Nganda knew nothing about pie-crust or they would doubtless have used it as a simile.

That afternoon Msuta came himself to the Englishmen's hut to ask them to attend a council in the cool of the evening. They were glad to have the invitation, for it would give them an opportunity to have the matter out, if the meeting had been called for the reason which they suspected, and they signified their willingness to attend. At the appointed hour they joined the circle which sat, as it had done fifty years before, though everyone of those who then formed it was dead and gone, in the shade of the look-out tree. If anybody had known they must have been struck with the similarity of the two scenes—twelve of the chief men of the village in a row, the *sarikin gari* alone slightly in advance, and the rest of the inhabitants ranged in the greater part of a circle before them. But nobody did know.

It became clear at once that things were as the trappers had feared. Msuta told them, without any beating about the bush, that the hunting of the gorillas must stop and the cages be pulled down and he even hinted broadly that the room of the Englishmen would be preferable to their continued presence. He had the grace to say, and it was plain that he meant it, that the necessity for this grieved him deeply. The Englishmen were his good friends, he declared, and he had a great affection for them. But the mind of the people was made up and they were no longer welcome in the village. Then he rose, not without some difficulty, owing to his size, from the low stool upon which he had been sitting, walked across to Passinger with that peculiar air of dignity which sat so oddly upon him and, with a courtly bow, returned the ancient gun by which he set such store. It must have nearly broken the old man's heart to do it but he managed to rake up a somewhat sickly smile somehow and returned to his seat without showing all he most surely felt.

It was up to Fearless to reply, for Passinger's knowledge of the language was very meagre, and he did it nobly. He began by thanking Msuta for his expressions of friendship, which he hoped might long continue. He said that he quite understood their point of view but stressed the fact that it was his men who had suffered and not any of the villagers. He insisted that the gorillas knew perfectly well that neither Msuta nor any of his people had done anything to injure them and that therefore Msuta and his people had nothing to fear. They were quite as intelligent as human beings, he declared, if not more so, and any risks that were being run were being run by him and Passinger and their men, and by them alone. Let Msuta remember this and alter his decision.

Unfortunately Fearless rather overdid the intelligence part of it. Old Msuta was no fool and he promptly countered by saying, in so many words, that if the gorillas knew such a devil of a lot they must also know that it was by his, Msuta's, permission that the cages had been erected in the village, that thus he must be assisting the trappers, if only indirectly, and that therefore they would have a score to settle with him as well. It was a pity that the gorillas were so intelligent, he said, or a pity, rather, that he had not known it before because, if he had, he would never have consented to assist his friends.

For two hours the ball of controversy was thrown backwards and forwards, but Msuta remained firm and the Englishmen were on the point of giving up the argument as hopeless and resigning themselves to the inevitable when what was nothing more nor less than a heaven-sent intervention of providence turned the tide of affairs in their favour.

Some weeks before Passinger had sent two men to Dualla on the plea that there might be important communications for him. The fact that the only communication of any sort which he expected was a letter from Mary Humberlayne does not concern us and he was at liberty to send his men to Dualla or to Jericho if he liked. At the same time he had given them orders to bring back with them about a dozen men to replace some who had left him for one reason or another and it had struck him that this would be a good opportunity to have the twelve guns and the supply of ammunition which he had promised Msuta brought up to Nganda.

By great good fortune the party, with the guns, marched into the village just at the critical moment, and Fearless was quick to seize upon the opportunity thus offered to him.

"White men never lie," he declared untruthfully. "Were you not promised twelve guns to be sent to you when we returned to Dualla? And did you doubt that they would come? To please you we sent men all the way to the sea especially to get those guns and behold! here they are. The gorillas I do not believe will ever attack you, but if they do what does it matter? Armed as you will be, with a large amount of ammunition and ourselves at your side, what have you to fear from a few gorillas? You can slay them in their dozens; you can drive them, if you wish, from your land forever and no longer have cause to fear them. And when we return to Dualla we will send you yet other guns and make you still stronger. Come, Msuta. Take back your weapon or choose anyone of these. And you, chiefs of the people of Nganda, come and choose. For each of you there is a gun and cartridges. Would you refuse them?"

They did not refuse them. In fact there was a somewhat undignified scramble for them and the day was won. But it had been a very near thing and if the party had not arrived from the coast at that very opportune moment the trappers must inevitably have gone elsewhere. As it was they had become extremely popular and nothing was too good for them. Msuta declared publicly that he and all he possessed was theirs and that his people would cheerfully die for them to the last man. So Fearless and Passinger were able to turn in that night with a great load lifted from their minds.

Early next morning they were on the warpath once more. They returned to the same spot in the forest where they had had their previous success and failures, and Fearless was relieved, and somewhat surprised, to find that the traps were uninjured. He had more than half expected that the gorillas would have broken them in pieces and that the work of building others would have to be commenced. He set them at once, only five now since the one in which the gorilla had been caught had not been brought from the village, and returned home hoping for the best, though he was rather afraid that now that one had been caught the gorillas were likely to avoid that part of the forest.

As on previous occasions, forty-eight hours were allowed to elapse before the traps were visited, and when the two men went at the end of that time to see if they had had any luck, they received the surprise of their lives. In the very first trap of all sat an adult male gorilla, and this in itself was more than they had dared to expect, though of course they had hoped for it. But it was not that which came as such a staggering surprise to them. It was that the animal was apparently quite docile. It made no grimaces, no attempt to force apart the bars of its prison. And from all appearances it had not done so previous to their arrival. It did not even trouble to get up, but just sat quietly in the trap and stared at them while they stared back in wide-eyed astonishment.

"It must surely be ill," Passinger suggested, and Fearless was inclined to agree with him.

"The first thing is to get it back to the village and into one of the cages," he said, "and then perhaps we shall be able to find out what is the matter with it. I cannot undertake to doctor sick gorillas in the middle of the forest."

Never did two similar animals behave more differently than their present captive and the one which had been so mysteriously rescued a few days before. The latter had stormed and raved and fought and bitten unceasingly except when it was sulking. It had beaten its massive chest, torn at the bars of its cage and put every possible difficulty in the way of its captors. This last one sat resignedly if not contentedly in the trap, almost as though it had entered it on purpose, knowing what it was. For a fleeting moment Passinger wondered whether this might not be so and suggested it, though rather shame facedly, to Fearless.

"Is it possible that this is some cunning scheme," he said, "and that it is we who are getting trapped? What I mean is, do you think that this gorilla has let itself get caught deliberately to see if we intended to keep on trying to capture one of its kind and, perhaps, what would have happened to the first one if it had not been rescued?"

"Don't be ridiculous," was the only reply Fearless vouchsafed to this suggestion, which certainly did sound rather foolish; but Passinger was not satisfied.

"You would have told me not to be ridiculous if I had suggested that the last one might be set free; but it was. I am beginning to wonder whether these gorillas are not a great deal more cunning than we thought they were."

But Fearless said nothing more and soon the idea was driven out of Passinger's mind by the work before him.

The long poles were slipped through the openings provided without difficulty and the trap with its occupant carried by relays of men, as before, to the village. There it was secured to the cage in the same manner as the first had been and Fearless prepared to exercise another long spell of patience. But no sooner was the door lifted and the way clear than the gorilla rose clumsily to its feet and walked quietly into its new prison. It seemed almost to be glad to get there and settled down at once amongst the plentiful bedding provided.

"I can't make this animal out," Fearless said as he climbed down from the top of the trap. "I do not pretend to know a great deal about gorillas but the behaviour of this one does not seem natural to me. It is altogether too accommodating."

"There does not seem to be anything the matter with it though, as far as one can see," Passinger replied. "I mean it looks healthy enough. I can't understand it at all."

At that moment Msuta waddled up with the information that one of his hunters had just come in and had some news for them. They sent for him at once and the news he brought was just what they had been wanting for weeks. Passinger's great ambition was to catch a very young gorilla, for he believed, and Fearless was of the same opinion, that the younger the animal was the more chance they would have of rearing it successfully and acclimatising it, provided always, that is, that it had been weaned. Msuta's hunter had located a female gorilla with a young one in a tree in a distant part of the forest in the opposite direction to that in which the traps had been set and he had come back to the village specially to tell them.

Thanks to the accommodating behaviour of their latest capture they had got it into the cage soon after mid-day and it was still quite early. So quiet was the captive that Fearless foresaw no trouble with it and, after he had consulted with Passinger, it was decided that they might as well take time by the forelock and set out at once to try to catch the young one. The necessary arrangements were soon made and within a couple of hours they had started. Fearless had detailed several men to take it in turns to watch the cage throughout the night, though he did not believe for one mo-

ment that there was any necessity for it, and he left the village with
a light heart.

Msuta was not quite so happy. He believed most of what the
white men had said and felt more or less secure in the knowledge
that he was well armed; but none the less his mind was more at
rest when he had posted sentries round the village at nightfall, and
even then he took the precaution of placing his gun within easy
reach when he lay down to sleep.

Fearless and Passinger with their two score or more of men
made good progress under the guidance of the native hunter, and
by the time their camp was pitched they had put a long distance
between themselves and Nganda. Their guide had told them that
the tree to which he was leading them was about two days' journey from the village, but as a matter of fact they did not reach it
until the evening of the third day, in spite of the fact that they were
travelling light and at their best pace. It was too dark then to see
anything clearly, so they retraced their steps for about a mile, in
order to lessen the risk of frightening the mother and baby away
by the nearness of their presence, and postponed any operations
against them until the morning.

Throughout their journey they had seen no sign of gorillas,
which had come as rather a surprise to them. The country through
which they passed was eminently suited to the requirements of the
creatures in every way, and Fearless had made sure that they
would have come across some. On the whole, he thought, it was
perhaps as well that they had not. It was on the capture of the
young one that they were bent and that would provide quite
enough to occupy their minds and their time without anything else.
Too many interests are just as liable to spoil as a re too many
cooks.

Soon the moon rose and looked down upon the sleeping world.
At Nganda it saw no movement save an occasional one from
Msuta's sentries or the men who had been left to guard the gorilla
in its cage. Some miles away, in the depths of the forest, it
searched out the sleeping camp of the trappers, the little white tent
which sheltered Passinger and Fearless and the motionless bodies
of their men. And a mile further on a wandering beam crept
through the leaves and lit up a platform of sticks in a tree-top and a
mother gorilla with her young one clasped tenderly to her breast.

CHAPTER X

NARROW ESCAPES

IT WAS SOON after dawn when Passinger and Fearless came out of their tent and yelled for Sam, who combined the duties of personal servant with those of cook, and an hour later they were on their way to the tree in which the gorilla had its home. Without the help of the hunter they would never have found the nest, and even after he had pointed out its exact position to them it was some time before they saw it. But at last the two men descried a platform of sticks high up amongst the topmost branches of a towering forest giant and, looking over the edge of it, the face of the mother gorilla.

It was the largest tree within sight and its smooth trunk ran up for nearly a hundred feet before the first branch was reached. To attempt to climb it was quite out of the question and Fearless could think of no possible way of capturing the young gorilla. To shoot the mother would be useless, for it would bring them no nearer to the young one than they were now and it began to seem as though they had made their journey in vain.

It was Passinger who had the great idea at last and, although Fearless was not enamoured of it he saw that it might be feasible and there was no other way that he could think of. It would involve a lot of work and must take some time, but that could not be helped and, as Passinger wisely remarked, the sooner they started the sooner they would finish. There was always the chance, too, that the gorilla might take it into her head that the nest-tree was no longer safe and move off with her offspring to some other part of the forest. So they set to work at once.

A score of men were sent to collect lengths of strong creepers and with them make a net with a two-foot mesh—that is, with a mesh a foot square. It was to be twenty-five feet in length each way and so constructed that it could be pulled together at the edges, like an old-fashioned purse, by means of a kind of draw-string. The remaining men had orders to clear a circle of the forest, with a radius of fifty yards or more from the tree in which the gorilla's nest was, of everything, large or small, which grew upon it, starting at the outer edge. This was not so heavy a job as it might have been for, luckily, there was but little undergrowth and the trees grew fairly far apart. On the other hand they were for the most part rather big trees which would have to be cut into many pieces after they were felled before they could be carried away.

The object of clearing the space was twofold—firstly, so that all avenues of retreat for the gorillas, except by coming down the nest-tree and out into the open, might be cut off, and secondly, so that their refuge when it came to be felled in its turn might fall without meeting any obstruction. What the trappers hoped was that when the tree fell the gorillas would jump clear just before the outer branches struck the ground. Men would be standing ready with the net stretched between them and it would be their duty to throw it over the animals before they could recover their equilibrium. It was an easy matter to calculate to within a very few feet where the top of the tree would land, and the rest would depend upon the quickness and dexterity of the men with the net.

There were admittedly many chances against the scheme proving successful. A miscalculation might be made; the tree might not fall in the direction in which it was intended to fall; the gorillas might omit to jump as they were wanted and expected to jump; or, finally, the fall might prove fatal to them. To minimise the risk of failure as far as possible Fearless arranged for a number of rehearsals to be held as soon as the net was completed, which was late in the evening of the day on which it was commenced. Several trees, each standing in an open space, were selected and measured. Men then set to work to cut them down and, when they were almost ready to fall, other men, holding the net, were stationed just beyond where the branches were calculated to strike the ground. As the tree fell they flung the net over an imaginary gorilla and after a little drilling became quite dexterous at the work.

The freeing of the men who had been making the net from that job helped very much to speed up the work of clearing the circle of forest. By nightfall on the first day a ring of trees had been felled; but there was still plenty of opportunity for the gorilla to escape with her young one if she wished and, to prevent this, Fearless deemed it prudent to post men with torches at intervals all round the cleared space. By the second evening most of the work had been done and the litter removed and by the third only the one tree remained standing and all was ready for the final scene to be played.

That night Fearless and Passinger talked long and earnestly over their future movements and it was unusually late when they at last turned in. By then they had decided that if the morrow's venture was a success they would return with all speed to Nganda, and that one of them, probably Passinger, should start at once with the baby gorilla for Dualla, while the other remained with the one they had already captured and tried to catch others. It was thought better to take only one at a time to the coast, and the baby, as the less heavy and cumbersome, would be the more convenient in view of the amount of clearing that would have to be done along the road. Subsequent journeys would be simpler for, once the tree trunks and other obstructions had been moved from across the path, travelling would be a great deal easier and quicker.

The first thing to be done on the following morning was to show the men in charge of the net exactly where they were to stand and to rehearse them once or twice in the throwing of their trap. When they had done this to the satisfaction of Fearless the work of cutting down the tree was commenced. It was considerably larger than any of those which had already been felled and the trappers knew that it would take a long time; but it was essential that the task should be completed by daylight and the men were kept hard at it, relieving each other at frequent intervals.

With the first blow of the axes the mother gorilla looked anxiously over the side of the nest and her anxiety increased as time went on. Several times she left the platform of sticks and climbed out amongst the branches, but the tree had been cut a great part of the way through before she made any sound. Then, all of a sudden, she gave a single barking roar and, after an interval, a second. They were so unexpected that the men jumped involuntarily.

"Did you hear the echo?" Passinger asked; but Fearless, to whom he had addressed the question, shook his head.

"Can't hear anything but the blows of these infernal axes," he grumbled as he wiped the perspiration from his streaming brow with the back of his hand for Fearless never failed to take his turn with the men, whatever the work might be.

A change had come over the behaviour of the gorilla after that second barking roar. Instead of climbing restlessly from one branch to another, returning every other moment to the platform of sticks and her baby, she was now jumping up and down on a stout limb in a state of extreme excitement rather than anxiety. Fearless had handed his axe to one of the men as he answered Passinger and strolled across to the edge of the clearing. He stood there, looking up into the branches of the now tottering tree, when the excitement of the gorilla and the sound which Passinger had thought was an echo were dramatically accounted for.

A shout from one of the men had made him turn round and there, within six feet of him, was a male gorilla, evidently the mate of the female in the tree and father of the baby they were going to such pains to secure. It was his answering roar which Passinger had heard and taken for an echo. Almost at the instant when Fearless caught sight of it the enraged brute sprang. He was unarmed. He had not the time to turn and fly even if he could have outdistanced the animal. There was only one thing which he could do and that was to match his strength against the gorilla's.

And then began one of the most extraordinary wrestling matches that mortal man can have ever seen. It made Passinger, who could do nothing but look helplessly on and marvel at the strength of the man, think of pictures he had seen of fights in the arena between wild animals and Christian martyrs, but he doubted whether even there such a fight had been seen as the one he was witnessing now. He dared not fire a shot for fear of wounding his friend. He could do nothing but watch. Fearless and the gorilla had each gripped the other by the upper part of both arms and they stood immovable, feet set wide apart, straining with all their mighty strength, the one to get at the man's throat, the other to hold his assailant off. For what seemed an eternity to the onlookers they moved not an inch. The veins on Fearless's forehead were swollen and pulsing, the muscles of his neck stood out like great cords and his chest heaved with the strain he was exerting.

The gorilla was a foot the shorter of the two but it was probably considerably the heavier. Its chest measurement and the massiveness of its shoulders were prodigious. It fought, not with set teeth as Fearless did, but with bared fangs and half-opened mouth as though ready to sink its yellow incisors deep into the man's throat. It seemed impossible that any man could stand up as Fearless was doing against such an adversary, but he did more than stand up, for very slowly the animal began to give ground. It had been in a half-crouching position, its stern thrust out like a Cornish wrestler's, but gradually it was forced upright and then began to bend backwards. It looked as though Fearless was to be the winner of that great contest, but unfortunately he made what might have proved a fatal mistake, for he let go of one of the creature's arms and grabbed it by the throat.

The arms of a gorilla are far longer than those of a man and in a fraction of a second the fingers of its free hand had closed round Fearless's neck. For the moment his thick beard saved him from strangulation but Passinger saw that it could be for a moment only and that the end was inevitable. Without waiting to think what the consequences of his action might be he gave a yell and dived for the gorilla's feet, as he had so often done for the feet of his opponents on the football field 10 years gone by. With a cry of rage and surprise it came crashing to the ground, dragging Fearless with it, and as it fell Sam, the cook, dashed in and drove a spear, once, twice, three times, into the black body, while the female shrieked her rage from the platform of sticks in the tree top.

It did not take Fearless long to disentangle himself from the corpse and scramble to his feet. Passinger had already risen and the two men joined in a long hand-clasp.

"Well tackled, old man," Fearless said. "I am grateful."

Those were the only words spoken, but there was a whole world of meaning in them.

Meanwhile Sam was strutting about with a wide grin on his black face, waving the blood-stained spear above his head, as proud and vainglorious as a peacock.

". . . good job . . . well done," he was saying. "Sam he kill um . . . brave man, Sam."

He was certainly deserving of all praise and he did not fail to get it.

The afternoon was by now far spent and not many hours of daylight remained so, as the work of felling the tree must be completed by nightfall, no time could be wasted in patting each other on the back. Accordingly the body of the dead gorilla was hastily dragged aside, the men with the net went to their appointed places, and the work was resumed forthwith.

With the death of her mate the gorilla seemed to have lost all heart and all interest, even in her baby. She sat on a limb at the side of the platform and whimpered dismally, and it was not until an ominous cracking announced the imminent fall of the tree that she moved at all. Then she snatched up her young one and clambered out amongst the top-most branches with it clasped in one of her arms. The cracking grew louder, and at last the great tree began to move slowly out of the upright and then to fall. The gorilla clung frantically to a branch with one hand and to her young one with the other, but she made no sound. The tree fell exactly as the men had intended and, as the outer twigs struck the ground, the animal was jerked from her hold and flung violently outwards. Even as she fell she managed to turn over on to her back so that her own body might break her baby's fall, and so she landed, with a dull thud that could be heard above the crashing of the branches. The two animals, mother and child, fell almost at the feet of the men with the net and in a trice it had been thrown over them and both were entrapped. But the devoted parent had sacrificed her own life to save her young one and lay helpless with her back broken.

A bullet from Passinger's rifle soon put her out of her misery, but the doing of that deed, act of mercy though it was, was a thing he was never to forget. It was through him, he could not help thinking, that the creature had been deprived of her life—and for what purpose? Simply to satisfy his own selfish desire to rob her of her child. He had not even the excuse of necessity, of the need to make money. And now that he had got the young one the chances, he knew, were quite ten to one against his being able to rear it. Even if he did rear it, it would do him no good. A gorilla was not the sort of animal to make a pet of. Notoriety, and very brief notoriety at that, was all he could ever hope to get out of it— a paragraph in The Times, perhaps his picture in the *Daily Sketch* or the *Bystander*— and what was the good of that? For this he had sacrificed the life of a devoted mother and he was thoroughly disgusted with himself.

The baby was quite uninjured and so frightened, which was not to be surprised at, that it made no resistance when Fearless picked it up in his arms and placed it in the light cage that had been prepared for it. It was made of slim but strong bamboos bound together, as the traps had been, with tough creepers. Every possible thing which would add to its weight had been dispensed with, and the cage was no more than strong enough to serve its purpose. Two men could have carried it with the young gorilla inside it, but a pole on either side enabled four to do so with ease. By the time the little captive had been safely housed, night had fallen and Sam, still swollen with pride at the part he had played in the day's proceedings, had finished cooking the evening meal. It had been a strenuous and eventful day, and it was not long before Passinger and Fearless turned in for a well-earned sleep.

Next morning the latter was so stiff about the arms and shoulders that he could hardly move them. The strength he had exerted in his struggle with the gorilla was prodigious and, talking it over after wards, he expressed the opinion that, had he been satisfied to retain his original grip instead of being so foolish as to loose one of the animal's arms in order to grasp its throat, he would have come off victorious without the assistance of either Passinger or Sam, and the former was rather inclined to agree with him. He admitted frankly that they had saved his life, that without their intervention he must inevitably have been killed, and he was most sincere in his expressions of gratitude. But he was very annoyed with himself for not having won the battle single-handed, especially when, as he believed, he had at one time had it all his own way. Every man born of a woman is vain about some one thing and Fearless's vanity was his strength.

Sixteen men were detailed to carry the cage and the young gorilla in relays of four and, as soon as camp had been struck, the cavalcade started on its return journey to Nganda, which they calculated to reach by nightfall on the third day if all went well and nothing unforeseen occurred. With the additional burden of the somewhat cumbersome cage, light though it was, their progress was of necessity slower than it had been on the outward march, but the going was good in this part of the forest and they got along at a very fair rate. They had no awkward torrents to cross, there were no tree trunks blocking the path, and the only real obstruction was a strip of marshy land about three miles across. It was fairly solid under foot but large areas of it were covered with water which in some places reached to well above a man's thighs. This difficult piece of ground came in their first day's journey and when once it was crossed, as it was early in the afternoon, they could comfort themselves with the knowledge that thenceforward all was plain sailing.

That night they camped on high ground in a little natural theatre and at an early hour next morning resumed their march without having met with any adventure beyond the ordinary trials of a day's travel and a night's sleep in the heart of the forest. It was soon after they had started that Fearless came across some tracks which, for a time, he failed to recognise. For several minutes he studied them before he realised that they had been made by the animal he had vainly sought the last time he had been in that part of the world.

Not only is the okapi one of the rarest, if not quite the rarest of living animals, but it is also the shyest. Very few white men have seen one at liberty in its native wilds and not a single specimen has ever been captured as far as is known. That so large an animal should have remained unknown to science until the birth of the

twentieth century is a fact that many people have found very puzzling and it is only when the kind of country it frequents and this
extraordinary shyness are taken into consideration, that such a
thing can be explained.

Fearless had his hands a great deal too full to trouble himself
very much about okapis at the moment, but he made a careful
mental note of the spot and resolved to try his hand at trapping one
of them before he returned to England. His idea was to get the
gorillas down to Dualla as soon as he could, after having caught
more of them if Passinger desired it, and then to return. If his present employer chose to engage his services for this new enterprise,
so much the better; if not, he would undertake it at his own risk.
The country hereabouts teemed with game and signs of elephant,
bush-cows and other creatures, as well as, sometimes, the creatures themselves, were seen almost hourly. It was a hunter's para-
dise.

The second day's march was no more eventful than the first,
but the third was destined to be full of thrills and nearly ended fa-
tally. They had been journeying for not more than two hours when
a small herd of elephants was sighted, amongst which was an old
bull with the most enormous tusks that either Passinger or Fearless
had ever seen, and the former decided that he must have them. The
party were on high ground when the great beasts were first seen
crossing a little open glade about a mile away and considerably
below them. They were travelling in a very leisurely manner,
stopping to feed every here and there, and what wind there was
was in favour of the hunters. So instructions were given for the
march to be continued towards Nganda, while the two Englishmen, accompanied only by Sam, started off at an angle in pursuit
of the elephants.

The trail left by the animals was easy to follow and within an
hour their pursuers knew that they must be getting very near to
them. They were then amongst thick undergrowth through which
the herd had trampled a passage-perhaps it would be more exact to
say, forced a tunnel-along which they were making their way, and
it was necessary to exercise extreme caution for, had they come
suddenly upon the animals and one of them taken it into its head to
charge them, the chances of escaping with their lives would have
been very remote. A veritable wall of green hemmed them in on
either side through which it would have been impossible for a
mere man to force his way with any speed, and the track itself was
cumbered with branches and broken saplings, trodden down by the

herd in its passing, over which nobody could have run for any distance without being tripped up.

They came to the end of the passage, however, without having sighted their quarry and found themselves on the edge of a considerable clearing on which only a few trees grew, and right in the middle of it was the herd, quietly feeding. The great bull was standing at some little distance from the others and nearer to the hunters, but it was not in a position to offer a convenient or an easy shot. Passinger saw a large tree at some little distance from beside which he felt sure he could place his bullet in a vital spot without difficulty and towards it he began at once to make his way by slow degrees, keeping behind the shelter of a convenient clump of bushes.

He reached the tree safely and found that his estimate had been correct, that he was now in an excellent position for a shot. Passinger, as has been said was an expert with the rifle—one of the best rifle-shots known, in fact. He was also a man of iron nerve with considerable experience of big-game shooting and never got in the least flustered. But on this occasion something happened. He hit the elephant, it is true, and in a mortal spot, but not in a spot that was immediately fatal, and the great brute charged. That there was no earthly chance for him unless a miracle were to happen he knew at once. He had a considerable space of open ground to cover, the bushes that had sheltered him during his stalk offered no protection, the tree beneath which he stood was unclimbable, and his rifle had jammed. Although he realised that it was hopeless he turned round and ran for his life. There was nothing else that he could do.

The elephant came pounding along behind him at a speed incredible in so ungainly a beast and would have caught him in another few yards had not Fearless come to the rescue. Very carefully, with a perfectly steady hand and eye, he covered the charging brute and pulled the trigger. There is one spot, no bigger than a saucer, in the front of an elephant's skull where the bone is rather thinner than elsewhere, and this spot the bullet from Fearless's rifle found and the great mountain of flesh came crashing to the ground not ten yards behind the flying man. Passinger's life was saved and again the two men joined in a long handclasp.

"Thanks, old man," Passinger panted a few moments later.

"That's all right," Fearless replied. "One good turn deserves another you know."

It was a long job cutting out the tusks, and late in the evening when they overtook the rest of the party, still some miles from Nganda, so they decided to camp and finish their journey on the morrow. Little did they guess as they crawled beneath their mosquito curtains what that morrow was to bring forth.

CHAPTER XI

THE VENGEANCE OF THE GORILLAS

I T WILL BE NECESSARY now to go back to the day on which Passinger and his party left Nganda, that the reader may know what had been occurring during their week's absence in the forest. On that first night Msuta did not sleep any too soundly. The possession of what seemed to him a very large number of guns and unlimited ammunition had set his mind at rest to some extent, but the belief that if the gorillas were injured or even offended they would wreak a terrible vengeance on the village was so deeply ingrained that he could not get it out of his head, and the recent death of the two watchers who had slept at their posts did not tend to help matters.

Msuta was not the only one in the village who was restless. It is doubtful, indeed, whether there was one of his people who was not, so the sentries and those men whose duty it was to watch over the captive gorilla had no difficulty in keeping awake. But as it turned out they might quite well have forgotten their worries and slept in peace—sentries and all. No sound disturbed the silence. Everything was as quiet and as peaceful as the grave. Never once throughout the night did the gorilla move, except to get into a more comfortable position, and dawn broke, as it had done thousands of times before, upon a village which nothing had come to disturb throughout the night except the unfounded fears of the inhabitants.

The next night was equally uneventful and by then the people were feeling at their ease again. They lay down to sleep on the third evening after the departure of Passinger with no fears as to what might happen to them, for no sign of a gorilla had been seen, even by the watchers in the forest, and though the sentries were still kept at their posts after dark by Msuta, they were not inclined to be so strictly on the qui vive as during the two preceding nights.

At that time Passinger and Fearless were in their camp a mile away from the tree which sheltered the female gorilla and her young one. They were quite content that all was well at Nganda, for instructions had been left with Msuta that if there was a recurrence of the raid on the cages or any attempt at another rescue he was immediately to dispatch a swift messenger with the news. Fearless did not for one moment expect that any such attempt would be made and was quite confident that, if it was, it would be on the night of their departure. This would have given any messenger more than ample time to have reached the camp ere this and he felt absolutely free of worry.

It has already been said that the bright moon looking down upon sleeping Nganda that night saw no movement but an occasional one from the sentries or the men whose duty it was to watch over the captured gorilla—and these were very occasional. Neither sentries nor watchers had been relieved with that meticulous care characteristic of well-organised societies. They were tired and believed, having been left for two nights in peace, that there was no need for them to have been posted a third time. Some of them slept deliberately without making any attempt to fulfill their duties and none of them kept a very keen lookout. The watchers were of the same opinion, they too considered their employment to be a mere farce. No lamb could have been more docile than the animal they were supposed to be guarding. It had never given one moment's trouble or anxiety since it had been caught had gone so far, even, as to take food gently from the hand of a greatly-daring watcher. What reason could there be for keeping men from their sleep all night to sit beside its cage? None, they decided unanimously; and so, like the sentries, they did not trouble to keep a careful watch.

It is probable that it would not have made any difference if they had. One man there was who saw them, those same dark, silent forms with their tall leader, creeping out of the forest towards the village. At first he did not believe his eyes, so vague and shadow-like were the advancing figures, and he realised that they had not deceived him too late to save his life, but, by chance, in time to give the alarm. As long, sinewy fingers gripped his throat the sentry convulsively squeezed the trigger of his rifle and its loud report shattered the silence of the night. It is doubtful whether he heard it himself. It is doubtful, even, whether he fired the shot consciously. But it had the desired effect and the village was roused.

There was no cautious advance now across a deserted market-place, no directing of stealthy shadowy forms by signs. That same double hoot, like the hoot of an owl, was given as soon as the rifle was fired and with a wild rush the attacking band swept into the village. It would have been abundantly clear to anybody watching that there was method in the way they advanced. Some spread out to the right, others to the left, and each individual seemed to know exactly where it was to go. A large body, in the centre of which was the leader, easily distinguishable by his greater height, made straight for the cages. These they surrounded as soon as they reached them in a serried rank, facing outwards, while their chief, as once before, fumbled with the bolts. This time he slid them back without so much difficulty, but the door did not open and it was some time before he discovered the two padlocks which Fearless had put on. When he did find them and had realised that it was they which were responsible for the unlooked-for delay, he wasted further time trying to open them and, failing in this, gave a sort of hissing grunt. One of his subordinates immediately came to his side and after what seemed to be whispered instructions, seized them one after the other and wrenched them off, strong as they were, with his bare hands, then he returned to his place in the ranks while the released prisoner and the leader threw themselves into each other's arms and stood for a long moment locked in a close embrace.

Again the double hoot was given, this time only loud enough for those in the immediate vicinity to hear, and the ranks surrounding the cages formed line in open order and advanced, not as steadily as Guards on parade, perhaps, but quite steadily enough, towards the main cluster of huts. None carried spears but each was armed with a heavy club held in the left hand, and very formidable they looked. All directions were given by the leader by means of those owl-like hoots, but otherwise no sound was heard, and the silence added to the strangeness and horror of the scene—a scene such as no living man has witnessed.

Amongst the people of Msuta there was no order, nobody to take command. Each man fended for himself backing up none, with none to back him up. For a moment the line of attackers wavered as the guns were fired, but only for a moment: Their discipline was marvelous, the power of their leader remarkable. One sound from him, presumably a command and the line became as steady as a rock and resumed its slow, relentless, irresistible advance.

Msuta was amongst the first to grab his weapon and scramble out of his hut when the sentry's rifle went off. There is some doubt, it must be regretfully admitted, whether this haste was inspired by any overwhelming desire to be in the forefront of the battle. If it was, that desire very quickly evaporated for, as soon as he saw the numbers and the determined air of the attackers, he turned and ran as fast as his age and obesity would allow him—and that was a great deal faster than he had run for many a long year—towards the darkness of the forest. But hardly had he disappeared from the market-place before he was back again and on his heels came one of the attackers with uplifted club.

As he reached the open space and found himself rushing straight towards that long, determined line, Msuta gave a shriek of utter despair and fell gibbering to his knees. Gone was the dignity that had once been his. He was a sweating, terrified old man, shaking like a jelly, breathless and hopeless, praying feverishly for life. But his prayers were to vain, for to a moment his pursuer was upon him, the great club came crashing down on the woolly head and Msuta's brains were splashing the dust of the market-place. The gun by which he had set such store, to obtain which he had dared so much had failed to serve him in his hour of need; and this is not altogether surprising, for so great had been his terror that he had never thought to fire it.

In every direction his people were suffering a like fate. The village was surrounded and all who attempted to reach the shelter of the forest were slaughtered by their enemies outside before they could reach it. Those who remained in the village had to face that inexorable, slowly advancing line. A few there were who put up some sort of a fight, but they were very few and their courage was the courage of despair. The vast majority were utterly cowed. What they had always feared, what they had been subconsciously certain of ever since the arrival of the Englishmen in their village, had come to pass. They had allowed the gorillas to be injured, had connived at the injury done them, and the gorillas were wreaking their vengeance on Nganda.

It is doubtful whether anything more orderly than that slow advance has ever been seen under similar circumstances, even amongst the most civilised and highly trained of peoples. As any part of the long line reached a hut the members in that spot, and in that spot alone, tore it to bits, smashed whatever it contained that could be smashed, killed every occupant that had sought shelter there or clung instinctively to their home, whether man, woman or little child, and then marched on. The remainder stood and waited until the work of destruction was complete. Never for one moment was the line broken, and this in spite of the fact that the attackers were armed only with clubs, had no shelter and were exposed to gunfire. It was not such shooting, admittedly, as is seen on the ranges at Bisley, but some of the shots were bound to tell and more than one of the steady line was hit. Never a sound came from the wounded, though, and unless they were dead or helplessly crippled they kept their places somehow.

There came a time when not a hut remained standing, not a living inhabitant of Nganda was to be seen. As a matter of fact only one, a young girl, had reached the forest and she was badly hurt. A club had smashed her shoulder and her father and brother had fallen across her body with their brains dashed out. There she had been left for dead, but she had not lost consciousness, and when a favourable opportunity had offered she had managed somehow to crawl out and slip painfully away into the surrounding gloom. When the last hut had been levelled the double hoot, like the hoot of an owl was given once more and those who had wrought the destruction faced about and returned to the market-place. There they formed a wide circle, facing outwards, in the centre of which their leader and the freed gorilla took their places. Then another hoot broke the silence and they stood waiting, their half-raised clubs gripped in their left hands.

They had not long to wait. In a very few moments there was seen advancing another long line, the comrades whom they had left to surround the village. They moved slowly and irregularly, searching every possible hiding place, making sure that every corpse was actually a corpse with no breath of life left in it. Nothing could have escaped them, save by a miracle, but only two living creatures did they find, a half-dead old man who was promptly brained and an uninjured baby girl. This last was picked up by her finder, thrown into the air and struck with the club as she fell, in the same way as a cricket ball is struck by the batsman.

In time the two circles met and the newcomers halted and faced about. Once more an owl-like hoot was given, two hundred clubs were raised as one in two hundred strong left hands and then the ranks broke. The attackers had been dismissed. Freed for a time from the restraint of discipline they began to behave like schoolboys who have been granted an unexpected holiday. They danced and capered; they ran aimlessly hither and thither; they made strange noises which were presumably their way of communicating with each other. When after a time their first exuberance had subsided somewhat they left the market-place in twos and threes and began to search amongst the ruins of the huts. All sorts of strange oddments they collected; bangles and beads torn from the bodies of their victims, loin-cloths, cooking pots, and a hundred others; but they behaved as little children behave, delighting in some new-found treasure for a few brief moments and then throwing it away and taking no further interest in it.

Everything that was edible, and many things that were not, found its way into their mouths and long before the signal which recalled them to the square was given not a scrap of food remained. At the command they fell in like veterans of some well drilled corps, doubling to their places, this time in four lines, one behind the other. At a word the first two lines laid down their clubs in a row, like men grounding arms, and went off towards the huts once more. Another word and the remaining two lines followed suit. After an interval they returned, some bearing woven platforms of sticks, very heavy and cumbersome, others the bodies of four of their comrades who had been killed, three of them by gunshot wounds, the fourth by a spear-thrust through the heart. These last and a few that were sufficiently badly wounded to make progress a matter of difficulty were placed on the rough stretchers, the ranks were re-formed and silence reigned once more. Then a command was given and two by two the attackers marched off towards the forest, each of the dead and badly wounded being carried by four of his companions.

And so once more destruction came upon that clearing in the forest after an interval of fifty years. It was destruction complete and horrible. Nganda was no more and only the ruins of huts and bloodstained corpses marked the spot where but lately a peaceful village had stood.

It will be well now to follow the attackers for a time. After leaving the scene of their vengeance they travelled, fast and without a rest, until some time after day had broken. By then they had covered a considerable distance and arrived at a part of the forest which was free of undergrowth and studded with great trees. Here a halt was called and the weary raiders gratefully laid down their weapons as soon as they had been dismissed and prepared to eat. Each one foraged for himself, and as there were many vines, to the leaves of which they seemed to be very partial, it was not a long or difficult business for them to collect sufficient for their immediate needs.

When the pangs of hunger had been satisfied they betook themselves to the tree-tops and were soon enjoying a well-earned sleep. They remained there until after nightfall, not leaving their airy perches until the friendly moon had risen to light them at the work which they had to do. Then they descended, snatched a few more mouthfuls of food, and fell in once more.

Their journey this time was not very long, for when they had been travelling for about two hours they arrived at a large clearing on high ground, in which were collected many of their kind—all of them females or young. They were greeted with low grunts, presumably of pleasure, but paid no attention to them until once more they were dismissed. Then they behaved as soldiers and their wives or sweethearts might behave on meeting once more after a separation. The females ran up eagerly to the males who came to greet them and they sat down in couples on the ground, their arms round each other. Sweethearts or wives they must surely have been, greeting their mates on their return from a dangerous enterprise. It was strange to see the way in which they behaved. There was no kissing as amongst humans, no whispering of sweet nothings. The way they sat with their arms round each other was strangely reminiscent of the way in which courting couples are wont to behave, but the only other marked sign of affection was shown by the females, who gently stroked the large hairless patch on the chest of the males, apparently in admiration. But it was not for long that they were allowed to dally like this. There was work to be done and, doubtless all too soon to please some of them, the order to fall in was given.

Again a large circle was formed by the males. Between each of them was a space and behind them, they were facing inwards, were ranged the females and the young ones. It was for all the world like soldiers lining the route of the Lord Mayor's show to keep the crowds back. Dead silence prevailed and there was not a movement. Presently one of those owl-like hoots was given and then there marched slowly into the circle a strange procession. First came a score of males, evidently chosen for their size. They were followed by the tall leader, walking alone. After him came four stretchers, each borne by four males, on which lay the bodies of those who had been killed on the previous night and behind them again a little company of females, presumably wives or mothers of the slain. Last of all came another score of huge males.

In the centre of the clearing rose a little hillock, not very high but steep-sided and having a flat top, and round this the funeral party, for that is what it was, ranged itself. One by one the stretchers were carried to the top of the hillock, and the bodies lifted off them and laid on the ground. The stretcher-bearers, as soon as their work was done, descended and left the circle, carrying the now empty stretchers with them, and the tall leader took their place. For a full minute he stood looking down on the four bodies, then raised his arms high above his head, his face turned towards the sky, as though praying or invoking the aid of some unseen power. His arms dropped to his sides again at last and at a sign the two score picked males mounted to the top of the hillock and it was soon clear that it was for their strength rather than their size that they had been chosen.

The flat top of the little kopje was littered with rocks and stones, most of them far bigger and heavier than could be moved by mortal man. But these giants of their kind made light of them. Single-handed they picked up things that would have taxed the strength of Samson. In twos they raised boulders to lift, or even to move, which the ordinary individual would have deemed a crane or a crowbar a necessity. They piled them over the bodies of their comrades, not roughly but with gentle care as though they were afraid of hurting them, and in a surprisingly short time a large cairn had been raised. Finally an enormous boulder was lifted by six of the strongest and placed on the top, a fitting crown to a monument raised by such mighty muscles.

As soon as the last great stone had been laid the builders of the cairn came down from the hillock and took their places in the ranks. Nobody remained within the circle but the female mourn-ers, if they may be so described, and the leader when once more he gave his owl-like hoot. Then as one man the males raised their great clubs high above their heads in their left hands, held them so for a long moment, then let them fall to the ground. It was the last formal salute to their dead and a minute later they dismissed.

After that all those who were present, males, females and young, filed slowly up one side of the hillock and down the other, and as each passed the cairn he or she laid the left hand on the crowning boulder. The upraised clubs had been in the nature of a communal salute; the touching of the cairn was a personal and in-dividual tribute to those who were gone. Before the last of the long line had descended the hillock the first flush of another dawn was beginning to paint the sky, but the clearing was deserted by the time the sun had risen. Far into the forest those who had just taken part in that strange, impressive funeral made their way and dawn was long passed before a halt was called for rest and refreshment; and a very welcome halt it was, especially to the children and those who had had young to carry.

The spot had been carefully chosen. As before large trees were predominant, there was but little undergrowth and a profusion of vines grew on every side, affording an ample supply of food for the entire company. When they had eaten they clambered up into the branches as on the previous day and slept till dusk. Then another meal was partaken of, the column re-formed and once more the strange band began their march. Soon they were hidden from sight and the last sound of their passage had faded in the distance. Nothing remained to tell of their passing but the torn tendrils of the vines and a litter of crushed leaves.

On the spot that had once been Nganda there had been no movement since the raiders had departed save those of marauding carrion eaters, mostly of the smaller kinds. The body of the obese Msuta lay where it had fallen, swollen now to twice its size by the unkindly sun but untouched by bird or beast. Other human bones lay about which had been picked clean and not a few had been carried away to be gnawed in greater privacy than that afforded by the shade of the look-out tree and the ruined huts. Msuta alone remained as though there was something distasteful about him.

The sole survivor of the massacre, the girl who had wriggled with a smashed shoulder from beneath the bodies of her father and brother, was in a sad way. She had conceived a weakness for Sam, the cook, or perhaps it was for the tidbits that he used occasionally to give her, and it was to Sam that her thoughts had flown as soon as the alarm was given. From the moment she had reached the forest she had made up her mind to get to him somehow and she had been fighting to do so ever since. But weakness and pain, constant fits of faintness and lack of food, had proved too much for her, and at last she had given up the unequal struggle in despair. Three times she had tried to rise when she had fallen from sheer weariness and three times her legs had refused to support her. The last time she had dropped flat on her face in the middle of the track and made no further effort to move. There she lay, moaning faintly, until blissful unconsciousness came to drive away her pain, and her last word was "Sam".

A mile away Sam lay peacefully asleep, snoring stertorously and dreaming of a lady in far Dualla.

CHAPTER XII

DELILAH

EARLY ON THE MORNING after Passinger's narrow escape from death he and Fearless started off to cover the few miles which now separated them from Nganda. Four of the men bore the cage and. the young gorilla, which seemed to be none the worse for its experience and was not fretting unduly for its mother, and four others the two great tusks of the bull elephant which had so nearly been the cause of a fatality. All were in the highest spirits. The expedition into the forest had been an unqualified success, they had not only got what they set out to get but some exceptionally fine ivory as well, and they were close to their journey's end and all in the best of health.

They had been so long at Nganda that all of them, masters and men, had come to regard it more or less in the light of home and they looked eagerly forward to being back there once more. Even Passinger and Fearless spoke of the comforts of their hut and were more than usually light hearted. They headed the procession, closely followed by Sam, who was never far from their heels, and it was the last-named who first saw the motionless form of the girl lying face downwards in the pathway.

At first they thought she was dead, for blood covered her from head to foot, but Fearless soon found that her heart was beating though but faintly, and that as far as he could see there was no flesh wound. The blood, therefore, must have come from someone or something else. With a total disregard of the proprieties Sam fetched water and proceeded to wash the lady from head to foot and it was then that the broken shoulder was discovered. Passinger knew nothing whatever about first-aid but Fearless, as might be expected of one who had spent so many years in the wilds, was very fairly well skilled in the setting of bones. The fracture, he found, was a bad one, but he set it as well as he could, and that was by no means badly, and thanks to her continued unconsciousness the girl suffered no pain from his ministrations.

It was not until he had finished binding up the shoulder that he allowed any attempt to be made to bring her round, and long after that before she opened her eyes and found herself gazing into the grinning face of Sam. Why he should have seen fit to grin at so inopportune a moment it is hard to understand—perhaps it was through nervousness—but the smile faded from his face with extraordinary suddenness when the patient slipped her uninjured arm round his neck and murmured the equivalent of "Sam, darling," before she lapsed into unconsciousness once more. He could not very well let her drop and there he had to remain, supporting her against his knee and muttering ". . . fine thing" at intervals in a mournful voice.

It was a long time before she finally regained her senses and a full hour after that before she was strong enough to make any attempt to tell her tale. Though he chafed at the delay the distance to Nganda was now so short—no more than half a dozen miles at the outside—that Passinger decided to stop where they were until the girl could give some account of herself. But there was to be another delay yet, for the bearers of the cage, which up to now had been out of her sight, decided for some reason best known to themselves to move it elsewhere, and no sooner did the injured girl catch sight of its occupant than she went into violent hysterics, screaming and raving like a maniac.

This gave Passinger some slight clue as to what might have happened, though no idea of the extent of the disaster. He walked aside with Fearless when she had quieted down and told him.

"The gorillas must have been to Nganda again," he said.

"What makes you think that?"

"The girl. Didn't you notice how the sight of our captive affected her? She would not have behaved like that just because she saw a gorilla in a cage, especially a baby one, unless she had had a great fright from one of them. I am ready to bet you any money you like that they have raided the village again and set the one there free."

"There may be something in what you say," Fearless admitted, "but I doubt it. If anything of that sort had happened Msuta would have sent to let us know, as he arranged to do. I am ready to believe that something else may have attacked Nganda, enemies of Msuta's for instance, but not gorillas."

"We shall soon know anyhow. The girl is much better and we may as well push on now."

A light litter had been made and in this the injured woman was laid. She was extraordinarily plucky as far as her injury was concerned but evidently dreaded the thought of returning to Nganda. The assurances of the white men, however, calmed her fears to some extent and before they had gone a mile she was able to tell Fearless who was walking at her side, something of what had happened, though by no means the full story.

The first thing she could remember was being awakened from her sleep by a shot and for the moment she did not connect the alarm with gorillas owing to there having been no sign of them on the two previous nights. None the less she had hurried out of her hut and turned instinctively towards the market-place in the wake of many others. There she had seen the ranks of the invaders forming round the cages and realised that another rescue party had come to free the second captive. The villagers were not interfering with them in any way, nor they with the villagers, so she had stood well on the outskirts of the crowd and watched, believing that as soon as their object was accomplished they would go away as they had done on the previous occasion.

It was not until the attackers had formed a long line and begun to advance upon the huts that fear conquered her curiosity and she began to think that there might be danger; and even then she was not greatly frightened. She had walked perhaps half way back towards her hut when another shot was fired and, turning round, she saw a club raised and brought down on the head of a girl whom she had known all her life. Then she had run for the darkness of the forest as fast as her legs would carry her.

It was probably due to the fact that she was not as speedy as many others that she owed her life As she reached the edge of the village she was overtaken by her father and brother, who ran one or either side of her and a moment later a dark form had sprung up in their path and, with a club, giver her the blow which had broken her shoulder. As he struck she had stumbled, which doubtless accounted for the blow having missed her head.

As to what had happened after that she was no altogether clear although she had never lost consciousness. She imagined that the same club must have dashed out the brains of her father and brother and she remembered their bodies falling upon her. She had had sufficient sense to remain motionless and feign death and when, after a time, her assailant moved away to do his bloody deeds elsewhere, had crawled out from beneath the bodies and made her painful way unseen to the shelter of the forest.

"That accounts for the blood that was all over her," Fearless put in. "What happened after that?"

But she could remember very little about subsequent events. She had a hazy recollection of struggling on and on along the forest track, of finding herself several times lying on the ground, though she had no remembrance of how she got there, of frequent falls, and of a time coming at last when she could rise no more. After that her mind was a blank until she found herself gazing into the eyes of Sam—and she smiled languishingly at that sadly embarrassed individual who, as ever, was walking on the heels of his masters.

"So I was right after all," said Passinger. "It was the gorillas. The girl's story is obviously true."

"True in the main, no doubt," Fearless admitted, "but there are one or two details I cannot stand for. Who ever heard, for instance, of gorillas forming line and advancing, as she appears to indicate, like a regiment of soldiers?"

"Ants will do it, so why not gorillas? And don't forget that she has had a very trying time," Passinger counseled, "and is in no fit state to remember exactly all that happened. Her nerves are very naturally overwrought and you must allow for a certain amount of unwitting exaggeration."

"Perhaps you're right. We shall know more about it when we get to Nganda and that should be within half an hour now."

Rather less than half an hour had passed when they filed out of the forest track and into the clearing. They had half expected to find a certain amount of damage done but never the scene of ruin which actually confronted them. They stopped aghast as they emerged into the open, staggered at the desolation before them. Not one single thing had been left standing except the look-out tree. Piles of ruins lay in untidy confusion where once neat huts had stood but otherwise the clearing had the appearance of having been swept clean. It was not until they reached the market-place that they discovered the body of Msuta, still untouched but more swollen than ever and making its presence most unpleasantly known.

"Now we know why he sent no messenger, poor old blighter," Passinger remarked as he gazed at the bloated body. "I suppose we ought to bury him, though it will not be a nice job."

"What I cannot understand," said Fearless, "is why some considerate carrion eater has not come along and done the business for us. There are cleaned bones here in plenty. Why should Msuta have been left to rot?"

"Don't know, I'm sure. It can't be because he was likely to be tough. On the contrary, one would have thought that he would have been a very delicate and tasty morsel to those who like that kind of thing. There is no accounting for tastes though."

The olfactory organs of the West African native would appear to be less sensitive than those of the average European, and Passinger's men raised no objection when they were asked, rather than ordered, to dig a grave for the dead *sarikin gari*. They chose to do so, indeed, close to the body so that when it was finished they had only to roll it in. This was effected with the help of two strong bamboos and the myriads of flies which had covered the corpse like a blanket were left lamenting. He had been very useful to them, had fat old Msuta, and the Englishmen were genuinely grieved at his death, but they drew the line at interfering with his rotting remains and were glad to have seen the last of them.

While all this had been going on camp had been pitched on the edge of the clearing as far as possible from the village and thither the two men now betook themselves. The girl, whom they had taken to calling Delilah—perhaps because of some obscure mental connection between Sam and Samson—was fairly easy and going on as well as could be expected. She was weak from her struggle through the forest and the pain she had suffered, but she was extremely plucky and seemed to be quite happy as long as Sam was near her. When he left her for a time to attend to his duties she began to fret at once and, as Passinger put it, "to get the horrors."

Blushing was not one of Sam's weaknesses—or accomplishments—but he became painfully embarrassed whenever either of the white men found him at the girl's side. She made no effort to hide her feelings for him even in public and he was not used to that sort of thing. Besides all which Sam was, in his own estimation, a first-class chef, a linguist of great merit, and an extremely important person, whereas Delilah was only a common nigger. At the same time he had to admit that there was something peculiarly attractive about the girl and could not conscientiously deny that he liked being near her.

". . . fine thing, s'pose she catch um," he muttered to himself as he left her to go and see to the cooking of the evening meal. "P'raps have to take um wife. Gorblimey!"

Passinger and Fearless retired into the comparative privacy of the tent that they always shared and settled down for a long talk.

There was much to be discussed and many plans for the future to be made. It seemed almost as though it would be impossible to keep any gorilla in confinement, however many they might catch, unless they slaughtered a great many more, and this both of them were anxious to avoid. It was true that they had the baby safe and sound and the question was whether it would not be wise if they were to be satisfied with that.

"It is probable that none of the others know of its capture," Fearless said. "Both its father and mother are dead and we saw no others in that part of the forest. We never even saw so much as the track of one, which makes it look to me as though they did not go in that direction, at this season of the year at any rate. I very much wish we had buried the bodies of the two dead ones, but it is too late to think of that now, and I honestly believe that the chances of their being found by any of their mates are very remote. They must be nothing but a heap of bones by now. Old Msuta is the only thing I have ever known to be left untouched in these latitudes for more than a couple of hours, and as often as not the scavengers are at work before the creature is dead, let alone cold."

"What do you suggest then?" Passinger inquired.

"I suggest that we get out of here as quickly as ever we can. Candidly, I don't like these gorillas. There is something about those two raids that I do not understand, something almost human, something the like of which I have never experienced in wild animals before. We have got the baby. Let us be satisfied with that. As I have said, its capture and the death of its parents are in all probability not known to any but ourselves and the chances of their being found out, for some time at any rate, are remote. By the time they are we ought to be well on our way to the coast if not actually at Dualla. But there may be no time to lose and the sooner we start the better chance we shall have of completing our journey without trouble. I propose that orders are given to strike camp at dawn and get away."

"I am quite ready, my dear old man, to bow to your vastly superior knowledge of all things connected with the animal kingdom," Passinger smiled, "but I cannot see that you have anything to fear from the gorillas. You say yourself that the greater part of Delilah's story must be grossly exaggerated, whether deliberately or not is of no consequence, and I agree with you. I do not believe any more than you do that a horde of gorillas drew up in a circle round the cages while their leader freed our friend and then formed line and marched through the village dealing destruction as they went. I do not for one moment believe that they had a leader at all and still less that they deliberately posted some of their number outside the village to cut off the retreat of fugitives. But I do believe Delilah's story in the main and, bereft of all its trimmings, I think if would be something like this.

"The sentry fired the first shot because he saw a gorilla, or perhaps two gorillas, or even three if you like, and got the wind up. Before he could recover himself one of them was able to spring on him and tear his throat out in that happy little way they seem to have and that was the end of him. Then the rescue party, for I do believe most implicitly that it was a rescue party, went to the cages to set our docile friend free, and if only the villagers had had the sense to keep quiet and not interfere we should have been the only sufferers.

"But unfortunately they did not keep quiet. The shot fired by the sentry had wakened them and very naturally they ran out of their stuffy huts to see what the rumpus was about. Seeing the three gorillas or whatever there were, and I shall never believe that it was more than half a dozen at the outside, some idiot fires off his rifle, probably by mistake, and one of them goes for him. The rest is as clear as daylight. There was a general panic, they had nobody to lead them, the thought that the vengeance they had always expected was now about to become an accomplished fact drove them crazy with fear, and they ran round and round the village, too scared to seek the shelter of the woods. While they ran the gorillas tapped them gently on the head one by one and that was that."

"Very ingenious up to a point," Fearless conceded, "but what about the blood that was all over the girl when we discovered her? What about all the bones we have found and buried? Why is there no living inhabitant of Nganda left except Delilah?

"There was doubtless plenty of blood splashing about anyhow and Delilah could have got herself smothered in it inside the village just as well as outside. As to the bones, I am quite ready to admit and have admitted, that a lot of the people may have been killed. Your last question does not seem to me sensible. You ask why only Delilah is left alive of all the inhabitants of Nganda. How do you know that only Delilah is left alive? I would like to bet that there are plenty more of them, too frightened to come back, and that if we wait here for a day or two we shall find them dribbling in by ones and twos."

"It is no use arguing about it because yours is the common sense point of view, I suppose," Fearless admitted. "All the same I am not happy. I do not like the business at all, and if it was not that I have a habit of seeing things through and carrying out my contracts I should set that baby free and get out of here this very night. However, except for the actual trapping, you are the boss of this expedition and your word goes. Whatever you may decide I shall not grumble and of course I will stick to you whatever happens. But I do advise you very strongly not to stop in Nganda any longer than you can help. I have got a feeling which I am unable to explain that if you do it will mean trouble."

"Thanks, old man," Passinger said as he rose from his camp-stool and stretched himself. "I will meet you half way and we will leave here at dawn the day after tomorrow. Post as many sentries as you like tonight if you think it wise. Now let us go and see how Delilah is getting on and whether she has succeeded in worming a proposal out of Sam yet."

Arm in arm they strolled across to the little shelter that had been erected for the girl and found Sam squatting at her side, busily carving some strange monster of his imagination out of a piece of soft wood with a jack-knife, a relic of his seafaring days. As Passinger stooped at the low entrance to the shelter he rose and hid his work shamefacedly behind him, but not quickly enough to escape the eye of his master.

"Hullo, Sam. Carving?" he asked.

"Make um beast," replied Sam, standing nervously on one foot like a child who has been found out.

"Let's have a look."

Very reluctantly the cook handed over the piece of wood and Passinger examined it with Fearless, who had by now entered the shelter, looking over his shoulder.

"Very nice. What is it, by the way? The dragon of jealousy?"

"No know um, jealously," was the reply. "Make um toy for chile when get back Dualla."

"I don't believe a word of it, Sam," broke in Fearless. "I believe it's a love offering."

"Make um toy for chile," persisted Sam obstinately.

"Well, can I have it instead of the chile?" Passinger asked.

Sam nodded his assent but this arrangement did not suit Delilah's book at all. It must be regretfully recorded that she flew into a towering rage. The carving was for her, she explained at considerable length and with unnecessary emphasis, and she strongly objected to the white men so much as touching it. Why did they think she had troubled to fight her way through the jungle, she would like to know? Was it for the sake of the white men? Very certainly not. The white men were the cause of all the trouble and deserved all that was coming to them. It was for Sam's sake; so that Sam should be warned. Sam was the only thing in the whole world that really mattered if they only knew it. He was worth all other men put together. He was wonderful; he was marvelous; he was beautiful; in fact he was hers. And with this last assertion she seized the unfortunate man, who had again squatted at her side, round the neck and dragged his head down onto her dusky bosom, glaring defiance at the world the while.

"This seems to be no place for us," Fearless said. "All right, Delilah. We don't want your toy; or your Sam for that matter, beautiful though he is. But we do want him to cook the supper; so get on with it, you old rascal, and if you behave yourself we will both be godfathers to the first."

Sam was all smiles again when at last he had succeeded in lifting his face from its tumultuously-heaving resting place and as soon as she understood that all was well, Delilah began to smile too, her outburst forgotten.

"S'pose Sam take um wife," that worthy grinned. ". . . fine thing. Now make um supper," and he scrambled to his feet.

"You are nothing but an old matchmaker, Fearless," Passinger protested as they left the shelter. You ought to be thoroughly ashamed of yourself."

"Oh, I don't know," he replied. "I have only hastened matters a bit. Delilah meant to have him anyhow and he might do a lot worse. She has plenty of pluck if nothing else."

Dawn broke and the sun rose in a cloudless sky. Already the little camp was astir and very soon it had been struck and all was ready to start the return journey to Dualla. Packs were picked up and balanced on woolly heads, the tusks of the great bull elephant were shouldered, Delilah's litter and the cage with the baby gorilla in it were lifted, and the word to march was given.

First went the two white men, then the litter with Sam in close attendance, and behind straggled the bearers with the cage in the middle of them.

"Good-bye, Nganda," said Fearless, turning round for a last look on the edge of the clearing.

"Good-bye, what was once Nganda," Passinger corrected.

The long journey had begun.

CHAPTER XIII

HOMEWARD BOUND

THE LAST OF THE LITTLE CAVALCADE had disappeared along the winding forest path and what had once been Nganda was left silent and deserted. Disappointed flies still buzzed over the grave of Msuta and occasionally a harsh-voiced bird screamed from a neighbouring tree, but as yet no four-footed animal had been so venturesome as to come out into the clearing. Except for the birdcalls there was no sound but the everlasting hum of the forest drowsing, even at this early hour, in the heat of the newly-risen sun.

Neither was there any movement visible until the bushes near to where the camp had been pitched were gently parted and two small brown eyes, set in a black face, glanced furtively and suspiciously about the clearing. For a long time no other part of the watcher was to be seen, but at last it gained confidence, the bushes were pulled further apart, and a male gorilla stepped out into the open space. It was still suspicious and kept looking furtively over its shoulder, but every moment it seemed to gain confidence until, at last, it had become completely reassured. For some little time it searched the ground where the camp had been with the greatest care, going systematically over it yard by yard and every now and then picking up some object for examination.

Whatever its suspicions may have been with regard to the camping ground they evidently needed confirmation and it was not until it came in its careful search to the spot where the cage containing the young gorilla had stood that this was obtained. When it reached that spot it became excited and gave vent to a succession of low grunts, running hither and thither far more rapidly than it had done hitherto. It appeared to rely less on its powers of sight and touch than on other senses for, though it frequently picked up different things, it invariably smelt and very often tasted them before its examination was concluded.

At last, an hour after the white men and their little company had started on their journey, it was fully satisfied and without

more ado left the clearing on the side opposite to that nearest to
Dualla. There were no slow, cautious movements now, no furtive
glances to right and left. The animal's mind was made up and
there was work to be done with all possible speed. It covered the
ground at a pace much greater than might have been expected,
sometimes walking or half running in an upright position, sometimes, when the going was good, on all fours. When travelling on
two legs it stooped and did not make very good progress but on all
fours it advanced in a sort of loping gallop, the hind legs passing
between the arms, and its pace was considerable. Occasionally,
when the conditions were favourable, and that was comparatively
seldom, it took to the trees and swung from branch to branch; and
never once did it stop for a moment's rest.

Long before midday it had passed the open space and the little
hillock where the four gorillas killed in the raid on Nganda were
buried and here it paused for a moment to climb the slope and lay
its hand on the cairn, as a man will pause in the reading of his
morning paper to take his hat off when he passes the cenotaph.
Then on, untiringly through the forest. Past the halting place of the
gorilla band it went, over hills and streams, skirting a big, slimy
bog from which the steam rose in thick, vapoury clouds and so to a
part of the forest where trees of exceptional size grew on ground
quite unencumbered by undergrowth. Here it halted for the first
time, an hour before sunset, and sent out a long, harsh, roaring
bark. Then it settled down on a stout limb and waited.

For ten minutes there was silence save for the call of the birds
and the chattering of an inquisitive band of monkeys, and the gorilla was almost asleep, wearied by the exertions of its journey,
when its call was answered at last. In a moment it was wide awake
and again its harsh roar rang out to be echoed almost immediately.
Again silence for a time and then the sound of something approaching, and a minute later a second gorilla swung itself up on
to the stout limb which supported the traveller.

For a moment they seemed to converse in low, grunting monosyllables; then they started off once more, this time together and
not at so great a pace. A quarter of an hour's travelling brought
them to an open space in the centre of which grew one giant tree
and in the tree sat the leader of the gorillas. On the edge of the
clearing they stopped and the weary traveller sat down to wait
while its companion waddled across and clambered up the tree.
Soon after it had joined the leader that owl-like hoot was heard
and the brief rest was over. Across the clearing and up the tree the

newcomer went and again those low, grunting monosyllables were heard, without doubt the speech of the gorillas.

For no more than five minutes the conversation lasted if conversation it may be called when practically all the "talking" was done by the new arrival when the leader put his hands up to his mouth in the shape of a funnel and three times that strange hoot, like the hoot of an owl, rang out. It was no gentle call this time but a booming roar that might have been heard a mile or more away. For a time there was silence after that, then at a signal the three began to beat their chests, rhythmically and in perfect time, sending forth a loud, rolling, hollow sound. It was like the reverberating beat of a tribal drum calling the men to war. It was a dread summons which, even to the uninitiated, seemed to bear in its very timbre the whole purport of the message it was intended to convey.

All this time no sign of life had been seen in the clearing except the three creatures in the tree, but soon after the last summons had been sent out the bushes began to be parted here and there and from between them stepped other gorillas. Each carried in its left hand a great club and each remained close to the bushes through which it had forced its way. One after another they appeared, coming suddenly and silently into view on every side, until not less than a hundred of them were squatting round the open space. The leader turned slowly on his branch and seemed to count them. Then that owl-like hoot rang out once more, almost quietly this time, and they all scampered across the clearing towards the central tree. Arrived there they formed a semi-circle, at a given signal every club was held high for a long moment, and then the strange company squatted down in dead silence and waited.

As soon as they were settled a stream of monosyllabic grunts began to issue from the lips of the leader and continued uninterrupted for several minutes. He was repeating to them the story told by their companion who that very morning had been searching amongst the ruins of Nganda, many a long mile away. If his monosyllabic grunts could have been translated into human speech he would probably have been understood to say that the "white apes" had again caught one of their number, in spite of the revenge that they had taken on Nganda and the people of Msuta; that a young one had been captured and imprisoned and was even now being carried away into captivity. He may have suggested the probability of the captive's parents having been killed in the defence of their young one in view of the fact that nothing had been heard of or from either of them. It is possible that he harangued them, asked them if they were content to stand idly by while they and theirs were taken away to what might well be worse than death, urged them to still further acts of bloodshed, to drive the "white apes" for ever from their land.

We do not know what he said. It is all pure guess-work. But whatever it may have been there came, when he had finished speaking, a long, low rumble from the semi-circle before him—whether of assent, disapproval, rage or what, who can tell?—and he was plainly satisfied with the effect of his words. For a short time again he spoke, then his hearers rose, gave the salute with clubs uplifted in the left hand, and shambled away across the clearing to disappear into the forest, accompanied by the one who had brought the message. Only the leader and the one other remained.

For maybe an hour silence reigned once more before the bushes were again parted and that strange company began to reappear, remaining as before close to the point at which they entered the clearing. As soon as they were all assembled a hoot brought them scampering out into the open, where they formed up in two lines. Another short address and they marched off, headed by the leader, and entered a wide forest track lined on either side by females and young. For a time these accompanied them on their march, but not for long, and before two miles had been covered the last had left them to return to wherever it was they had come from.

Shortly after they had started the moon rose and helped to some extent to light their way, but it was still very dark. None the less they made good progress, mostly at that loping gallop which looked so ungainly. The white men with the captive gorilla would have a good twenty-four hours' start of them by the time they reached Nganda, and if they were to be overtaken there was no time to lose. The forest did not last forever and it was only in the forest that they might be taken at a disadvantage; therefore it was in the forest that they must be caught.

On the other hand they were encumbered with the cage, Delilah's litter and a vast number of smaller loads, which would tend to make their progress very much slower than that of creatures carrying no more than a club. Again, even if they had been equally laden or, rather, equally free of burdens, gorillas were far more experienced and expert at making their way over obstacles or travelling through difficult country, and this was much in their favour as, also, was their greater strength and staying power.

Some such thoughts as these may have passed through the mind of the leader as he hurried along at the head of his formidable band. For the most part he travelled alone, but from time to time he was joined, at a signal, by one of his subordinates, a sort of sergeant-major perhaps. He was a huge creature, about five feet eight inches in height, with a fifty-inch chest and an arm-spread of over seven feet. Except for the bare breast he was covered with coarse grey hair and, like those of his companions his face was black, its repulsiveness being added to by an almost white streak, the relic of a wound received at some time. At intervals he would grunt an order and he was evidently in a position of some authority, though he never gave a loud command.

With this sort of non-commissioned officer the leader had long and earnest conversations and there can be but little doubt that they were discussing the plan of campaign. The gorillas were vastly superior in strength, both physical and numerical, but it is probable that any creature so enlightened as their leader appeared to be must have had some idea of what a rifle was. Not of its mechanism or how to use it, that would be too much to expect, but of the fact that it killed or wounded from a distance. It had taken him only a short time to discover how the bolts on the cage were worked and it is unlikely that, having seen some of his companions shot during the last attack on Nganda, he would have failed to grasp the significance of the reports and, in all probability, to trace them to their source.

Assuming this to be the case it is not too much to suppose that he was puzzled as to the best way to deal with them and it is only natural that he should have seen fit to talk the matter over with the only other member of the band with whom he seemed to hold any converse. He evidently trusted the creature implicitly and relied on it greatly. It was the same as had been sent to meet the bearer of the news from Nganda in answer to its call, the same that had remained behind with him in the tree after his first address to his followers. But there was no "palliness" about their friendship and mutual trust. It was a clear case of master and man—of a master who exacted implicit obedience and a man who was accustomed and willing to obey.

All that night they travelled without a pause and dawn was breaking before a halt was called for food and a brief rest. By then they had passed the cairn on the hillock and it was there alone that they had slackened their pace while they climbed up one side and down the other, laying their left hands on the stones as they passed. A bare two hours they were allowed to have their meal and snatch what rest they could before they were off again, at as great a pace as ever and apparently as fresh as when they started.

They crossed the clearing where Nganda had stood, pausing only for a few minutes while the leader went to investigate the spot where the cage had rested and, possibly, satisfy himself that he was not out on a wild goose chase, that the information he had received was correct, and plunged into the winding path along which Passinger and Fearless had started not much more than twenty-four hours before. The journey so far had been made in record time.

At noon another halt was called and this time a longer rest was allowed. In spite of the disadvantages of darkness they could travel better at night. The heat of the day made the going far more wearisome and they could afford to spare a few hours. So they fed at their leisure and then climbed up amongst the branches for a well-earned sleep, from which they were not disturbed until the shades of evening were beginning to fall. Then off again, rested and refreshed, through the darkness of the night.

Again they travelled unceasingly, except for two hours at dawn, until midday, and by then they had gained many miles on the white people. While the gorillas foraged for food their leader, accompanied by his second in command, made an exhaustive examination of the track. He did not seem to be so good at deducing facts from the signs left by the travellers as was his companion, which was perhaps why he took him with him. His eyes were better than the gorilla's but his sense of smell was far inferior and he did not rely on taste at all. The result of their careful search must have been satisfactory for that night the sleeping gorillas were not awakened until some time after dusk and the moon was high before they resumed their journey.

In the meantime Passinger and Fearless had been getting along but slowly with their party. Here and there they were able to make fair progress, but there were more tree trunks across the track than there had been when they had come from Dualla and they found it a far more difficult job than they had anticipated to get the cage with the young gorilla in it over or round them. As a general rule they found that the simplest way was to cut their way round, long and tiresome business though that was, and the necessity of doing so many times a day delayed them greatly. The sunken bridges over the many streams, too, were a source of great difficulty and annoyance and more than once on the first day's march the gorilla narrowly escaped finding a watery grave.

Added to this their captive did not seem to be in such good health. Fearless ventured the opinion that this was due not so much to its confinement in necessarily close quarters or to heart-sickness, as to the succession of frights that it received when its cage was being got over the various obstacles in their path, particularly the streams, and the severe bumpings that it was subjected to on those occasions. It stood to reason that such rough treatment should have an adverse effect upon so young a creature's health. To Passinger's suggestion that it must have got pretty severely bumped about in its mother's arms when she was moving from place to place or about her arboreal home, he turned a deaf ear.

Fearless was admittedly worried about the young gorilla but he was far more worried about other things. He had a sort of sixth sense and was sometimes in that state which Scotch people are accustomed to call "fey". What he had said to Passinger in their tent at Nganda had not been said because his was a nervous or a panicky disposition. It was not. Never had a man been better named, for he was absolutely fearless and had proved it again and again during the many years that he had pursued the calling of a trapper of wild animals. Something told him that there was trouble threatening, and that something refused to be denied. His one great hope was that they might be able to keep ahead of it, that they might reach Dualla before it overtook them.

He tried hard to look at things from a common-sense point of view, to convince himself that what he feared could not possibly come true. It was quite ridiculous, he argued to himself, to suppose that one gorilla should be born with a brain so far more fully developed than those of its fellows as to enable it to band them together and take command of them. Passinger was right and Delilah's story, although Fearless was confident that she believed every word of it herself, must be a gross exaggeration of the facts. Gorillas did not drill, he told himself, like soldiers and obey words of command. They did not post some of their number in strategic positions to cut off the retreat of their enemies while others attacked a village and massacred its inhabitants. They did not go about in bands fifty or sixty strong, as old Msuta had suggested they did, and exact swift vengeance for every injury, real or imagined, that was done to them or theirs. Gorillas were overgrown monkeys, with considerable intelligence, he admitted, but they did not do such things as these, and that was the end of it. None the less that insistent, warning voice, that second sight which is, perhaps luckily, the gift of so few, kept telling him that they did, and had, and would again.

With considerable hesitation he had confided his fears to Passinger but, outwardly at any rate, that young man refused to be convinced or even greatly impressed. He did not openly laugh at his friend because he knew that he was in earnest and really worried, but he did make light of the matter and tried to chaff him into a brighter frame of mind. In this he was partially, though not wholly, successful. Fearless shrugged his shoulders and said he supposed it was all right, but he never once relaxed his vigilance. Not only were two sentries posted every night on the track on either side of the camp and relieved every four hours, but when they were on the march four were sent on some distance ahead and four others kept an equal distance behind. Thus, if an alarm was raised, the main body would have time to form up in some sort of order and put up a good fight.

They had just camped after the fifth day's march and sat down to their evening meal outside the door of their tent. It had been a day of difficulties greater even than the ordinary, and both the men were what is vulgarly known as "fed up".

"To-morrow," Fearless said, "we shall cross that range of hills. Thank heaven for that. There are a good two miles of open country and the going will be easier. Also I do not mind admitting that I shall be glad to have that treeless ground between us and this part of the forest. It may act as a sort of barrier. Gorillas do not care to come out into the open more than they can help and I am hoping that they will hesitate to cross it."

"You and your old gorillas," chaffed Passinger, but without any malice. "I dare say you are right though. I shall be glad enough to get over the hills myself if only because, if I remember rightly, the road is better on the other side of them. How is Delilah, by the way? I have not had a chance to speak to her all day and you have, I know, because I saw you attending to her shoulder."

"Delilah is on the high road to recovery and quite wonderful considering the short time that has elapsed since she received her injury and the state she was in when we found her. She had the effrontery to want to get out of her litter and walk for a bit today and I believe she would have done it, too, if it had not been for the pleadings of her beloved Sam and a little cunning work of my own. He has promised to marry her, you must know, as soon as we reach Dualla, and I jeopardised my chances of everlasting joy and felicity by swearing that it was impossible for anybody to get married unless all their bones were whole, and that if she did not do exactly as I told her that her shoulder might remain broken for months. After that she was as good as gold."

"Sam seems quite resigned to his fate now, I think."

"Sam is not only resigned to his fate but he glories in it—and not as a martyr glories in going to the stake either, but because he is supremely happy. The sooner we get to Dualla the better pleased he will be."

"I am very glad the match is so likely to come off. He is a very good and faithful chap even if he is a rotten cook and I am sure Delilah will look after him well. They deserve to be happy, both of them, and I think they will be."

If anybody could have seen round the corner of the screen of branches which sheltered the litter they would have agreed with Passinger's last remark at any rate. Delilah was nothing but a big child and, if the truth was known, Sam was no better. At the moment when his employers were talking about them he was squatting on the floor by the side of the litter and she was trying to fix a number of gaudy feathers which he had picked up for her in his woolly hair. Whether such domestic felicity was likely to last was another matter, but for the time being they asked for nothing better than to be allowed to play together like children.

Passinger had disappeared into the tent and he, too, was soaring in a dream of love, though he had no fair lady to play with his hair; he could only close his eyes and think about her. On the day before they left Nganda he had sent a messenger with two long cablegrams to be dispatched by Mr. Rogers, one to the captain of his yacht, the other to his fiancée, and he was thinking that very soon they would both be making their preparations to come out to him. Rogers should marry them at once, he decided, and they would spend their honeymoon on the yacht, going from one place to another as the spirit moved them, staying wherever they wished for as long as they liked.

He rose from the camp-stool on which he had been sitting with a sigh, half of happiness, half of impatience, and as he did so Fearless entered the tent.

"I am going to turn in," he announced. "I am absolutely worn out and tomorrow's journey will include a long uphill climb, even if the going is better in the open."

"I was just thinking the same thing," Passinger replied, and half an hour later the two men were asleep.

Two hours before dawn they were still sleeping soundly, as also were all the others in the camp. The sentries on the track on either side were wide awake but they heard no sound. Yet only a short distance to one side of the path a band of dark forms a hundred strong, led by one taller than themselves, drew level with the sleeping camp and then passed tirelessly on, as silent as the night itself.

CHAPTER XIV

THE FIGHT IN THE FOREST

NOTHER MILE and we ought to be in the open at the foot of the hills."

"And jolly glad I shall be too," Fearless replied to Passinger's remark. "It may sound foolish but you have no idea what a relief it will be to me to know that we have that stretch of open ground between us and this part of the forest. I shall feel more or less safe then."

Camp had been struck soon after dawn and the two men, with their followers, had been on the march for about four hours. For the last two miles the track had been rising steadily and it was this, rather than any recognition of landmarks, which had prompted Passinger's remark. The nervous condition of Fearless was beginning to become painfully apparent in spite of his efforts to conceal his thoughts and feelings and there was some indication that it was beginning to spread, in that strange, unaccountable way in which such things will spread, to other members of the party.

Passinger himself was not altogether unaffected, but he persuaded himself that this was only through sympathy with his friend. When he took the trouble to think things over in the cold light of reason he was absolutely convinced that there was nothing to worry about. It was only when he did not think them out that a vague fear seemed sometimes to grip him. With scouts ahead and a rear-guard following on, all picked and trustworthy men how could any enemy approach the column without the alarm being given?

In and out the track wound between the great trees, for the most part hemmed in on either side by a wall of verdure, though here and there comparatively open spaces were encountered. So much did it twist and turn that sometimes those in the centre could see neither the head nor the tail of the column, short though it was. As usual Passinger and Fearless walked in front and as they turned one of the many corners a dreadful sight met their eyes which made them grip their rifles and halt suddenly. In the middle of the track, not six feet from where they stood, lay the bodies of the four men who had been acting as the advance guard, their heads smashed to a pulp.

"Good God!" cried Passinger as he caught sight of them. Fearless said nothing. It was no more than he had expected; but now that what he had feared and foreseen had come to pass all traces of nervousness left him.

"Keep the others back," he ordered. "We will stop here for a while. Our patience is sure to be greater than theirs and in a minute or two they will show themselves. Then we can have a little rifle practice."

For ten long minutes, which seemed to Passinger like ten hours, they waited; but not a leaf stirred, not a sound broke the stillness.

"Where the devil are they?" Fearless muttered impatiently into his beard at last. "I expected to have seen them before this."

Before his companion had time to reply a shot rang out from the rear of the column.

"Ah ha!" the trapper continued. "They have got behind us, have they? Well, that leaves the way clear in front, which is all to the good. Come on, old man. Let us go back and fight a little rear-guard action while the rest make for the open. It must be quite near now."

Back the two men went, but at the rear of the column they found exactly the same state of things existing as at the head. In the centre of the track lay the bodies of all four of the men who had been left to protect the rear, their heads smashed to a pulp; but of the attackers there was no sign.

"This is getting beyond a joke," Fearless grumbled. "The best thing will be for you to go back to the head of the column and lead on towards the open ground while I remain at the tail in case any more of our friends turn up there. You need not worry that I shall get caught napping. I am far too old a bird for that. Get on as quickly as you can, old man. The sooner we are out of this and in the open the better for everybody concerned."

Fearless had taken command automatically, as it were, and obediently Passinger retraced his steps. He knew which of the two of them was the better fitted to take the lead and was quite content to obey without comment. Neither did he do so reluctantly, but with a good will and, in a way, gratefully.

For a hundred yards the party marched on unmolested and then, turning a corner, they saw, not a quarter of that distance away from them, a tree trunk lying across the track and beyond it, through a gap in the foliage, the open hills for which they were making. It was the worst of bad luck that they should have encountered this new difficulty when what they had come to believe meant safety lay so near. Passinger cursed roundly, but luckily it was not a very big tree and he decided that the quickest way would be to cut a passage through it, and it was obvious that the sooner they set to work the sooner the road would be open to them. So the axes were brought into play and in a few moments great chips of wood were flying right and left.

Half the work had been done and no sign had come from Fearless when there was a crashing sound somewhere towards the centre of the column followed by cries of pain. Leaving the men to continue the work on the fallen tree under the directions of Sam, Passinger hurried back along the track and found that a great bough had fallen on the pathway, killing one man and severely injuring another. He could not understand either why it should have fallen or where it could have fallen from, for the trees overshadowing that particular part of the path were of a different kind.

While he was gazing upwards, trying to solve this mystery, he thought he caught sight of a movement in the branches and something prompted him to fire at it. The report of his rifle was followed by a scream of mingled rage and pain, there was a violent disturbance amongst the branches, and a moment later a black, hairy form fell with a crash onto the track. For a few seconds it lay twitching convulsively. Then it was still and the first of the attacking gorillas was no more.

There being no further sign of any of their pursuers Passinger returned to the fallen tree; and he only got there just in time. As he turned the corner there was a shout and he saw a dozen gorillas rushing awkwardly but swiftly along the path on the further side of the trunk, waving their clubs and evidently bent on annihilating the workers. They had apparently realised that in a few more moments the path would be clear and that it was the tree that had been keeping the men back. Perhaps, Passinger thought as he hurried along, they had known it all the time and deliberately chosen this spot to attack them for that very reason. It was a good thing that so large a number of the men were armed with firearms. Ten out of the twelve weapons presented to the people of Nganda had been found unharmed amongst the ruins of that ill-fated village, probably because the raiders had been afraid to touch them, although the other two had been smashed up. These had been allotted to ten trustworthy men and in addition to them there were four others who had been armed from the start as well as Passinger and Fearless, making a total of sixteen.

Before the hurrying white man could reach the fallen trunk the first of the gorillas had clambered up on to it, but only to be met by a charge of shot in the face, from the gun which had been given to Sam, which blew half its head away. Another shot tore a hole in the side of the next arrival and the remainder, deeming discretion the better part of valour, turned and ran even more quickly than they had advanced. They had five and twenty yards to go before they could turn aside into the undergrowth and Passinger was in time to get in a shot at the last of them.

The bullet passed through both the animal's thighs, smashing them, and never, surely, was anything heard approaching the thundering ferocity of the roar it gave as it fell. It sat on the ground, tearing up the earth with its hands, grimacing hideously and beating its great, bare chest with its fists, while again that appalling roar of mingled rage and pain rang out until the whole forest trembled with it. It was such a noise as one would expect would be made by the foul fiends of hell and yet there was something of a human intonation about it which only helped to make it the more horrible. But it did not last, very long, for a well-directed bullet through the brain soon put an end to the animal's sufferings.

Barely had this attack been driven off when the sound of Fearless's rifle was heard for the first time. Passinger dared not leave his post, so he sent Sam to find out if all was well. In less than five minutes he was back again—Sam was not usually a fast traveller but it may perhaps be presumed that he did not like being away from the side of his lady love—with the information that everything was O.K. and that all Fearless wanted was for them to get on as quickly as possible towards the open.

Very shortly afterwards Passinger was able to send back word that the way was clear and ask for instructions. When these arrived he pressed forward, keeping as compact a formation as he could, and another fifty yards were covered without incident. He had been very cautious as he passed the spot where the attackers had turned aside into the undergrowth and the body of the gorilla he had killed lay, but it was passed in safety and he began to think that the havoc wrought by the rifles had finally driven off their pursuers and that they would have no more trouble.

In this he was mistaken for, all of a sudden, with a roar such as he had never heard before, a band of the brutes full fifty strong crashed through the undergrowth onto the track and charged. At this point the path was straight but narrow and it was almost impossible for guns or rifles to miss, in however inexperienced hands they might be. The execution they did was terrific and very terrible to see. As such close quarters as they were the guns tore great holes in the bodies of the animals, while the bullets from the rifles crashed their way through two or three or more, one after the other. At the first discharge nearly a dozen of the creatures fell and as many again at the second. They waited for no more but burst their way back through the bushes at the side of the track and disappeared. Those of them that could do so, that is. Fourteen lay motionless where they had fallen, five more crawled painfully away, and there was reason to believe that there were others less severely wounded.

As there was no bend in he track just here to obstruct his view, Fearless made his way to the side of Passinger and they stood for a time talking, one looking either way.

"This can't go on for ever," he said. "There must be some limit to their numbers. I have killed one, one you got up in the trees, there were three other bodies this side of the fallen trunk, and I can count fourteen here besides the five you say are badly hurt and probably hors de combat. That makes exactly two dozen of them put out of action. I doubt if we shall have any more trouble with them now."

"I am not so sure," Passinger replied. "There must have been quite fifty of them in this last lot, so we shall have at least as many more to account for before they are wiped out."

"You take my word for it; they won't wait to be wiped out," and as he spoke another roar, even more terrible than the last, made the forest shake.

Not only was it more terrible but it was very much more serious, for it came from both front and rear. Fearless ran back to his place and began firing at the advancing horde at once. The same thing happened at the head of the column and again the execution done by the firearms was terrific. But this time the gorillas were not to be stopped so easily. A tall figure standing on a stout limb of a tree urged them on and, try as he would, Passinger could not hit him. He seemed to bear a charmed life for the white man, as has been said, was a first-class shot. Several times he could see where his bullets struck branches within a few inches of him, but always he moved slightly just as the trigger was being pressed, and presently the immediate need of driving off the attackers gave the marksman other things to think of.

So determined were they that a few broke through the first line of men, but they all fell before the axes of those in the second rank. The track was cumbered with their bodies before at last they drew off once more and Passinger had time to turn round to see how Fearless was faring. He saw him kneeling, with his shoulder against the trunk of a tree, a smoking rifle in his hands, and at that moment he rose.

"Get on," he shouted at the top of his voice. "Get on before they have time to collect themselves again. I will look after this end of the business all right."

Passinger gave the word and the column moved once more. The open ground was very near now, not more than a hundred yards away, and the open ground might mean safety. Twice again the gorillas attacked from the front, striving to keep the men in the forest, but the attacks were very halfhearted compared with those that had gone before, and easily repulsed. Yard by yard the open ground was approached and at long last the head of the little column had reached it. Passinger stood aside to allow it to file past, for he felt instinctively now that Fearless was right and that the gorillas would not leave the shelter of the trees.

When half of it had passed Fearless sang out to him to go on with it and he did so, marching at the side. Their progress was quicker than it had been at any time since leaving Nganda, for they had so little now to carry. Nearly all the loads had been dropped and they had abandoned the young gorilla in its cage long ago. There was one man, wounded by the branch, to be carried, and Delilah's litter, in which she had had the foresight to have the two tusks placed. Otherwise there was nothing.

It was not until all were safely out except Fearless that any further sign was seen of the gorillas, and then one of them, bolder than its companions, charged him. He dropped coolly on one knee, put his rifle to his shoulder and squeezed the trigger; but there was no report. The magazine was empty and long before he could hope to slip in another cartridge the gorilla, he knew, must be upon him. With a bound he was on his feet, then he clubbed the now useless weapon and brought it down with all his strength on the brute's head. The rifle snapped off short at the stock but his assailant fell and, as it did so, dropped its club. It was the work of a second for Fearless to seize this new weapon and brain the creature and a moment later he had turned and was following the others, who were by now some little distance off.

Fearless did not hurry himself. He strolled after the column as though he was sauntering down Piccadilly instead of in the wilds of West Africa. He was like that. Highly strung to a degree he would fret himself to fiddle strings anticipating anything, but as soon as it came to the point he was coolness personified. The little column was a couple of hundred yards away at the moment when he had brained the gorilla and he was at about the same distance from the edge of the forest when a shout from Sam caused him to turn round and look back. Half way between himself and the trees, racing along at that loping gallop, was a single gorilla. That it meant business was plain, for its great canine teeth were bared and the tuft of hair on the top of its head rose and fell as it wrinkled its forehead in rage.

Fearless gripped the club, which he had retained, tightly and prepared to meet the attack. Never had he seen so horrible looking a beast, he thought to himself, or so big a gorilla. The length of its arms was enormous, the muscles on its shoulders rippled like baby waves on a sandy shore as it ran, and its hideousness was added to by a livid, almost white scar which ran diagonally across its face. Why it should have chosen to attack him alone, why it should have dared to come into the open at all, Fearless could not understand. But its reasons were of no consequence. It had come, it was intent upon killing him and there was every probability that it would carry out its design.

"Leave this to me," he found time to shout to Passinger, then prepared to meet the attack.

This would be the second time that he had met a gorilla on equal terms. The first time both had been unarmed; now each had a club. The first time both had been fighting in a good cause, the one for his life, the other for its mate and her little one. The first time he had been saved from certain death by Passinger and Sam; what was going to happen now?

When it was within a few yards of him the gorilla rose on its hind legs and advanced slowly in a stooping attitude, its club swinging loosely in its left hand. Fearless gripped his own weapon in both of his and stood, his feet planted wide apart, waiting for the attack. It was long in coming, for the creature circled warily, looking for an opening. The column had halted and stood watching at a distance of about two hundred yards. Almost the same amount of open ground lay between Fearless and the forest, on the edge of which had collected every gorilla in the band which could stand on its legs. Passinger counted over forty of them and in the centre noticed one taller than the rest, the one that he had seen urging them on and had so frequently missed as it moved about on its branch. He would have liked to have fired now, but dared not, at the one that was attacking Fearless. From the moment when he had first seen the creature his friend had been almost in the line of fire and it had been too risky to shoot.

Round and round the brute circled, its yellow fangs gleaming between drawn back lips and the scar on its black face showing whiter than ever owing to its rage, while Fearless turned slowly on his heels and followed every movement. Twice it raised its club as though about to dash in, but thought better of it and circled on. The man was getting impatient but he remembered the mistake he had made on the last occasion on which he had engaged in single combat with a gorilla and he did not mean to make another. He balanced lightly on his toes, like a boxer in the ring, ready for instant action, and never for one moment did his eyes leave those of his opponent.

It was a strange sight, reminiscent of the days of old when champions of opposing armies would come out and fight single handed under the eyes of their comrades. On the one side stood Passinger and his men, on the other that extraordinary company of gorillas leaned on their clubs or squatted on the ground, and in the centre the two combatants circled round one another. Nobody on either side came to their assistance. It is doubtful whether anybody ever thought of doing so. This was a fight, as of old, between two champions, and the onlookers would take no part in it. It was not their business to interfere. Not a sound was heard. Nature herself seemed to have stopped breathing, waiting for the battle of giants to begin.

Of a sudden the gorilla dashed in and the sound as the two clubs met was like the crack of a pistol shot. The animal had aimed a terrific blow at Fearless's head and he had parried it, but the force of the impact jarred his left arm to such an extent that it went numb and for the time was useless. The second blow came from the man, but that, too, was parried and Fearless nearly lost his balance, which would have been tantamount to losing his life.

And so it went on—ding-dong, ding-dang—first one delivering a mighty blow and then the other, but neither of them with any success. It could not last forever, this titanic struggle. The pace was too great and already Fearless was beginning to feel the effects, in first-class training though he was. The gorilla was apparently as fresh as ever and seemed as though it would never tire.

The end must come soon, the man thought to himself, and in his mind's eye he saw his smashed skull and his brains untidily bestrewing the ground. He wondered whether it would hurt or not, whether there would be any feeling after that last blow was delivered. He wondered what Passinger would do when he was dead, whether he would shoot the animal that had killed him; and he hoped he would not. It was putting up a fine fight and a fair fight and deserved to live if it was good enough to win.

Whether it was that his thoughts momentarily distracted his attention or what is of no consequence, but somehow the gorilla managed to half get past Fearless's guard. Anyone of the blows given by either of the combatants would have been enough to fell an elephant, let alone an ox, and this one of the animal's was the heaviest yet. It crashed onto the man's upraised club with the force of a steam hammer and drove it against his own upper arm. Luckily the blow was turned aside or Fearless would have surely died, but there was a sharp crack and his arm dropped useless to his side with the bone snapped.

But instead of stunning him the pain seemed to put new life into the man. With his right hand he raised his club high above his head, ignoring the chances of leaving himself exposed, and with all his great strength brought it sweeping down. Never before, surely, was such a blow given or received. Instinctively the gorilla raised its own club to ward off the attack but it might as well have raised a piece of straw. Down onto its own head it was forced with a strength utterly irresistible, there was a sickening sound like the crushing of an eggshell and the animal dropped—brained by its own weapon.

Fearless had won, and this time without assistance, but it was only just in time. Another minute and the fight would have gone the other way, for he fell unconscious upon the body of his victim, utterly worn out. His legs refused to support him, his arms and even his eyes to do his bidding. He had come to the end of human endurance and could do no more.

As the gorilla fell a cheer came from the throats of the watching men, which turned to a groan when Fearless collapsed. Passinger had started to go towards him when a roar came from the edge of the forest and one of the opposing side, the tallest of them, rushed out into the open with club held high. His object was self-evident. Fearless was to be murdered where he lay. It would be impossible, Passinger knew, for him to get there in time to be of any assistance, so he dropped on one knee and carefully sighted his rifle.

It was a long shot, not less than two hundred and fifty yards, when he pressed the trigger, but this time his aim was true. The running figure threw up its arms, flinging far its club, stood for a moment motionless, then crashed to the ground. And immediately every gorilla turned round and disappeared into the forest. Their leader was dead, they thought. His second in command, too, was dead. There was nobody now to give them their orders, to tell them what to do, so with one accord they started for home. Neither were they seen again.

PETER

CHAPTER XV

T HE COLLAPSE of Fearless was only temporary. A few moments after Passinger had reached his side he began to stir and opened his eyes, and a little later, when he had had a draught from a flask, he was able to sit up and even to smile, though rather faintly. The setting of the broken bone was a difficult matter, for Fearless himself was the only one who knew anything about that sort of thing, but between them they managed it in the long run, though not without causing the chief· actor a good deal of pain.

"I managed without your help all right that time," he boasted, with a rather sickly grin, when he was feeling a little more comfortable, "but it was a near thing and I don't want any more of it if I can help it. It is altogether too much like hard work."

"I made sure it was all over bar the shouting when your arm got broken," Passinger replied. "That was the most awful moment I think I have ever experienced. I suppose, now I come to think of it in cold blood, that I ought to have come along to help you at the start, in spite of your shouting to us to leave it to you."

"I don't think I should have ever forgiven you if you had not left us to fight it out alone. How did it actually finish up? I can remember getting this crack on the arm and also slogging back with all my strength, but what happened after that is a blank."

"Your last blow would have been enough to flatten the Pyramids, so it is small wonder it flattened the gorilla. Your club drove his, which he had raised to guard himself, right into his skull and he went down like a log. Hardly had the body touched the ground before you fell on the top of it and you were still there when I reached you. Just as I started one of the gorillas, which is taller than the rest and seems different in some way, came dashing out of the forest, obviously intent on braining you where you lay, but I was lucky enough to drop him with a long shot. I was a bit afraid that the others would have followed when they saw him fall but instead of that they turned round and disappeared into the forest and we have not seen a sign of one since.

"I cannot make out that tall gorilla. During the fight amongst the trees I saw him standing on a bough urging them on and incidentally I missed him clean about half a dozen times. And he runs differently from the others, does not stoop nearly so much. Do you feel strong enough to stroll across and have a look at him Strong enough? Good heavens, yes," replied Fearless. "I am as right as rain now except for this blasted arm. Come on."

They walked slowly across to where the body lay on its face about fifty yards away and stooped over it.

"Turn him over," Fearless said. "I am so jolly helpless with only one hand"; and when this had been done, "Ha! I thought so. He is still alive. Prop him up somebody and let me have a look."

Sam, who had torn himself away from Delilah's side to follow his employers, put his arm round the creature's neck and propped him against his knee, and it was then for the first time that they got a really good look at him. Instead of being black they saw that his face was dark brown, as also was the bare chest. The hair which covered the rest of the body, though thick and coarse, was also brown in colour, almost ginger in fact. The head was quite a different shape to that of the average gorilla and boasted a well formed if somewhat negroid nose. But the most remarkable thing about the creature, the thing that made the two Englishmen gasp with astonishment when Fearless lifted one of the lids, was the eyes. Instead of the wicked little brown eye of the anthropoid ape, here was a large orb as blue as the white men's own.

"Good heavens above," exclaimed Passinger. "It's a man!"

"Good heavens above indeed," echoed Fearless, "but it is not a man. Did you ever hear of a man with a seven-foot spread of arms and covered all over with hair like this? Strange things happen in the forest and I will not deny the possibility of some native woman having been carried off by a gorilla at some time with results that you may guess. If this creature's eyes had been brown I would not hesitate to say that that was what had happened, but their blueness makes it impossible. If any white woman had disappeared it would most certainly have been heard of."

"I know," cried Passinger. "Mrs. Hillier!"

"I am afraid that won't do, old man. Mrs. Hillier died when her own baby was only a few months old and you have yourself seen that fact recorded on her grave-stone. She could not have had another child, so she may safely be ruled out."

"I did not mean that exactly," Passinger explained. "What I meant was that this might be Mrs. Hillier's legitimate child, the one that disappeared when she and her husband were killed and was never heard of again."

"Unfortunately that theory will not hold water either. Just because a baby is carried off by gorillas, as you suggest that child was, it is not reasonable to suppose that it will grow hair like its foster parents and develop a seven-foot reach. And there is another objection. Mrs. Hillier died over fifty years ago and therefore her son would of necessity be over fifty now if he was alive, whereas, unless I am much mistaken, this creature cannot be much more than half that age. It is very difficult to judge, I admit, but that is my impression."

All this time Fearless had been carefully examining the animal and dressing the wound which he had found in its chest. The bullet had entered below the right breast and come out near the shoulder blade, but as far as the amateur doctor could discover it had touched no vital spot, and he thought that with care the sufferer's life might be saved. The chief difficulty was going to be transport, he thought. To make another litter it would be essential to return to the forest to cut materials and this nobody appeared to be over-anxious to do. It was now admittedly some time since any sign of a gorilla had been seen, but they might quite well be lurking amongst the bushes ready to pounce out upon anybody who was so foolish as to take such a risk.

Fearless, however, was convinced that there was nothing to be afraid of. He had guessed, and as we know guessed rightly, that it was the leader of the animals whom he had been tending and that without him to guide them they would be lost. So Passinger and Sam, the latter very much against his will, seized a couple of axes and set off towards the trees. They saw never a sign of the enemy and in twenty minutes were back again with all that was required. It did not take long to make the litter on which the still unconscious form was laid, and then they rejoined the main body.

They had brought with them from the forest sufficient material to make a second litter, for the man who had been hurt by the falling branch, and as soon as this had been constructed the little procession started on its way once more, Fearless insisting upon walking with the rest. But they did not go far. The afternoon was already well advanced when they resumed their march and, though they might have made a few miles through the forest, it was thought advisable to camp in the open. Not that the white men had any further fear of the gorillas. They were quite convinced that they had seen the last of them. But the natives were evidently not so confident and, as they approached the forest again, began to get fidgety. Taking everything into consideration this was not altogether surprising. The matter which was worrying Fearless chiefly at the moment was the problem of the leader of the gorillas.

"It may seem an inhuman thing to do," he said to Passinger, "but I am going to tie that chap down to his litter. And I am going to do it now, before he comes back to his senses again. I do not trust him. Badly wounded though he is he might find the strength to get up and attempt something desperate. It would probably kill him, but he would take no count of that."

The patient was still unconscious when the two men reached its side and Passinger set to work to tie it down to the litter. It certainly did seem a rather inhuman proceeding, but he saw the wisdom of taking the precaution. As Fearless had said it might make a last, desperate effort to get its revenge by killing one or more of the party even if it realised, which it probably would not, that it would be its own final act in life.

"I have got a sort of idea," Fearless said as they strolled back, "that my doughty opponent must have been a particular pal of our friend. Why else should he alone have troubled to leave the forest with the obvious idea of avenging its death? From what you tell me the killing of other gorillas did not seem to affect him much, if at all. Not that it really matters. I am far too tired to think of arguing about things tonight. What do you say to turning in?"

"Turning in" was a simple matter, for the tent had been lost in company with nearly everything else. Luckily a certain amount of food had been saved and Sam was able to get together a somewhat scratch meal which fulfilled the requirements of the moment. In spite of the pain in his arm Fearless was such an old campaigner that he managed to make himself fairly comfortable and get a certain amount of sleep, while Passinger was frankly worn out and in the land of dreams the moment he closed his eyes. To the natives the conditions under which they had to spend the night were in no way out of the ordinary.

The sun was already above the horizon when Sam woke the two white men with the information that their breakfast, such as it was, was ready. They ate sparingly and as soon as they had finished hurried across to see to the wounded prisoner. He was conscious now and lay on his back, unable to move owing to his bonds, glaring at them with a look of concentrated fury. He snarled with rage, drawing back his lips over teeth neither so large nor so yellow as those of a gorilla, and savage hate flashed from his big, blue eyes, opened now to their fullest extent.

"I wish he could talk," Fearless sighed: "or that I could speak gorillese or whatever his language is called. He must have had some means of communication or he could never have led and ruled that savage horde in the way he did."

"I am sure he must," Passinger agreed. "When we were fighting in the forest I several times heard him give what were certainly orders. I wonder if he could be taught to speak a civilised tongue if anybody had the patience to try?"

"He might be in time, I suppose, but it would be a long job. There can be no possible doubt that he is gifted with considerable intelligence—far more than the average village idiot, I should say, and he can always talk enough to make himself understood. By the way, don't you think that for the sake of convenience we ought to give him a name? What about Peter?"

"Why Peter, if it is not a rude question?"

"Why not? If you can think of a better name, spit it out. Peter seems to me to be a good, honest, straightforward appellation. It also means 'rock', I believe, and this chap must be as hard as one or your shot would have killed him for certain."

"Very well," laughed Passinger. "Peter let it be if it pleases you": and Peter it was from that day forward.

Passinger's suggestion that Peter might be taught to speak made a deeper impression upon Fearless than he had been willing to admit. The more he thought about it the more he came to believe that it was possible, and the idea fascinated him. What a tale he would be able to tell, he often thought to himself. Every moment that he could spare, and they were many, he spent at the creature's side and by degrees, though very slow degrees, he began to get over his violent tempers. Fearless had not dared to loose him altogether, but his arms were free now and he would take food from his hand. He had even allowed him to examine his wound without protest, though the white man risked much in doing so and would certainly have had his throat torn out if his patient had happened to turn nasty. "Good morning, Peter," was his invariable greeting and the name was on his lips a hundred times a day. His delight when the creature showed that he recognised it was extreme, though really it was no more than might have been reasonably expected from any animal kept in captivity and made a fuss of day after day.

His marvellous vitality made the task of curing him a comparatively simple matter and after only a few days Fearless had known that he would recover. All his patients were doing well. The native, some of whose ribs had been stove in, was cheerful and thoroughly enjoying the unaccustomed experience of being carried instead of carrying. Delilah was so much better that she was allowed to walk for a little every now and then, and she made her weakness an excuse to do so with one of her arms round Sam's neck and one of his round her waist. Lastly, Fearless himself had nothing to complain of in the way his breakage was going on and felt happy that the bone had been correctly set.

They had expected to have considerable difficulty over the matter of food but their fears proved to be unfounded, for never once through all the days that followed did they run short, thanks to Passinger's skill with gun and rifle and the presence of an unusual amount of game. The track seemed to be less cumbered with obstructions than it was when they had traversed it before, the tempers of all the men were good, and the goddess of fortune was certainly smiling on them once more.

"The only thing I regret," Fearless said one day, "is that we have had to come back empty handed; without a gorilla, I mean. Don't you dare to start telling me that Peter is a gorilla because he is nothing of the sort. We are becoming very good pals, Peter and I, and one of these days I shall make quite a little gentleman of him. You will see us dining at the Savoy together yet. With a shave and a hair-cut and a decent dress-suit, Peter would be far more presentable than some of the people I have seen—and heard—drinking soup there, and he would certainly make an impression."

"With your last remark I agree entirely," Passinger laughed, "though I am not so sure about the rest. He might want to eat the waiter."

"Don't talk so ignorant, my friend. He would want to do nothing of the sort. Peter will be a perfect gentleman before I have finished with him. You wait and see. But none of that alters the fact that I very much regret having come back with no gorilla, though I should feel it much more if we had not caught any. In fact I should have felt then that, unlike the proverbial labourer, I had proved unworthy of my hire. But we did catch one—or, to be more exact, we caught three. There was nothing wrong with my methods and there fore I feel that my conscience is fairly clear. I have been trapping, as you know, ever since I was a boy, which is a long time, and once I have got my animal out of the trap and into the cage I have always counted on all my troubles being over—until this time. With these gorillas that appears to be the moment when the troubles begin. It is a new experience for me."

"Don't you worry about bringing home no gorillas, old man. We have had plenty of excitement and seen a bit of life which has been well worth the trouble and expense, from my point of view at any rate. As for coming back empty handed, that is ridiculous. What about the tusks from that elephant that was so fond of me? They must be nearly a record and your precious Peter is surely a unique specimen."

"Peter is not destined for any menagerie, believe me. I would rather shoot him with my own hand than that such a thing should happen and risk what you might say or do. As to the tusks, they are yours—not mine. Your shot would have proved fatal in a very few more seconds without any interference from me. The tusks are certainly yours."

"A fat lot of use they would have been to me dead, wouldn't they? My shot might have proved fatal in a matter of seconds as you say—indeed I think it would have done—but I should have been squashed flat first."

"Well, we shall have plenty of time to argue that out when we are safe in Dualla," Fearless wound up. "In the meantime where is that lazy rascal of a cook of ours? I am hungry."

One after another the days passed with but little to relieve the monotony. Passinger was kept fairly well occupied in the pursuit of game, for the whole company had to rely very largely on his rifle for food. Occasionally Sam was able to catch a fish in a sort of wicker trap which he constructed, shaped more or less like one kind of eel-trap, and there was generally some fruit to be had, though not always. As Dualla was approached the spirits of the travellers rose and there was great excitement when one evening, just before the usual hour for camping, a figure was seen approaching along the track. It turned out to be the messenger whom Passinger had sent off the day before they had left Nganda with the telegrams to Mr. Rogers, and he brought letters with him.

A halt was made for the night at once and as soon as he could Passinger tore open the two envelopes that had been handed to him. The first contained a number of closely-written sheets from Mary Humberlayne, the import of which was for the most part for her fiancé's eyes alone. For the moment he only glanced hurriedly through it to assure himself that there was no bad news before turning to the other package. This proved to be from the Reverend Rogers and enclosed in it were two telegrams, one from the captain of the yacht to say that he would be ready to sail on a certain day, the other from Mary with the welcome news that she was coming and would bring her father with her, as he had been able to arrange for a *locum tenens* to take over his duties for a time.

In his own letter Rogers mentioned that he was looking forward eagerly to their return, that he had taken upon himself to engage an empty house close to his own for Passinger's use until the arrival of the yacht, and that the thought of meeting his old friend Humberlayne once more after so many years had done him more good than six months' leave. The only bit of local gossip told of the death of the Landeshauptmann soon after their departure and the recent arrival of somebody to take his place. He had been discovered with a knife in his chest and a native woman, murdered in the same way, lay at his side. Her husband, who was without doubt the culprit and who had the sympathies of everybody in Dualla, had entirely disappeared.

The new Commissioner, Rogers said, was a much younger man than his predecessor, a strict disciplinarian, but just to a degree and excellent company. Even in the short time he had been there he had made himself very popular with all classes and the missionary had already found that his coming had made things a great deal easier and more pleasant for him.

The messenger, in answer to questions, said that he had left Dualla only three days before. He had, of course, been travelling light and fast, but Fearless calculated that, in spite of having the three litters to carry, they ought to be able to do the journey in four full marches, or five at the outside. On the receipt of this news Sam went nearly crazy with delight. He danced round and round Delilah, who was as radiant as he was, and invited everybody in the camp to his wedding which, he vowed, should take place within an hour of their arrival on the coast. When Passinger explained that this would be impossible he became somewhat subdued, but only for a moment or two. He was far too happy at the thought of getting back to the place of his birth, apart altogether from his approaching marriage, to be depressed for any length of time.

His devotion to Delilah was the joke of the whole company and he had a great deal of good-tempered chaff to put up with. Every moment that he had to spare was spent at her side and he was forever trying to find something to please her, forever bringing her little presents—the bright fallen feathers of a bird, or flowers, or some specially luscious fruit.

". . . fine wife . . . fine children like Sam," he was wont to say, and she was no whit abashed at his outspokenness.

The unwonted excitement kept everybody up later than usual that night, but they were on their way as early as ever in the morning. There was new life in their bearing as they swung along the track and it was with some difficulty that the more lightly burdened could be persuaded not to outstrip their companions. Fearless was compelled to slow them all down more than once, for the litter carriers were inclined to travel so fast that their occupants suffered from many a jolt, and he was afraid that their injuries might be adversely affected. But the best of good temper prevailed throughout and there was no grumbling at his orders.

On the first day after meeting the messenger they travelled considerably farther than on any since they had left Nganda, and the two succeeding marches were almost as long. Quite early on the afternoon of the fourth day they fell in with some people from the town out for a day's work in the forest, and four hours later they filed out of the track and into the open. The long journey was an accomplished fact and except for the eleven casualties mentioned—nine of them during the fight in the forest—all those who had set out so many weeks before had returned safely.

Rogers had been warned of their approach and was there to greet them with the new Commissioner, a tall, fair, typically Prussian man with blue eyes, a small up-turned moustache and very white teeth. His first action after greeting them was to apologise for the behaviour of his predecessor and express the hope that they would look upon him as a friend, eager to do all in his power to help them in every way.

Under the guidance of Rogers they went straight to the little house he had taken where, somewhat to Sam's annoyance, they found a meal already prepared, to which Passinger, Fearless, the missionary and Fritz von Zugend, the Commissioner, sat down together. They had barely finished when there was a tap on the door and in walked Sam with Delilah on his arm, grinning all over his face. Straight across to Rogers they went, and at the man's signal, which consisted of what must have been a very painful dig of the elbow in his lady-love's ribs, flopped down on their knees.

"Good gracious me," gasped the reverend gentleman. "What on earth is the meaning of this?"

"Make um wife," grinned Sam, who had evidently not believed all that Passinger had told him.

"My dear man, that is impossible. As soon as ever I can I shall be most glad to marry you to this lady. But not tonight; not tonight. It is impossible for me to do it tonight."

"No . . . difference," Sam almost chuckled as they rose to their feet, "but sad, very sad, because sure to do wrong."

"Sure do wrong," smiled Delilah in entire agreement; and a moment later the door had closed behind them.

CHAPTER XVI

"MABEL HILLIER"

THERE WAS SOME considerable time to wait before Passinger could hope for the arrival of his fiancée and he was not unnaturally impatient. But there was much to be done and Fearless, knowing what his state of mind must be, made a point of keeping him fully occupied. The house that had been taken for them was roomy and allowed of their allotting an apartment to Peter. By the simple expedient of taking out the doors on to the verandah and replacing them by strong bars they turned it into an effective cage, while at the same time preserving a certain human touch about it.

Fearless had been secretly convinced from the first that Peter was the offspring of a gorilla and a human being, though which of its parents was which he made no attempt to decide, and Rogers agreed with him. Stories of native women having been carried off by anthropoid apes, though possibly unfounded, were by no means unknown, and both the men would have been ready to believe that that was what had occurred in this case. But never had there been so much as a rumour of such a thing having happened to a white woman, and the natives did not have blue eyes.

Like the trapper, Rogers was struck with the possibility of teaching Peter in time to understand speech and perhaps to speak, and he spent many an hour with him, patiently repeating the names of objects which he held up in his hand. His name he had learned to know before the expedition had reached Dualla and since then his progress had been remarkable. After three days he would take first a knife and then a fork from a plate, or vice versa as he was ordered, and there were many objects between which he could differentiate when they were mentioned. Even Passinger, who had hitherto shown only a passing interest, began to be intrigued, and used to take an occasional spell as teacher.

One evening, after a lengthy sitting in the cage like room, Rogers came in in a great state of excitement while the others were having their dinner.

"Sit down and have something to eat," invited Passinger. "We are only just beginning. I thought you were over at the Mission enjoying your own food."

"So I ought to be; so I ought to be," Rogers replied, "but I could not tear myself away from Peter. I am perfectly convinced that he has been trying to say something to me this afternoon. He has been pursing up his lips in the most peculiar manner and there has been just the same look in his eyes as I once saw in the eyes of a man who had been suffering from temporary loss of memory and was trying to bring something back to mind. I do not mean to suggest that Peter is trying to remember anything, but I do think he is trying his utmost to articulate."

"Well, sit down and eat something now," Fearless said, "and then we will all go and see him."

"As you are so pressing I will, thank you, though indeed I ought to be going back to the Mission."

As soon as the meal was finished the three men went in a body to "Peter's room," as they called it. They found the occupant, sitting in a corner pursing up his lips, as Rogers had said he had done while he was there, in a most peculiar manner. As soon as they entered he rose, walked across the room, and took one of the clergyman's hands in both his own while his mouth worked painfully. For a long time he stood thus until the tears which had welled up in his blue eyes overflowed and coursed down his cheeks. Then, with a sob that was heartrendingly human, he flung his arm across his face, walked back to his corner, and threw himself face downwards on the floor. There he lay with his shoulders heaving, and there the three men left him, closing the door softly behind them.

"Now do you believe what I told you?" asked Rogers when they were back in the other room.

"Absolutely," replied Fearless without a second's hesitation. "To my mind there can be no possible doubt about it. Peter is doing his very utmost to articulate and his failure is breaking his heart. If he does not succeed soon it will break his heart."

"I have no doubt that you are right," Rogers agreed. "The question that I am inclined to ask myself is whether it would not perhaps be best that he should die. What sort of a life is he going to lead if he survives and learns? Women and children will fly from him. Men will despise and jeer at him."

"I had an uncle," Passinger broke in, "from whom men used to fly, if they had done anything to displease him or that he did not approve of, and women and children worshipped, and he was a damned sight uglier than Peter. I beg your pardon, Padre. I should have said very much uglier."

Rogers smiled. Even though he may not have used them himself he was not one of those people who will pull up ordinary mortals for every harmless swear word.

"Then perhaps there is a chance for him," he said. "Let us at least hope so. And now I really must go home. This is not the time for a respectable and self-respecting pillar of the Church to be drinking whiskey in bachelor apartments. And besides I have work to do before I can go to bed. So good night."

While he was sitting over a final cup of coffee with his breakfast next morning Fearless saw the missionary coming up the verandah steps. Passinger had gone across to the Commissioner's office to see if by chance there was any message for him, so the trapper hailed Rogers and together they went to pay Peter his morning call, inwardly praying that he was all right.

"Good morning, Peter," greeted Fearless as the door was opened.

"Gor, Peter," came in a deep bass voice from the corner where he had been sitting.

There was the light of triumph in the creature's eyes now. "Peter, Peter, Peter," he repeated every time he was spoken to. The two men were as excited as he was and there can be no doubt that he saw how pleased they were. "Good morning" was a terrible stumbling block, but by degrees it got to "Goming," and eventually to the two full words. When Passinger opened the door, looking for them, five solid hours later, he found the three sitting in a row on the floor, Peter in the centre, like three gossiping old salts on a cast-up spar. It was not until Peter had said "Good morning" to him several times that he was allowed to tell his own bit of news and by then it was lunch time.

Passinger, it appeared, had spent the whole morning in the Commissioner's office on the chance of a wireless message coming through for him, and he had not been disappointed. He had been receiving fairly frequent reports of progress, for the yacht was equipped with her own radio, but this was the first time that he had been in direct communication with her and it seemed to bring her, and his wedding day, suddenly nearer. The message had been brief but very acceptable, for it had given him the yacht's exact position and the assurance that, barring accidents, she would anchor off Dualla on the fourth day from then.

Sam had somehow come to know that this other wedding was in the wind and was vastly intrigued. Having been married to Delilah for considerably over a fortnight and engaged for many weeks before that, he flattered himself that he knew exactly how his young master felt and sympathised with him accordingly. He had been ousted from his post as cook, not without a struggle, soon after the return to Dualla, and for a time was rather down in the dumps until he had been persuaded that his appointment as valet was a big promotion. There after he had become as cheerful as ever again and the only drawback to him as a personal servant was his everlasting chatter.

Sam felt that he was quite an old married man now and competent to give expert advice to anybody about to embark upon the stormy seas of matrimony. The immediate result of this was that Passinger was daily bombarded with directions as to what he should do—some of them distinctly embarrassing. But it was all very kindly meant and the man took such evident delight in giving his bits of advice that his master had not the heart to say very much to him. Oddly enough most of them were pretty sound and might have been quite useful if embodied in a pamphlet for the use of callow young men just going out into the world.

Sam's great ambition was that Delilah should be "valet" to Mary Humberlayne when she arrived and he was for ever worrying Passinger to promise that this should be so. He had eventually to satisfy himself with the assurance, given somewhat grudgingly and in self-defence more than for any other reason, that she should at least have a chance to show how she was likely to shape at the job—if Miss Humberlayne would agree to that arrangement, which Passinger could not guarantee—and thereafter Delilah spent much of her time, under the tuition of her lord and master, folding and refolding the garments of his employers—sadly, be it said, to their detriment.

To Passinger those last four days of waiting for the arrival of his fiancée seemed to drag along in the most wearying manner in spite of the fact that Fearless and Rogers kept him as fully occupied as they could. Much of his time he spent in the office of the Commissioner, with whom he had become very friendly, waiting for wireless messages which seldom materialised. Fritz von Zugend had a girl of his own of whom he dreamed and was inordinately proud. In a confidential mood he one day took the Englishman into his bedroom to show him her photograph, and Passinger thought that he had never seen such a plain dumpling of a woman in his life. He naturally did not say so and gave a rather transparent imitation of gushing over her charms which delighted the Landeshauptmann and helped to cement their friendship.

All preparations for the wedding were made in the most approved and correct style. The banns were published in the little mission church, Fearless was informed that he was expected to be best man and coached, entirely wrongly, in his duties, and a number of small children were drilled in the art of throwing flowers at the feet of the bride. The question of reserving certain seats for relatives and friends of the lady and others for those of her husband-to-be was brought up by the latter as being most important, until it was pointed out to him that Francis Humberlayne would be the only relative present of either party and that his daughter as yet had no friends there at all. The wedding breakfast was arranged for, various people were invited, quite unnecessarily, to attend the ceremony, and all was in readiness long before the yacht was due to arrive.

The doing of so many things kept Passinger fairly busy, largely because he did all of them many times over, but Rogers had no more than his ordinary duties as head of the Mission to attend to and Fearless had nothing to do at all. Consequently the two last named, and more especially Fearless, were able to spend much of their time with Peter.

On the afternoon of the day on which he had first spoken, a table and two chairs had been taken into his room, for the men had not found it comfortable to sit on the floor and Rogers had been anxious to write down all that Peter might say. These had been left, together with a pencil and some sheets of paper which had been carelessly thrown down on the table, and when the two men came into the room to pay their morning visit they had found Peter sitting on one of the chairs making marks with the pencil. They were mere haphazard lines that he had drawn, with no sense or meaning to them, but Fearless was as delighted as though they had been a picture worthy to be hung on the line in the Royal Academy. And it certainly did go far to show that Peter's intelligence was as great as they had thought it was. When the point of the pencil broke he came directly to Rogers to have it sharpened, having seen him perform that operation on the previous day, and he never once attempted to use the wrong end.

"I believe we shall be able to teach him to write in time," Rogers exclaimed.

It was the first word that had been spoken, beyond the conventional "Good morning, Peter," which had been responded to with as clear a pronunciation as that of any man. Peter stopped scribbling at once and his lips began to work in the strange, painful manner they did when he was trying to make some new sound.

"Wite," he got out at last, and his blue eyes lit with triumph at the approval he saw in those of the two men.

Hour after hour and hour after hour Fearless and Rogers spent in Peter's company. When one of them was not with him the other generally was, except at meal times, and often they were both there together. From the time they first found him in the chair he refused flatly to sit on the floor and they soon understood that he wanted a chair for himself. Thereafter the three of them might often be seen seated round the table, for all the world like three men discussing some knotty problem.

The progress that Peter made was quite extraordinary and his pronunciation excellent. It is true that any word beginning with the letters TH floored him and was spoken as though it commenced with a V, but that, after all, is a common failing amongst human children and even adults. Every day he added largely to his vocabulary, and every succeeding day more largely than the preceding one. The making of sentences must be beyond him for some time yet, his instructors knew, but they were quite confident that in the not too distant future he would be able to converse like an ordinary human being.

Early on the morning of the fourth day after receiving his first direct communication from the yacht, Passinger was awakened from a sound sleep by the long-drawn hooting of a siren. He was out of bed in an instant and within a quarter of an hour his figure might be seen dashing at full speed along the path to the beach. His chin was bleeding from a gash given by a too hastily wielded razor, one of his shoelaces was undone, and he was struggling into his coat as he ran. But the yacht had arrived and what did the spilling of a little blood matter? Another ten minutes and he was being warmly greeted by the captain, but so great was his impatience that he was hardly civil to him. His only thought was to hold the girl he was to marry in his arms once more and he demanded to be taken to her immediately.

"It is only just half past five," Captain Redfern smiled. "It will be contrary to her usual custom if Miss Humberlayne is about for nearly three hours yet."

"But that is ridiculous," Passinger stormed. "How the devil do you think I am going to wait three hours?"

"Might I suggest that you should come below and attend to the cut on your face. I can fix you up with a jacket to replace that one which ought to be about your size. It is all over blood. Or perhaps it would be better still if you were to go ashore again and get one of your own. That would help to fill in the time of waiting. Breakfast is served at half past eight."

In spite of his impatience and excitement Passinger had sufficient sense to appreciate the wisdom of Captain Redfern's suggestion. It was not reasonable, he realised, to suppose that Mary should want to get up at that hour of the morning. He saw, too, that there was indeed a great deal of blood on his white jacket and that he was in no fit state to appear before the lady of his heart especially, perhaps, after so long a parting. So he swallowed his impatience as well as he could and moved towards the gangway. Before clambering back into the boat which had brought him across he turned for a moment.

"Of course you are perfectly right, captain," he acknowledged. "I was in too much of a hurry. Did not stop to think, you know. Was wondering if everything was all right. I will be back at half past eight. You might tell Mary, Miss Humberlayne I mean, that I shall be coming, will you?"

"She shall know as soon as she is awake," Redfern promised.

It was well short of half past eight when Passinger once more reached the yacht, but there was a slim figure in white waiting for him at the top of the gangway. They shook hands formally, almost nervously, and it was not until they had reached the saloon and the steward had discreetly retired that their shyness relaxed. Over what happened then let us draw a veil. It is no business of ours and it cannot have been anything very serious, for when the steward returned once more and entered the saloon, having paused for some time after his knock, they were standing one on either side of the table. It is true that they both seemed to be rather flushed and that Mary's hair was unwontedly ruffled for so early an hour, but that again is no business of ours.

Close on the heels of the steward came Francis Humberlayne, and almost immediately afterwards Fearless and Rogers arrived. They had expected to come with Passinger, and that was the arrangement that had been made, but he had been too impatient to wait for them. Introductions were soon effected and immediately after breakfast the whole party went ashore. Rogers and Humberlayne strolled off together at once. They had many things to talk about concerning days gone by and their experiences since last they had met. Passinger and Mary had no eyes or thoughts but for each other and Fearless was consequently left out in the cold.

"I am going to visit Peter," he announced. "I have not seen him yet this morning."

"Righto, old man," Passinger responded. "Mary and I will go for a stroll. See you at two o'clock."

They waved him farewell and turned away along the beach.

"Do you realise, sweetheart," Passinger began as soon as they were out of hearing, "that this is our wedding day?"

"Don't be so ridiculous, Jack," she laughed. "Why, I have hardly got here yet."

"But you have got here. That is the main thing. And I am not being ridiculous. All the arrangements have been made and the wedding will take place at two o'clock precisely."

For a little longer Mary protested, but not very much. She was only too willing to be persuaded and her lover found it an easy and a very pleasant task. When once that important business had been successfully arranged he told her of their long journey into the forest and of all that had befallen them there. Much of it she knew already from his letters but there was much more that was altogether new. She had not previously heard any mention of Peter and was interested beyond measure when she was told that he was actually learning to speak.

"Perhaps one day he will be able to tell us who he is," she hazarded, "and how he came to live in the forest."

"That is one of the things we are hoping for," her lover replied. "I have not taken a very great interest in his education myself— not so much, perhaps, as I ought to have done. Rogers and Fearless have been seeing to that and they spend every moment they can with him. I have had something else to think about."

"What else have you had to think about, I should like to know?"

"What else but you, darling," he replied, and the rest of their conversation was for their own ears alone.

By midday Mary Humberlayne had returned to the yacht in spite of Passinger's protests. She had five thousand things to see to, she explained, and if she did not attend to them the wedding would have to be postponed. He could not expect a girl to get married at four hours' notice and for the whole of those four hours keep her tied to his side. It was not reasonable. And so at last he was persuaded to take her back to where the boat was waiting and allow her to go on board alone.

"You have got a lot to do yet and very little time to do it in," was her parting remark. "I shall be at the church at two o'clock and mind you are not late because I shall not wait for you and you will have to find somebody else to marry."

"Don't you worry," was the reply. "I shall be there."

Punctually at two Mary Humberlayne reached the entrance of the little mission church accompanied by almost the entire crew of the yacht, to all of whom she had endeared herself during the voyage. She walked up the aisle on the arm of her father and soon, as in a dream, Passinger found himself making the responses that he had so often silently repeated during the last few days. Then the ring, which had belonged to his mother, was slipped on to her finger, there was a short address from Rogers, and the simple service was finished. Mary Humberlayne and John Passinger were man and wife. The days of waiting were over.

Down the aisle they walked arm in arm and out into the sunlight. She was delighted with the children who strewed flowers before her—dusky little creatures with very few clothes and very fat tummies. She was delighted with the attentions of Sam and Delilah. She was delighted with the wedding breakfast. She was delighted with everything. It was so much nicer, she declared, than a smart wedding at a fashionable church in London could have been, with all its attendant worries and ceremonial.

Humberlayne had arranged to stay for a time at the Mission house and Fearless to remain where he was until he should start on his projected trip after okapi. The newly-married couple were sailing that night on the yacht for an unknown destination, but before they went on board Mary was anxious to be introduced, as she put it, to Peter. So what luggage there was was put in the care of Sam and Delilah, who, to their immeasurable delight, were to accompany the bride and bridegroom, with instructions to see it safe on board and wait for them there, and the others went to call upon Peter as Mary had wished.

"Don't be afraid of him whatever you do," Fearless begged. "It would hurt him dreadfully if you showed that you were and he is as gentle as a child."

As they entered the room Peter rose from his chair. Mary was the first woman he had ever seen dressed in European clothes but he showed no surprise or undue interest. He walked over to her and shook hands as he had been taught, then started suddenly as he caught sight of a little golden crucifix hanging from her neck. For some moments he stared at it intently, fascinated, his visitors thought, by its brightness. Then he put up his hands, dragged something, which had hitherto been hidden by the long hair, from about his own neck, and held it out to the girl.

Mary Passinger reached forward and took it from him—a little ivory crucifix on a thin gold chain. Too astonished to speak she turned it over in her hand and there on the back, scratched but lightly and so much rubbed by long wear as to be barely decipherable, was a name—Mabel Hillier.

CHAPTER XVII

THE EDUCATION OF PETER

"MABEL HILLIER!"

For a long moment after the name had been read out by Mary Passinger then was a deathly silence broken only by the heavy breathing of Peter, who was clearly in a state of extreme tension.

"I cannot believe it," Rogers gasped at last taking the crucifix in his own hand. "It is true though," he added when he had examined it and passed it on. "There can be no possible doubt that that is the name scratched there, worn though it is. Mabel Hillier! What can it mean?"

"One thing at least you may be sure of," Fearless broke in, "and it should be a comfort to us in a way. Mabel Hillier was not, could not have been the mother of Peter. We know the date on which she and her husband left Dualla on that ill-fate expedition into the interior, we know the date on which she died, and we know the age of her child on that date. He was still a baby at his mother's breast and it is quite impossible for her to have had another. That is a plain, incontrovertible, scientific fact."

"What explanation do you suggest then?" asked Passinger. "Do not forget those blue eyes. They rule any theory of native women out of court altogether. It seems to me that the date we have both seen on her tombstone must be incorrect."

"I will stake my life it is not incorrect," Fearless exclaimed. "Those tombstones were put up by somebody who was interested and that somebody was a European. I would not mind going so far as to bet that it was he who chiselled the lettering on them. They were not carved by an expert and it is equally certain that they are not the work of a native craftsman. In my spare time since our return here I have wandered around a good deal, as you know, for the most part trying to pick up information which might be useful to me on my okapi trip, and I have heard some strange bits of gossip. One of them was about the Hilliers, and I paid so little attention to it that I had almost forgotten it until now and would certainly have never believed it. To-day's events have altered my opinion and I will tell you what I heard.

"There is a man who lives right on the edge of the forest at the back of the Mission Station who has made several trips into the interior and has gained quite a reputation as a hunter. I went to him in the first place because I thought he was more likely to be able to give me the sort of information that I sought than anybody else in Dualla, and I was right. He has been very useful and is coming with me when I start as my head man. Besides giving me information that was useful he told me many other things, some of which were interesting, and amongst them that he had been to Nganda. His father, it appears, was the personal servant of the Commissioner who was in office at the time of the Hilliers' murder and, knowing that he was going in the direction of Nganda, he told him to visit the grave of Mabel Hillier and see that the stone was in good repair. He did as he was asked and on his return to Dualla found his father on his deathbed.

"He seems to have reported that Mabel Hillier's tombstone was all right except for some of the letters having become clogged with moss or something and that he had cleaned them out, at which the dying man was vastly pleased. He then appears to have added that he had performed the same service to Hillier's stone, and immediately his father began to curse him roundly. When his rage had subsided somewhat he explained the cause of it. Remember, please, that I am only repeating what I heard second-hand after a lapse of nearly half a century from the lips of a native. I do not vouch for the truth of one word of it and, as I have explained, did not believe it myself at the time. I tell it for what it is worth.

"According to the dying man's story—and I suppose even West African natives are not much given to telling lies on their death-bed—he had been wakened one night from sleep by the sound of voices in his master's office. Curiosity had prompted him to creep up to the window to find out what it was about, for it was then past midnight, and he had seen the Commissioner talking to Mrs. Hillier and holding her baby in his arms. He was assuring her that he would look after the child and she, with the tears streaming down her face, had hung a crucifix which she took from her own neck round that of the baby. Then she had kissed her boy and said that she must go, and at that moment the watcher had heard footsteps approaching and been compelled to leave his post of vantage.

"But he was too interested to go far, and though from his new position he could see nothing and only hear a word now and again, he lingered on.

"He had seen, as he passed through the beam of light which shone through the opened door, that the new-comer was Mrs. Hillier's husband, and shortly afterwards the voice of the Commissioner was raised in anger. The replies, in a lower voice, evidently that of Hillier, were quite incomprehensible, but the eavesdropper could make out much of what his master was saying. The last thing he heard was an announcement that he was going to arrest Hillier immediately and he waited for no more, expecting that the Commissioner would be coming to rouse him and the other men at once. But he never came. For a long time the native lay awake waiting for the summons, but when he heard the Hilliers go he supposed that his master had changed his mind and went to sleep.

"Next morning the Landeshauptmann was found lying unconscious on the floor of his office, nearly killed by a blow on the back of his head. It was many days before he regained his senses and during all that time his personal servant never left his side. It was thus that he learned, from his master's ravings, that it was Hillier who had struck him down from behind—and Hillier was gone away with his wife and child. The forest had swallowed them up.

"It was many weeks after that that a native of the name of Abu had come with news of the murder. Another white man arrived at Dualla about that time and he had set out at once for Nganda to inquire into the matter. He came back having found the grave of Hillier and the body of his wife, which he had buried. Then he had gone away again.

"Abu had had many tales to tell of the cruelty of the missionary to his young wife, of how he had refused to use his medical skill and left her to do what she could in that way for the natives, of how he had brought lying accusations against one of the people of Nganda, and of how that had been the cause of his death—though not of his wife's. That, and the disappearance of the boy, had always remained a mystery.

"The Commissioner knew that his body servant was aware of the whole truth of what had occurred on the night of the Hilliers' visit to his office. He knew, too, that he was to be trusted to keep the knowledge to himself, and had a very strong suspicion that he had guessed at the love which his master bore, in all purity of thought, for the dead woman. Therefore he had confided still further in him and one night, some weeks after the departure of the other white man, they two had set off alone for Nganda, each of them carrying a flat stone.

"Those two stones were the tombstones which Passinger and I have seen. The Commissioner and his servant both hated Hillier, both knew him for what he was, and the only reason they took a stone for his grave was because his wife had set up a little wooden cross over it and it was thought that that was what she would have wished. That is the story, the unbelievable story if you like, as I heard it from the lips of that servant's son. You must make what you like of it and disbelieve what you can."

Fearless stopped speaking and again there was a long silence. It was broken at last by Rogers.

"Even if that tale were true," he said, "and I find it very difficult to believe, it does not seem to get us any nearer to the solution of Peter's parentage. All it does is to prove conclusively that Mabel Hillier was not his mother."

"That is all I meant it to prove," Fearless rejoined. "Who or what his parents actually are I am as fully convinced as I am that I am standing here we shall one day learn from his own lips. But that he has some connection with the story is surely proved, is it not, by the presence of Mabel Hillier's own crucifix round his neck? I have no least doubt in my own mind that it is the one which she hung round the neck of her baby in the Commissioner's office on the night before she left Dualla."

"It would certainly seem to be so on the face of things," agreed Humberlayne. "It is all a very complicated and a very sad story and I am inclined to agree with Mr. Fearless that the solution of it must rest with Peter."

Peter looked up at the sound of his name. He and Mary Passinger had been standing hand in hand throughout Fearless's narrative and it was only now that she realised this. She made no move to free herself, however, but remained as she was, clasping her husband's hand in her other one. There the three of them stood— the man, his bride, and the patient, sensitive creature that was half man and half ape. They were a strange trio.

"Peter is our only hope," Rogers agreed, "and I have every confidence that we shall not be disappointed in him. Already he knows sufficient words to make some of the more simple of his wishes understood and the meaning of many phrases is clear to him. Fetch the lady a chair, Peter," he added, as though to prove his assertion; and obediently Peter placed his own chair for the girl to sit on.

She accepted it with a smile of gratitude, for she was tired from standing, as they had been ever since they had entered the room, and glad of the opportunity to sit down.

"Thank you, Peter," she said, laying her hand affectionately on his hairy shoulder.

The instinctive action seemed to remind her of something and she turned to Fearless.

"The ivory crucifix," she said. "Ought it not to be given back to Peter? It is his, after all."

"I think one of us ought to keep it," her father put in before the trapper had time to reply. "It might prove to be a very valuable clue and help towards the solution of the mystery."

"I do not see how it could well do that," Mary replied, "but if you think one of us should keep it I propose that that one should be me. None of you will deny that it must have belonged at one time to my great-aunt, Mabel Hillier, and I doubt whether anybody living is more nearly related to her than I am; so in a way it is mine by right of inheritance. In exchange I propose to give Peter the one I am wearing. You have no objection, father?"

"None whatever, my dear. Do whatever you see fit. In fact I think it is a very good idea."

So Mary unclasped the little golden cross from about her slender neck and hung it round Peter's. Then, round her own, she placed the broken chain on which hung the ivory crucifix which had once belonged to her great-aunt, Mabel Hillier.

"There, Peter," she said when the transfer had been effected. "You shall wear that in memory of me while I am away, and I will wear this in memory of you. Perhaps we will change over again when I come back to Dualla."

The hours were slipping by and it was time for the newly-married pair to commence their leave-taking if they intended to sail that night. It was Francis Humberlayne who reminded them of this, little as he relished the idea of losing his daughter. She shook hands solemnly with Peter before they left his room and when they reached the verandah stood aside with her father for a while, talking softly. This would be the first time that they had been parted since her mother had died, while she was still a little girl at school, and both of them felt it keenly.

Mary, however, was happy in the love of her husband and visions of this new life that was opening out before her, and her fa-

ther realised that he, too, had much to be thankful for, more especially for her sake. Passinger was a thoroughly upright, conscientious English gentleman, honestly devoted to Mary, and one who
would do his utmost to make her life a happy one. He had great
riches, which he used wisely, he was looked up to as an honour-
able man, and he was a fine sportsman. What more could any father desire for his only daughter, especially when she so whole-
heartedly returned her husband's love? So he swallowed the tears
that would keep coming so near to his eyes, and soon they rejoined
the rest of the party.

In a body they went down to the beach and so on to the yacht.
There an unwritten rule was broken by many, for everybody on
board joined in drinking the health of the bride and bridegroom.
The sun was sinking before they left and as it dropped below the
horizon the graceful yacht steamed slowly away, while from her
bridge two white-clad figures—a man and a girl—waved a long
farewell to their friends on the little quay. The four men—Rogers,
Humberlayne, Fearless and van Zugend—stood watching until she
was lost to sight behind a jutting point of land. Then they turned
and walked slowly away towards the Mission Station.

Fearless slept badly that night. He missed Passinger keenly after so many weeks of close companionship. They had lain down
within a few feet of each other every night since they had left London—months before. In the morning he missed him even more,
although since their return to Dualla they had not been seeing so
much of each other during the hours of daylight, and everything
seemed to go wrong. Sam had been a terrible chatterbox and
Fearless had cursed him roundly for an incompetent fool many a
time and oft, but he had always got through his duties somehow
without making too many blunders and he had grown used to him.
The new boy who had come to take his place could do nothing
right and the white man put him down as being a born idiot. To
crown all the cook contrived to send up a thoroughly bad breakfast.

There was more than a chance that both of them had spent a
large part of the previous night indulging in the equivalent of our
"looking upon the wine when it was red" and in time this possibility occurred to Fearless. Popular weddings were far from common
in Dualla and there may have been some excuse for them. When
he had managed to consume part of his unappetising meal he went
across to pay his morning visit to Peter, but even Peter failed to
distract him satisfactorily. He was not so bright as usual, almost

distrait, as though he had something on his mind that was puzzling him and he was trying vainly to find a solution. He constantly fingered the little golden crucifix round his neck which, being on a longer chain than the other one, hung lower and was not hidden in his coarse hair, and he did not show his usual interest in learning new words.

Whenever the sound of a footstep reached his ears he got up restlessly from his chair and looked eagerly towards the door, as though he was expecting somebody. This continued when Rogers and Humberlayne had arrived, which they did about an hour after Fearless, and at last the men realised that it was Mary for whom he was watching. On the next day he was better and he continued to improve day by day. He took a greater interest than ever, if possible, in his education—for that is what it was—but a footstep never failed to distract his attention and bring his big blue eyes to the door, and this trick he had not lost when, some weeks later, Fearless started on his trip after okapi.

Never since he had seen the tracks of these shyest of animals on the far side of Nganda had the thought of them been far from the trapper's mind. No man, as far as was known, had ever yet succeeded in catching one—certainly no white man had ever done so—and to break this record, to triumph where so many others, the most expert in their line, had failed, would be the crowning glory of any trapper's career. Fearless had fully made up his mind that he should be that man, and ever since his arrival at Dualla he had not ceased to make careful inquiries from all and sundry and still more careful preparations for the expedition he contemplated.

Now he had learned all he could and his arrangements were completed so, one fine morning, he tramped away, back into the forest, at the head of his men, leaving only Humberlayne, Rogers and von Zugend, who had been there to wish him farewell, of all those who had gathered round the table to eat that wedding breakfast. Three weeks later Humberlayne too had gone, back to the daily round in his little Leicestershire village, and there were no strangers left in the land. Only the Commissioner continued to fulfill his duties as the representative of his Government and the missionary as the representative of his Church.

But all this was not until a long time after John and Mary Passinger had sailed away on their honeymoon, and in the meantime none of them had been idle with regard to Peter's education. Before Fearless left he had been able to form short sentences on his own initiative and to make use of them. Thus, he would ask for more water if he was thirsty and had run out of that commodity, or for more food if he wanted a second helping. The food question, for a time, was rather a problem. At first Peter had been content to eat greenstuffs and fruit—indeed he would eat nothing else—but in time he began to yearn for more solid food, though this his keepers did not know. Whether it was the appetising odours which chanced to reach him from the near-by kitchen that were responsible or what, Fearless never learned, but one day, when the servant came in with a jug of water on his way to the dining-room carrying a dish of hot cooked meat in his hand, he was given quite clearly to understand that if he did not hand it over it was likely to be the worse for him. So, very wisely, he did hand it over and then hurried away to tell his master of the fate which had befallen his midday meal.

When Fearless reached Peter's room, which he did in a very few moments, he found him discussing the food, tentatively at first but soon with evident enjoyment, and thereafter he refused to be satisfied or to eat at all unless he was given meals more or less similar to those served to Fearless himself.

The time came, not very long after the yacht had left Dualla, when it was deemed safe to give Peter his freedom. This was not done until after long and earnest consultations between the trapper and the two clergymen, but once the step had been taken they never had any cause to regret it. He roamed where he would about the house but always returned of his own free will to his room at nightfall, as well as at meal times, and remained there until the morning, though his door was never locked. In time he began to make himself useful, carrying water for use in the house and lifting anything which it was desired to move that was beyond the strength of ordinary mortals. Sometimes he was taken out to gather fruit and on these occasions his tree-climbing capabilities proved invaluable. Shortly before the departure of Fearless his quarters were shifted to the Mission house and thereafter he was the constant attendant of Rogers, seldom leaving his side.

Contrary to general expectations the forecast of the clergyman was not fulfilled. Far from running from him in terror women and children delighted in Peter. The last-named worshipped him and were never so happy as when they were in his company. Many and many a time he might have been seen with a baby hand in each of his big ones, a tiny tot on either shoulder and half a dozen others dancing round him, making his slow way to the edge of the forest. There he would bring them flowers and bunches of fruit from the topmost branches of the trees and their mothers were happy in the thought that they were safe with him. Neither did the men despise or ridicule him. One or two there may have been who showed a certain amount of contempt when first he began to move about freely amongst them, but popular opinion soon compelled them to sing a different tune.

He spent some hours each day with Rogers, improving his knowledge of speech, and could soon talk as well as a six-year-old child. For a time an attempt was made to teach him to read and write but those accomplishments appeared to be altogether beyond his powers and, though much to his regret, his tutor gave up all hope of his acquiring them. None the less his education improved daily until Rogers felt that very soon the time would arrive when he might start to question him at length and try to learn his history. He had been sorely tempted to begin ere this, but had decided that he would be unable to get a connected narrative until his pupil had made further progress. So, though impatiently, he had waited for the psychological moment.

In the meantime John and Mary Passinger had been sailing the seas, moving from place to place as the spirit moved them, staying for a day or a week or a month, now here, now there, and thoroughly enjoying themselves. They were as happy as the day was long and the days could not be long enough. Nothing that John could do or say or buy or think was too good for his wife. She was his whole world and he lived only to serve her. Her love for him was as great as his for her and their constant question was "how did we ever live so long without each other? How could we have ever thought that we were happy before we met and loved?"

They had steamed northward first, then sauntered through the Mediterranean, leaving the yacht for a week at Alexandria to visit Cairo and the pyramids. Then down through the Red Sea to Colombo, Bombay and the ports of India, and so on to Japan. Sydney they had visited and other parts of Australia; New York and San Francisco. It was a wonderful experience for a girl who had hardly left a little Leicestershire village in her life before.

But riches entail responsibilities and the time came when John Passinger had to return to London. Mary hated the idea but there were compensations. She would see her father again for one thing and there was something else which seemed almost more important, for both she and her husband wanted their son—they were sure it was going to be a son—to come into the world under the most favourable conditions possible.

So back to London they went and in due course the son was born and a very fine, healthy baby he was. Some day, they decided, they would take him to Dualla to see the church where they were married, and Rogers and Peter.

"Dear Peter," Mary used to say sometimes. She often thought of him, often wondered whether his story would ever be known to anybody but himself. Did he ever think of her, she asked herself, and of her husband? Would he be fond of her baby boy? She thought he would. She was sure he would. They must certainly go back to Dualla one day.

CHAPTER XVIII

PETER'S STORY

IT WAS A MONDAY MORNING in June. Seated round the break-fast table in a bright room, through the open french windows of which the summer sunlight was streaming, were three people—Francis Humberlayne the vicar, grown a little older and greyer than when we last saw him, John Passinger and Mary his wife. Breakfast was over and presently they rose, the clergyman to go and attend to his correspondence, his son-in-law and daughter to amuse themselves as they saw fit until he could join them. They strolled through the open windows on to the lawn and across it to the same rustic seat beneath the lime trees where they had plighted their troth. John reminded his wife of this as they sat down.

"Do you regret it, dear?" he asked.

"How could I regret it, darling?" she countered. "Think how happy we have been, how happy we are. Nobody could have been more devoted than my husband. And how little Jackie loves his daddy! I am almost jealous of him sometimes."

"Goodness knows I love him enough too," John replied, "but as for your being jealous let me tell you that I would rather lose him ten times over than be parted from my Mary."

It was very peaceful in the vicarage garden. Bees hummed amongst the lime blossoms, a blackbird, waiting for a late brood to hatch, sang a song of love to while away the time for his patient sitting mate, a flycatcher made repeated little flights from the top of a post, returning after each to the same perch with some luck-less fly in his beak, a water-wagtail ran busily, in rapid jerks, about the lawn, hunting food for his young.

Presently the sound of childish laughter woke John and Mary from the reverie into which they had fallen, and round the corner of an arbour toddled a little two-year-old boy with the sunlight glinting in his curls. His steps were very uncertain but he had a goal in view. That goal was his mother and he was determined to reach her. And reach her, too, he did in the long run, though not until after more than one tumble. She lifted him up on to her knee, making out that it cost her an effort.

"What a lump you are getting, Jackie," she said. "You will soon be as big as daddy. Why, look! Here comes grand-dad."

Francis Humberlayne walked quickly, as was his wont, across the lawn and sat down at his daughter's side.

"You have got away from your stuffy old study early to-day, daddy," she smiled as she moved nearer to her husband to make room for him. "That is very nice of you."

"It so happened that there was not very much for me to do in the way of correspondence," he replied, "and there is a long letter from my old friend Rogers which I thought we might all enjoy together," he held out a bulky package as he spoke, "so I brought it out here into the fresh air. It is lovely under the trees."

"That will be delightful," Mary agreed; "and it certainly is quite beautiful out here. I love this seat."

John vouchsafed no more than "Good egg. How's Peter?" but he looked forward no less than his wife and father-in-law to the reading of the letter. Rogers was a good correspondent and had written regularly by almost every mail ever since Humberlayne had left Dualla. He knew well how interested his old college friend was in Peter and had kept him fully informed as to his progress. For several mails now he had been hinting that he had been getting Peter's story from him piece by piece and reducing it to writing with the greatest care, and in his last letter had said that it was then almost complete and that he would be sending Humberlayne a copy of the entire narrative very shortly.

That, he explained, had seemed to him a better plan than sending it bit by bit as though it was a serial story—"the most tiresome and unsatisfying form of literature that the mind of man has ever conceived, fit only for housemaids and office boys." The thought had come simultaneously into the minds of all three of them in the vicarage garden that here might be the promised story, and they looked forward to the reading more eagerly than ever.

"My dear friend," the Vicar began to read in his clear, well modulated voice. "There is, I fear, but little to tell you in the ordinary way concerning events in Dualla; it is not, as you know, a place very prolific of events of any kind. Indeed I may as well admit at once that nothing has occurred here which might fairly be called exciting or even noteworthy since your charming daughter's wedding over three years ago. How is she? And her husband, and the boy? All very well I hope.

"I think the only thing that might be of interest to you since my last letter was mailed is the return of Fearless about ten days ago. This, as you know, was his third trip after okapi since your departure and he came back more crestfallen than ever. It appears that he was successful in trapping two of the creatures, a female and her young one, and getting them to within a week's journey of the coast alive and seemingly healthy. Then, for no apparent reason, they died. He left them as fit and well as ever they were late one evening and when he went to look at them in the morning they were both dead. It must have been a very great disappointment to him, and a great financial loss too, but he has the skins to console him to some extent, and that of the young one, I understand, is unique. Of gorillas he saw no sign on any of his trips, not so much as the track of one.

"And that brings me to Peter, about whom I know you like to hear. He is in the very rudest health and most useful to me, especially with the children, who love to be with him. I have never been able to teach him to read or write one word but he loves me to read aloud to him and takes a really intelligent interest even in good books, such as Ivanhoe, for instance, which we have just finished, and some of Charles Kingsley's. Now and then, of course, I have to go into explanations, but for the most part he understands them quite well. His powers of speech, and indeed of conversation, are as good now as I suppose they ever will be and far better than I had dared to hope.

"For many months past I have been making the fullest and most careful notes of everything he has told me connected with his past life, going so far as to take down his remarks verbatim as nearly as I could. I have not hesitated to question him, jog his memory, and even make suggestions in my efforts to obtain a complete, connected and comprehensive history of the years he spent in the forest, but I am fully satisfied that he has not told me one word that he does not believe to be true. A short time ago I came to the conclusion that he had nothing more to tell, so I collated all the notes I had made and from them wrote as connected a story as I could, putting it more or less into narrative form. The result I handed to Fritz van Zugend—he sends you all sorts of kind messages, by the way—and he was good enough to have a few copies of it made on the office typewriter, one of which I send you herewith. Please overlook any literary short-comings that it may contain. Writing, I fear, is not my forte.

"I feel sure that you cannot but agree from what you will read in the very first pages of Peter's story that the mystery which has puzzled us all so much is satisfactorily solved, and surely a stranger tale was never imagined. The remainder is only interesting as being the personal history of one whom I, and I think you, call a friend. I would suggest very strongly that you keep the story to yourselves. I am very fond of Peter indeed and he is so dreadfully sensitive that I fear that notoriety of the kind that the publication of his life history would assuredly mean would be the death of him. An agitation would be started to bring him over to England and, failing that, Dualla would be over-run with reporters if not with so-called scientists. You are of course at liberty to act as you may think best in the matter but it would be a very great comfort to me to think that you would tell the story only to such as you knew you could trust to let it go no further.

"I have not been at all well lately which, perhaps, is not altogether to be wondered at in view of the fact that I have been here now for nearly six years without so much as a week's holiday. If only I could find somebody whom I could trust to come out and take over my duties for a few months I should be sorely tempted to leave Dualla for a time and go home to see if England looks anything like it used to when I left there. But it is not easy to find anybody at all who is willing to risk this climate and I would not accept anyone whom I did not know a good deal about. The general idea seems to be that a man who goes to Dualla goes to his grave, that he is deliberately committing suicide, so people not unnaturally fight shy of the experiment. Though that may have been more or less true at one time, you know what a mistaken belief it is now. But then you are one of the few, and nobody will take your word for it.

"I have just been reading through my letter and am forced to the unwilling conclusion that you are bound to say you have never received so uninteresting a screed, so I will write no more. I hope Peter's story may make up for it. He sends all sorts of messages to you and yours, as also do I, my dear Humberlayne. Perhaps, in God's good time, we may meet again. I pray that we may. Yours very sincerely, HENRY ROGERS."

The Vicar laid the letter aside as he finished and picked up the considerable packet of typed sheets which had been enclosed with it, smoothing them out upon his knee.

"He need have had no fear that we should consider his communication uninteresting," he said. "Rogers's letters I always find most entertaining. And now for Peter's story. I seem to have been looking forward to reading this for years."

Again the vicar smoothed out the typewritten sheets, then settled himself more comfortably on the rustic seat, cleared his throat, and began to read.

"The first thing that I can remember clearly is a wide-open space surrounded by dense forest with a single large tree growing in the centre of it. We only went there on special occasions when there was some important meeting or our chief wished to address us, and that was not very often, but it is probably the very importance of those occasions which was responsible for the spot making such an impression on me when I was very young. Our homes were in the forest near by, in a place where very big trees grew, near to the top of one of which my mother had built a nest. It was nothing more than a platform of interwoven boughs, but I had never known any greater comfort, and to me it was perfect.

"I can remember my mother well and, though she was a gorilla pure and simple, I loved her very dearly and often wish that I could see her now. My father was a white man like you, but he wore no clothes. He had no hair on his body, like the rest of us had, and his eyes were big and blue like mine are. The gorilla whom he called mother was not his mother at all really, as I will explain in due course, but she was very devoted to him and looked upon him as her own. My mother's mother was, of course, a gorilla like her, but my father's father, or rather his foster father, was not. At least he was not quite like the others. He had a black skin like they had and brown eyes, but otherwise he was more like me. It was he who was our chief and he alone was allowed to use the big tree in the middle of the open space.

"His father, I was told, had been very much like mine when he was alive, but quite black. How he came to be with us I never knew, for he died long before I was born, and the memories of gorillas are not so long as those of men. I was told, however, that he was responsible for us all living together, as we did, instead of more or less separately, and that he had also instituted the drills which were a feature of the education of the males, and held regularly in the open space.

"When he died his son, that is my father's foster father, had taken his place as chief of the band and carried on the work that his father had commenced. He drilled his troops, if I may call them so, regularly, and enforced the strictest order and obedience. His word was law and nobody ever thought of questioning it. It was not often that we went out on the war-path, and when we did it was invariably on a punitive expedition. It was after one of these, I was told, that my father first appeared amongst us. The mate of the chief had lost her young one, killed by some accident, and she was feeling her loss so keenly that its father, who was devoted to her, had gone contrary to all the unwritten laws and permitted her to accompany him on this particular raid.

"What the exact object of the expedition was I do not know, but I believe it had something to do with the death of one of our number at the hands of a black man. The village was the same as that in which you were camping for so long, and I imagine, from what I heard, that it was treated in much the same way as when it was raided under my own leadership. It was not our custom to leave anybody living to tell the tale of our raids. Every soul in the village was certainly to be slaughtered, none must be left alive. My father's foster mother, happening to go into one of the huts just before the end, found there a woman, a white woman, with a child at her breast. The mother she killed with her own hands, but the child, who was to become my father, she took to replace the young one which she had recently lost. After the raid she carried him back to her own nest-tree, nursed him at her own breast, and brought him up as though she had borne him.

"He throve exceedingly and grew up to be a fine man, far taller than any of the gorillas. In all our games, racing on the ground, or, even through the trees, wrestling and fighting with the club, there was not one of the band who was his equal. His foster father grew to be as proud of him as though he was his own son, and as soon as he was old enough put him with the troops and had him taught to drill. So apt was he that in a surprisingly short time he was as fit to command as the chief himself and far cleverer when it came to tactics. It was he who first resorted to ambushes and other ruses of warfare. It was he who first took to stationing some of his company outside the village, or whatever it was that was being raided, to cut off the retreat of those within, as I did on the night when we wiped out Nganda; and when the old chief died it was my father who took his place, not only because, in a way, it was his right to do so, but also at the earnest and unanimous desire of every member of the band.

"He did far more to instill discipline than either his foster father or his foster father's father had done before him. He also greatly strengthened and increased the numbers of our band by having the tale of its deeds spread far and wide. He sent trusty individuals to great distances with the sole object of ingratiating themselves with other gorillas and impressing upon them the advantages to be gained by living in a community and fighting in a common cause. Little by little the band grew until the time came when over a hundred trained men, ready and willing to obey his word of command, could be put in the field at an hour's notice. His great ambition was to drive all men, black as well as white, from the forest and keep it for the gorillas alone. By that I do not mean that no other animal should live there, but none that were not under the dominion of himself and his band.

"My father was very much more clever than any of his predecessors in office had been. Indeed I think his own father and mother must have been exceptionally well educated people of some position in life, though of this, of course, I have no proof. So highly was he thought of by his foster father that before he died the old chief had given him his own daughter by another mate and it was she who became my mother. She was supposed to be the most beautiful female of her kind ever seen and, though that estimate of her looks might not have agreed with human ideas and the arrangement was what I suppose would be called amongst civilised creatures the equivalent of a *mariage de convenance*, he loved her very devotedly and never took another mate.

"It was not long before the old chief's death that he gave her to him and he was carried to his grave some months before I came into the world. By then, of course, my father had taken over the reins of government, so to speak. This necessitated his living, according to custom, in the big tree in the centre of the clearing, so that during the first few years of my life I saw him but seldom, for none but the chief was allowed to live in that tree or even to approach it except upon urgent business. The only exception to this rule was the one who acted as what might not unfairly be called his second in command, and even he might only go there by invitation.

"But though each family lived in a different tree, and often at some distance from one another, I was not lonely. It was the common custom for the youngsters to meet and play together in some open glade while their mothers sat looking on and, I suppose, gossiping. And even without them I should not have been lonely for long, for within eighteen months of my coming into the world my mother took into her nest the baby of another female, who had been killed by native hunters and whose father joined his mate as a result of the punitive expedition which resulted.

"With this foster brother I grew up and we were inseparable. As soon as we were of an age to carry a club we were enrolled in the little army and, like my father, I must have showed a great aptitude for the life, for I soon rose to a position of some responsibility at the head of a line. On the rare occasions when we set out on a raiding expedition I was invariably given a post in which a certain amount depended upon me and I suppose must have fulfilled my duties to my father's satisfaction or otherwise he would not have promoted me, as he did, to the envied rank of second in command.

"That was an event I shall never forget. We had been to destroy a village which was so small and unimportant that the usual care was not taken, with the result that the then second in command and several others with him, including my foster brother, Mguru, were cut off and surrounded by three times their number of men armed with spears. The leader of the little band had fallen and Mguru was putting up a great fight at the head of the others, but there did not seem to be a chance for any of them when I happened to catch sight of them and realised what had happened. It was not bravery on my part, but love for my foster brother which prompted me to charge them single-handed in the rear. I could not stand idly by and see the playmate of my childhood's days butchered by those black men and I suppose I must have lost my temper.

"At any rate I charged them blindly and, being taken in the rear, they must have thought that I was only one of many and they turned and ran for their lives. My foster father, although I did not know it at the time, had seen the whole thing, and he promoted me to the position of the dead gorilla, whose fault it had been, on the spot. Not only that, but he allotted Mguru to me as my personal attendant, an arrangement which suited us both admirably.

"As second in command my duties were greatly increased. I had to do all the drilling and I took a pride in making my little body of troops smart and efficient. I was given a good deal of latitude, too, and permitted to introduce innovations which I thought would be advantageous, though I never actually did this without consulting my father first. One thing I tried hard to do was to find half a dozen amongst the troops who could be trusted to drill the others in batches, but in this I failed dismally. The only one that was of any use at all was Mguru, and even he was not much good.

I could have picked out two score or more who knew their drill every bit as well as I knew it myself and could obey any order without a second's hesitation; but when it came to giving one they were hopelessly lost. It almost seems as though no creature without some human blood in its veins could ever be a leader except by right of physical might. There is no doubt in my own mind that that is what happened when I was shot down. My followers had nobody to tell them what to do, so they did nothing. They probably straggled homewards. But I am anticipating.

"Towards the end of his life, and it is not so very long since he died, my father grew to rely on me more and more. It was very seldom that he took command of the troops himself, even if we were attacking a place that was quite near, and when my mother was killed he seemed to lose all interest in life. I was away at the time on a diplomatic visit to some gorillas who did not belong to the band. A great gale seems to have arisen in the night which did much damage and, amongst many others, my mother's nest-tree was blown to the ground. She was in it at the time and the fall broke her neck. When I got back home she was dead and Mguru was very nearly so. A branch of the tree had snapped off and fallen, and the jagged end had cut his face open from forehead to chin right down to the bone. How he ever got over it I do not know and he carried the scar all his life. It was like a white streak across his black face.

"My father was absolutely broken hearted and could do nothing but sit and mope. He took no further interest in his little kingdom, if I may call it so, and one day he called a meeting in the big open space and publicly proclaimed me leader in his stead. I was well received by my new subjects, although such a proceeding was unprecedented, and things went on very much as they had done, except that my father retired to the forest while I moved to the tree of honour in the middle of the open space and Mguru, as soon as he was well enough, took my place as second in command.

"Within six months of my appointment my father died, I think of a broken heart, and I missed him almost as much as I had missed my mother. It is a fallacy to believe that men and women are the only creatures who have feelings of affection which last for more than a few days. Gorillas, at any rate, suffer just as much as humans when they lose somebody they love, and there is no reason that I can see why there should not be other animals who feel the same.

"Just before he died my father sent for me and, contrary to established custom, I went to him in his nest-tree. He was very weak, but he pulled himself together sufficiently to impress upon me once more the necessity of driving all human beings from the forest and winning it for the gorillas alone. He made me swear to do my best and then, with his last strength, he unloosed the ivory crucifix from about his neck and clasped it round mine. Then he whispered my mother's name twice, sighed deeply, and died."

CHAPTER XIX

BACK TO DUALLA

A T THAT TIME I did not, of course, know that it was a crucifix that my father had given me. Neither, I am sure for
that matter, did he. I thought then, and until long after I
saw the one which I now wear round Mrs. Passinger's neck on her
wedding day, that it was a sort of badge of office, and I have no
doubt that it was as such that it was looked upon by the whole
band. Indeed I was more than surprised that my father had omitted
to give it to me at the time when he had publicly appointed me
chief in his place and I rather think that there were others who
were equally puzzled that I should be allowed to rule without it.

"I wore it with great pride and it was a constant source of
annoyance to me that the shortness of the chain on which it hung
caused it to be hidden by the long hair on my neck. My father, being hairless, was not troubled in that way and the cross rested
openly on the upper part of his bare white chest for all to see. But
everybody knew that I was the chief and it was only on very rare
occasions that I found it necessary to show my badge of authority
to some newcomer to the band.

"The death of my father, as I have said, was a great blow to me,
more especially, perhaps, because it came so soon after that of my
mother. If it had not been for Mguru I almost believe that I should
have left my people, so broken hearted was I, for a time at any
rate, but when my moods were at their worst he never failed to
remind me of the promise I had given to my father to do my utmost to drive all human beings from the forest and this, eventually, I made up my mind to do with as little delay as was consis-
tent with the chances of success. For the present I would continue
to drill my troops, practise them in mimic warfare, teach them new
manoeuvres. I would send more and more trustworthy individuals
to distant parts of the forest, as diplomatic envoys and propagan-
dists, to teach the gospel of 'the forest for the gorillas' and impress
upon their hearers the necessity of banding together and working
for the common cause if ever that dream was to come true.

"I had visions in those days. I could see my little army doubled, trebled, increased to four times its number perhaps. I went so far as to dream of organising the lesser apes and the monkeys and making use of them for my own ends and the ends of my people. The chimpanzees are strong and cunning and they would have been very useful. The monkeys, too, would have been of the greatest assistance owing to their speed and I meant to use them as scouts and messengers. I foresaw the time when I should have thousands under my command, but until that time came punitive expeditions should be all that we would undertake, as had been our custom heretofore. No injury must go unpunished.

"That was three years ago and, as you know, my dreams did not materialise. I see now that they never could have done. What could two or three hundred, or even two or three thousand, gorillas have done with nothing but clubs or, perhaps, spears in their hands, though I admit that strangely enough I never thought of them as a weapon, against a tenth of their number of men armed with rifles? And I doubt whether there are a thousand gorillas in the whole of the forest. It was only a dream, a crazy dream, but at the time it seemed to me more than feasible; it seemed inevitable. Gorillas, like men, may make their plans for the future and, like men's, their plans may come to nothing. 'It is human to err,' I have been told. Why human? Every creature that comes into the world is equally liable to make mistakes and it is a merciful dispensation of Providence that this is so. Nearly every death in the animal world is due to some error of judgment or carelessness. It is through an error of judgment or carelessness that the fly fails to elude the bird or the spider that seeks to catch it. It is through an error of judgment or carelessness that the ape misses its hold as it swings through the trees and crashes to its death on the ground below. It is the same with nearly every fatality that occurs in the forest. But to return to the death of my father.

"It was the custom of the people whom I ruled to bury their dead, though whether the habit was introduced by the first chief, three generations before my time, or was older, I do not know. We did not bury them in the ground as you do, owing perhaps to the lack of the necessary implement wherewith to dig graves, but carried the body to some place where loose stones lay about which were piled over it. Except in certain cases there was no ceremonial about the funerals, the corpse being merely carried to the chosen spot by its relations and friends and often but carelessly covered.

"But special honour was paid to the remains of certain of our number, notably those who were killed in battle and the chiefs of the band. The bodies of all those who died fighting were brought home, or to some special burying place near home, however great the distance might be, and a common cairn raised over them in the presence of the entire populace, after which everybody saluted their memory by filing past and laying the left hand for a moment on the stones. From that day forth none would pass the spot without repeating the salute and no other body might be buried there.

In the case of the chiefs it was different. There is a high and very steep hill near to where I used to live, on the summit of which, with infinite labour, a great heap of rocks had been raised in such a manner that it was hollow in the centre. This monument was called 'the grave of the chiefs,' and in it the bodies of all those who held that rank were laid, access to the vault being gained by rolling aside a great stone. It was to the top of this hill that the body of my father was carried, followed by the entire band. My little army was drawn up round the tomb with an interval between each, so that the females and young who stood behind them might be able to see, and when the body had been laid in the vault and the stone rolled back into its place, I mounted to the top of the cairn and prayed that he might find peace, rest and happiness in that land to which he had gone. Then the troops gave the salute that was given only to the dead, by raising their clubs high above the head in the left hand, holding them there for a long moment, and then letting them fall to the ground. Finally everybody filed past the tomb in the way I have indicated, each laying the left hand on the stones in passing. It was an impressive ceremony and one which I shall never forget.

"For two years or more after the death and burial of my father I was very busy trying to increase the number of my followers and making plans for driving all men from the forest. From time to time something occurred which called for reprisals, but on the whole things were unusually quiet and, in my ignorance, I began to believe that men had guessed what my intentions were and, having seen the way in which we meted out punishment for injuries received, had thought discretion the better part of valour and decided at least to leave us alone. Then I got news from one of my scouts that traps had been set up near Nganda.

"Though this was the first time as far as we were aware that any attempt had been made to catch one of our number alive, we knew well enough hat the traps were and I considered the matter of sufficient importance to go and visit them myself. I went alone except for Mguru and we had very little difficulty in finding out how they were worked. Once that was discovered it was an easy business to spring them and this we did. Shortly afterwards they were set again and this time I sent Mguru and another to see to them, not deeming it necessary for me to go a second time myself.

"He seems to have forgotten some of what I had taught him about their mechanism, and twice he got caught, but with the help of his companion was soon able to free himself and smash up his temporary prisons. After another short interval exactly the same thing happened again, but there after there was peace for several days and I thought that no further attempt on those lines was going to be made; but I was wrong. Again one of my scouts came with the information that the traps had been set and again I sent Mguru and one other to spring them, he having assured me that even if he did get caught it would only be for a few minutes. As a matter of. fact it was not he who got caught at all, but his companion, and the traps had been so much strengthened that their combined efforts to set him free were in vain and he had perforce to be left there.

"It so happened that I was out in the forest with a party of young males, practising them in mimic warfare, and early the next day we fell in with Mguru on his way home. We were not far from Nganda at the time, much nearer than we were to home, so I decided to attempt a rescue with what companions I had. They were far too few to think of making any reprisals, but I thought that we might be able to achieve our object by strategy, and with this end in view we lay hidden on the outskirts of Nganda until far into the night, and then entered the village as silently as possible.

The rescue proved to be a far easier matter than I had dared to hope. There were two men sleeping by the cage in which our companion was imprisoned, both of whom we killed before they could utter a sound, and with some little difficulty I found out how to slide the bolts. I was sorely tempted to attack the village, few as our numbers were, but second thoughts prevailed and we left as silently as we had come.

"If the traps were set again, I decided, I would adopt different methods, and when I was brought word that they had been I acted on a plan which I had thought out. I instructed one of our number, who was gifted with considerably more intelligence than the others, to allow himself to be caught and taken to the village where he would remain for two or three days. During that time he was to behave as though he was resigned to his fate and learn all he possibly could, especially about the white men. At the end of it I would come with the entire army, set him free and kill every living soul in the place, then destroy it utterly as a lesson to any others who thought they might trap gorillas with impunity.

"He was a brave and faithful creature, devoted to me and my cause, and performed his difficult task with the utmost fidelity. He was caught and carried to the village and remained there for some days, as I had arranged. Then one night I swept down with every male in the band who was capable of carrying a club to set him free and take our revenge. Unfortunately sentries had been posted and the rifle of one of these went off accidentally while he was struggling for his life, thus giving the alarm. This added to our difficulties but not, as it turned out, greatly. We freed our companion and then made our way systematically through the village, killing every living thing and destroying everything that could be destroyed as we went.

"Many there were who attempted to flee, but the village was surrounded by troops under the command of Mguru, and no single soul escaped our vengeance except the girl Delilah. It was only the accident of their having received some message which took them away into the forest that saved the lives of the white men and their servants, and had it not been for that message I should have been sitting now in my tree in the middle of the open space, dreaming dreams of conquest, instead of on a verandah in Dualla. What little things may change the course of life.

"That raid was the most expensive we had ever engaged in, for it cost us the lives of four of our number besides others badly wounded. We carried them away with us, buried them after our custom and then returned home, I secure in the belief that now we should be left in peace. So sure was I of this that I began to make arrangements to take a mate. It was not that there was anyone of the females whom I fancied or that I was growing tired of my bachelor existence. On the contrary, I rather dreaded the thought of wedded bliss, having seen the way some of even the strongest and bravest of my companions were treated, and visions of paternity had no attractions for me. But my people expected it of me, were becoming somewhat persistent and restless indeed, and I saw, too, that it was my duty to mate in order that there might be someone to carry on my work when the time came for me to die.

"Everything was arranged and the day had been fixed on which I was to take the chosen female from the nest-tree of her parents and run with her deep into the forest, as was our custom, when news was brought to me that the white men had returned to Nganda and left again, carrying with them the girl who is called Delilah and a young one of our own species. For a moment I decided to let them go, for the parents of the young one did not belong to my band, but then it struck me that, if we were to rescue it, it would make a very favourable impression on others who had not joined us, and very likely result in a considerable addition being made to our numbers. So that very evening we started off in pursuit.

"The white men had a long start and we had to travel fast and far. We reached Nganda on the following morning and had made such good speed that thereafter we rested most of the daytime, travelling only after dark. Some hours before dawn one night we passed the camp not far from the edge of the forest and lay in wait beyond. Of the fight that resulted you know, and nobody who saw it, I am sure, will attempt to deny that my troops bore themselves well and bravely. But clubs and numbers, I learned then, are useless against rifles and men who know how to use them, and we failed. How many of my faithful companions must have died in the forest on that day I do not dare to think even now: and all for the sake of a young one who had nothing whatever to do with them.

"Once our enemies were clear of the forest I knew there was no hope. I stood watching them, thinking that I would climb to the top of a high tree and throw myself to the ground, for I could not bear the thought of returning home with the sorry remnant of my little army, when Mguru left my side and dashed out into the open. I knew what his object was and that the opponent he sought was armed like him with no more than a club, and I was certain in my own mind what the result would be. But that man had the strength of a lion and I was wrong. When Mguru fell dead before my eyes I think I must have gone made with rage. My one thought was revenge, for I loved Mguru as a man loves his brother.

What happened then you know. I was shot and unconscious before ever I could reach his side, and the next thing I remembered was lying bound to a litter. At first I only wanted to die but they were kind to me, my captors, and somehow that wish passed. In time I grew happier and now I know how lucky I have been. My one regret, and that is a regret which will be with me always, is that through me so many brave creatures should have lost their lives in a hopeless and a foolish cause."

"That is the end," Humberlayne said as he refolded the pages. "It explains much that was dark to us. In its way it is a great moral lesson. I am more sorry for Peter than I can say. He says at the end of his story, you will notice, that he knows how lucky he has been, and so he has in a way. But I cannot help feeling that he must know and constantly grieve over the fact that, directly or indirectly, there is the blood of scores of innocent men and women on his hands. Had he remained in his native wilds he would never have realised that."

"No doubt you may be right," Passinger put in, "but, on the other hand, he may comfort himself with the reflection that whatever he did contrary to human standards of right and wrong he did because he knew no better. I am inclined to believe that he regrets it deeply and would undo it if he could, but I do not think that he feels he is to blame, any more than a Mohamedan who turns Christian need blame himself for having previously taken, or thought of taking, more than one wife. *Autres pays, autres moeurs.* All those little things are a matter of what one is brought up to."

"I, too, am dreadfully sorry for dear old Peter," Mary chimed in, "but I must confess that what interests me most is the first part of his story. Do you realise, John, that he is a sort of cousin of mine, and therefore of yours by marriage? There can surely be no doubt that his father was Mabel Hillier's son and her brother was my grandfather. Isn't that right? Therefore Peter and I have a common great-grandfather. Doesn't it seem strange?"

"Who do you suppose the foster father and his father were?"

"That seems fairly clear, I think," said the Vicar. "I should imagine that the foster father was the offspring, like Peter, of a man and a gorilla. In this case the man was black and there is no reason why he should not have been stolen, in the same way as the little Hillier boy, by a gorilla who had lost her own young one and yearned for something to take its place."

"That would certainly seem to be a reasonable explanation," Passinger agreed. "Not the least strange part of the whole story, to my mind, is that very fact—that two men, a white and a black, should have been stolen by the same band of gorillas with a generation between the two events."

"And what makes it stranger still," Mary added, "is that it should be the mate of the offspring of the first who stole the second. I wonder whether the perfect organisation which seems to have existed would have continued if Peter had become the father of young ones instead of being wounded and caught?"

"I wonder," said the Vicar.

For a time there was silence. They were all thinking deeply, not perhaps so much of Peter individually as of the strange sights he must have seen. Mary could visualise the scene in the open space when the troops were being drilled. In her mind's eye she could picture the funeral of Mabel Hillier's child, the ranks of gorillas round the stone tomb on the top of the hill giving the salute that was given only to the dead with clubs raised high and then dropped to the ground, the procession filing slowly past the cairn and touching the stones as each one passed, the females and young ones craning their necks to see between the files of troops. She could see Peter and Mguru as quite little ones, playing under the shade of the nest-tree. She could imagine that nest-tree falling, carrying Peter's mother with it to her death. She roused herself with a start and shuddered.

"Don't let us talk about it any more just now, daddy," she begged. "It frightens me somehow; I don't know why!"

"I think you are quite right, my dear," her father replied. "And I understand exactly what you mean. There seems to be something uncanny, something unnatural, something, if I may say so, almost unwholesome about it. Let us go for a stroll round the garden before lunch. It would seem to be time for Jackie's already. Here comes Nurse."

Jackie suffered from a particularly healthy appetite and he made no protest against being carried off to his meal. The others moved away through the trees but, though they tried to talk of less unusual things, the history of Peter was in all their minds and they soon came back to it. It was Mary who was the culprit.

"What do you think would happen if Peter was to go back?" she wanted to know.

"Peter never would go back, my dear," her father answered. "You may remember that he intended to kill himself before he was shot down and I feel sure he would rather do that now than return to his old life. Even if he did I do not for one moment believe that he would ever again hold the sway over those creatures that he once held. You must remember that they have been without a leader for three years and more now. Peter has explained in his story that they are helpless without somebody to tell them what to do and I have no doubt that by now his band is scattered far and wide. It will be far better if they are, and I am convinced that they will never again be organised. As Peter says, a creature must have a certain amount of human blood in its veins to be able to give orders and surely it is not every child brought up by gorillas that would undertake the work of ruling them on its own initiative; besides which it must be very, very seldom that a child is so brought up—not more than once in many years."

"I did not mean to imply that I thought Peter might go back," Mary explained; "I was only wondering what would happen if he did. I am afraid I wonder about a lot of things that you would very likely think silly. For instance, I wonder what happened to all those widows and orphans that were left after the fight in the forest and whether the males who were not killed ever found their way home again without a leader."

"What I am wondering," John broke in, "is what you will have to say to a plan that I have been thinking out. You have been grumbling for months, father, that you never get a holiday. Oh, very well then; not grumbling—hinting, if you like it better. Well, what I have been thinking while you two have been gossiping and speculating about things of which you are both painfully ignorant is that Rogers's letter is a heaven-sent blessing meant to point the way to our future movements. You want a holiday, Mary wants to take the boy to Dualla, Sam and Delilah want to see the land of their birth, Rogers wants somebody to take his place for a month or two, and the yacht wants using. All those various wants can be supplied at one fell swoop by the simple expedient of getting on to the yacht and going to Dualla. What about it?"

"Oh, do let us," Mary cried eagerly. "Shall we, daddy?"

"It would be very delightful, my dear, very delightful indeed; but I fear there are difficulties as far as I personally am concerned, though they need interfere in no way with you. It will not be easy for me to find a *locum tenens* for one thing, and for another Rogers might not care for me to take his place."

"What poppycock," John snorted. "You ought to be ashamed of yourself, father, for talking such nonsense. You know perfectly well that there is nobody Rogers would rather trust at his job than you and as for finding a local demon—well, my experience is that all men are much the same when it comes to business, except that some are cleverer than others, and I am willing to bet that if you offer a man a decent screw to take over your job for a bit he will jump at it, even if he is a clergyman."

"I do not quite see, my dear boy, how I can at this juncture afford . . ." the Vicar began, but he was interrupted.

"Nobody is asking you to afford anything. Mary and I can do all the affording. You pop off to your study after lunch like a good little boy and write a nice letter to some anaemic curate telling him that if he is not here by Thursday week and prepared to stop here for at least six months he will get the sack from whoever it is that gives the sack in your profession. In the meantime Mary and I will motor into Leicester and wire to Captain Redfern to say that we shall be sailing next week or the week after at the latest and to Rogers telling him that we are coming and that you are taking over from him for a bit. There goes the lunch bell. Come on, I am ravenous."

Humberlayne really did need a change of air and when his daughter added her entreaties to the commands of her husband it was not long before he gave way. He wrote his letter obediently and another to the bishop of the diocese for his sanction, while John and Mary went off to send their telegrams. Two days later he had satisfactory answers to both of them and Mary went at once up to London to indulge in an orgy of shopping and packing. When Sam and Delilah, who happened to be together at the time, were told that they were off to Dualla for a visit almost immediately, they frankly wept for sheer joy and their excitement was so intense during the days that followed that they were practically useless. But at last all was arranged and one lovely evening, just before sunset, the great white yacht steamed slowly away from the shores of old England with the whole party on board.

It was early morning at Dualla and on the little quay stood three men—Rogers, Fearless and Fritz von Zugend. Fearless had a much-travelled gladstone bag in his hand and his two friends were just giving him a last handshake and wishing him a pleasant journey back to the old country, when a boy came running down from the Commissioner's office with a folded sheet of paper, which he handed to Rogers. He opened it at once and jumped back in surprise.

"Good gracious me," he said, "this is from Passinger. He and his wife and boy and her father are coming out at once for a long stay. What a pity you are just going, Fearless."

Fearless picked up the battered gladstone bag which he had set down at his side.

"I'm not," he said. "I'm stopping here." Then the three men turned and walked slowly away from the quay towards the Mission house.

CHAPTER XX

BEAST OR MAN?

T HERE WAS GREAT EXCITEMENT in Dualla when the *S.Y. Moonbeam,* John Passinger's yacht, steamed slowly and gracefully in and dropped anchor at a short distance from the quay. Before she had finished doing so a boat had put off from the shore and was hastening to her side under the powerful strokes of four natives. It was a government boat, reserved for the exclusive use of the Commissioner, and in the stern sheets sat three men—Rogers the missionary, Fearless the trapper, and Fritz von Zugend the Landeshauptmann—while in the bows crouched no less a person than Peter.

In a surprisingly short time they had clambered aboard and the travellers found themselves enjoying the sort of reception accorded only to those who are really welcome. It was interesting to watch the different ways in which the three men greeted the new arrivals. Rogers bustled up to them with both hands outstretched murmuring, "My dear friends; my very dear friends"; Fearless strolled across the deck and shook hands with no more than, " 'Morning Mrs. Passinger; 'morning John"; von Zugend marched across like a soldier on parade, halted smartly in front of the lady, clicked his heels sharply together and bowed stiffly from the waist without saying a word. But all were equally glad to see the visitors.

Peter was the last to approach them and he did so diffidently. It is possible that he would not have done so at all had Mary not called to him and he may have wished that he had stayed ashore and waited for them to land. He was used to moving about freely amongst those who knew him, and everybody in Dualla knew him, as though he was one of themselves; but he was dreadfully sensitive, feeling what he considered his inferiority to human beings acutely, and was nervous in the presence of strangers, especially of white strangers. On more than one occasion sailors, for the most part, though not always, half drunk, had made fun of him and once gone so far as to throw mud and filth, and he dreaded going through such an ordeal again. He minded the missiles less than the insults, but what bothered him most of all was the fear of losing his temper and that, if his aggressors had only known it, would very certainly have resulted in murder. So whenever strange sailors landed at the quay it was his custom to keep out of the way as far as possible until they went aboard again.

It was Rogers who had persuaded him to come to the *Moonbeam* by assuring him that he would be well received and that Mrs. Passinger would be deeply hurt if he failed to do so, but the astonished stares of such members of the crew as saw him made him feel uncomfortable. At Mary's call, however, he came forward from his place in the background of the little group, and when she laid her hand on his shoulder, as once before, and said, "Dear Peter; how glad I am to see you," all his fears were swallowed up by a great and overwhelming joy which was only increased when Jackie stretched out his little arms to him with the un-appropriate exclamation "Good doggie". He was not offended, for he loved children as few human beings love them. Mary Passinger held her boy out to him with no slightest misgivings and a moment later he was perched on Peter's shoulder and thoroughly enjoying himself.

The *Moonbeam* had come to anchor a short time before midday and the visitors to the yacht were persuaded without much difficulty to lunch on board, Rogers deciding that the Mission could get on without him for an hour or two and von Zugend that on such an occasion as this government business might go hang, while Fearless, having nothing whatever to do, was thankful for something to fill in his time. There was much to talk about and it was not until the cool of the evening that a move was made for the shore. Only Jackie and his very competent Scotch nurse, who was horrified and not a little alarmed at the sight of the crowd of "naked heathens", remained on board besides the crew.

Mrs. Hester Macfarlane, as Jackie's nurse was designated, was a character. She had adopted the "Mrs.", it would seem, only as an appropriate adjunct to her age, for she held, or pretended to hold, all men in abomination and had certainly never enjoyed the delights of connubial felicity. In return all men were inclined to be somewhat afraid of her, and more especially of her tongue, and to keep out of her way as far as possible. She had deep-rooted ideas about religion, which she was fond of expounding to anybody, man or woman, who would listen to her, and had been known to smack Sam's face for daring to sing upon a Sunday. She always dressed severely in black, even in the hottest climes, and never failed to wear black cotton gloves when she "went out". But for all her vinegary ways she loved her charge devotedly and he was equally attached to his "Nanny".

Rogers and Humberlayne retired at once to the former's sanctum when they reached the Mission house, giving instructions that they were on no account to be disturbed. The missionary could hardly believe that his old friend had indeed come to Dualla with the intention of taking over his duties for a time and his gratitude was pathetic. When he was further informed that Passinger and his wife intended to live ashore and that it was their hope that he, and Fearless if he wished, should return to England or wherever it was they wanted to go to on the yacht, instead of incurring the expense of an uncomfortable journey under ordinary conditions, he very nearly broke down.

"I have never received such kindness," he exclaimed. "I would not have believed that such kindness could exist. And I can give nothing in return but my sincerest gratitude and the promise of my daily prayers for your happiness. It means more to me, this chance of getting away for a time, than you may perhaps realise. I love my work here, but I have not left Dualla for six years, and six years is a big slice of life at my age. I was beginning to fear that I should never see England again."

It was eventually decided that Rogers and Fearless should leave in three days' time and that Humberlayne and the Passingers should take up residence in the Mission house on the day of their departure. If they sailed in the evening this would give ample time for the luggage and things to be transferred and in the meantime the visitors would remain on the yacht. Fearless's little house should be kept on for the accommodation of the servants, as all the rooms at the Mission house would be needed for the incoming party, and thus everything would fit in nicely.

The next three days passed all too soon, even for the returning wanderers. There was so much that Rogers had to explain to the Leicestershire Vicar, so many people that he must be introduced to. And there were his farewells to be said and his packing to be done. He thought he would never get through all he had to before it was time to say good-bye. The offer of a passage on the Moonbeam was a perfect godsend to Fearless. During his three trips after okapi he had not confined his attentions entirely to those elusive animals. He had been working for himself and so had taken everything which came his way that might repay him for his expenditure, which was of necessity considerable. The consequence was that he had accumulated a large number of skins and heads besides a certain amount of livestock, chiefly monkeys.

But somehow the last duties were performed within the allotted time and by late in the afternoon of the appointed day the final pieces of luggage had been carried to and from the yacht, steam was up and all was ready for departure. Last time it had been Rogers and Fearless who had waved goodbye to John and Mary. Now the positions were reversed. Humberlayne and von Zugend were also on the quay as, too, was Jackie, perched in his favourite place on Peter's shoulder. Soon the graceful yacht had disappeared round the jutting point of land and the new tenants returned to the Mission house to settle down for their six months' stay at Dualla.

It was a very peaceful life that they led after the first rush of getting their belongings arranged to their liking. There was a little trouble at first with Sam and Delilah, who showed a disposition to discard the major part of their clothing and revert to the extremely scanty garments they had been wont to wear before they journeyed to distant lands, but they were persuaded that the wearing of apparel added immeasurably to their dignity and marked them as far superior to their fellows, and thereafter they wore as many clothes as they could.

Hester Macfarlane clung tenaciously to her high-necked black dress and continued to look with marked disfavour on the more flimsy garments of her mistress, but she went about her duties efficiently and appeared to be just as much at home as she had been in Berkeley Square. Mary interested herself deeply in the work which her father was doing and was of great assistance to him, thanks to her early training in the old vicarage, by taking Sunday School classes and things of that sort.

Passinger went for frequent shooting expeditions, on many if not most of which von Zugend found time to accompany him. Peter never failed to join them on these occasions and his knowledge of the forest and the ways of its inhabitants was invaluable. Though not so gifted in that way as pure-bred gorillas, his sense of smell was remarkable and often helped to lead them to game of the existence of which they would otherwise never have known and, as he made more use of it, that sense developed greatly. It was three years, it must be remembered, since he had entered the forest except in search of fruit or something of that sort, so it was only natural that his powers of smelling should have become to some extent impaired, in the same way as a man who had not used his eyes for so long a period would no doubt be unable to see clearly at the end of that time.

In the cool of the evening John and Mary would often go for a ramble along the beach or into the forest a little way, sometimes accompanied by Humberlayne or von Zugend or both, but more often alone. She never tired of strolling beneath the great trees, gazing at the blossoms that were so strange to her and watching the big gaudy butterflies flitting from flower to flower. There was one little open glade particularly in which both he and she loved to sit on a fallen log in the cool of the evening and while away an hour. It was their favourite spot above all others and when they were alone they used to turn towards it instinctively.

To this fairy glen, as Mary called it, they wended their way one evening just before sunset. The day had been exceptionally hot and the coolness which came with the gentle evening breeze from the sea was like a breath of life. Mary had taken her hat off as soon as they reached the shade of the trees and was sitting on the fallen log with it beside her while her husband lay at her feet. He had not long returned from a day's shooting with von Zugend and was tired.

"Do you realise," Mary said after a long silence, "that we have been at Dualla for nearly four months? It hardly seems credible, does it? In another three Mr. Rogers will be back again and it will be time for us to go."

"I know," her husband replied. "And Redfern may be here with the yacht almost any day now. Shall you be sorry to go?"

"In some ways, very, in others I shall be glad. I think six months in this climate is more than enough for a child of Jackie's age, though he certainly seems to thrive in it. How fond Peter and he are of each other. They are never so happy as when they are together. I am afraid Jackie will miss him terribly."

"I know he will. I have been thinking about that and wondering whether we could not take him back with us, but I have come to the conclusion that it would be a mistake, if not impossible. For one thing I very much doubt whether, in spite of his powers of accommodating himself to circumstances, he would ever be able to put up with more clothes than that sort of bathing-drawers concern he wears, and what would Hester have to say to that when we got back to civilisation? For another I am greatly afraid that the cold of an English winter would kill him, and if it did I should feel that it had been my fault. What do you think about it?"

"I agree with you, dear, absolutely; especially as regards the last part. I am sure it would be fatal to Peter to change this climate for another. And besides what could we do with him in London? He would be mobbed every time he put his nose outside the house and miserable in consequence."

"Yes, I am afraid it will be impossible to take him with us, much as I should like to; but there are three months left for us to think it over. At the moment it is getting late and unless you want to get into serious trouble with your cook we had better be making a move, Come along, dear."

Arm in arm they walked back along the winding forest path, chatting of this and that as they went. At the edge of the trees they stopped to look at the little stretch of open country and the calm sea which lay beyond.

"What is all that smoke?" Mary asked, pointing in the direction in which the Mission house lay.

"Having a bonfire in the garden, I expect; burning weeds or something like that," her husband replied. "Wait a minute though. My God! I believe it's the house. It is! It's on fire"; and without another word he began racing down the path, leaving his wife to follow as best she could.

Mary Passinger was a country girl who had swum and ridden and run with the beagles all her life. She was quick to think and quick to act and in less than a second she was after him. "Jackie, Jackie, Jackie," she panted half audibly as she ran. She thought of nothing else, not even of her father. Jackie was the only thing in the world that mattered to her then.

She reached the gate and ran across the garden close on the heels of her husband and they got to the house almost at the same moment. It was a raging mass of flames and a great crowd of natives stood round, staring helplessly. In front of them she saw her father and Hester Macfarlane and she thanked God that he, at least, was safe as she forced her way through to his side.

The nurse was behaving like a lunatic, tearing her hair and fighting to get into the house, but her struggles were of no avail against the two men who held her. She had been downstairs to warm some milk for the boy, who was in his cot, and somehow the little oil-stove had been overturned. The flames had run along the floor and by the time she had snatched up a bucket of water the stairs were impassable. Once, twice, three times she tried to force her way through the tongues of flame but in vain, and at last she had been dragged screaming away. Nobody, men said, could enter there and live.

John and Mary did not learn these details until later. At the moment all they knew was that the Mission house was a burning, fiery furnace and that their boy, their little Jackie, was trapped in one of the upper rooms.

"Save him, save him," the distracted mother kept shrieking again and again. "For God's sake save my boy."

With a curse John tore off his coat, snatched a kiss from his half-crazed wife, and made a dash for the door; but Sam, who was standing near, put out his foot and tripped him neatly ere ever he could reach it. Before he could rise two men fell on him, but it took all their strength to hold him. He was mad with rage and misery. At last Humberlayne succeeded in soothing him a little.

"Think of Mary, my dear boy," he begged, while the tears streamed down his face. "If it is God's will that our Jackie should die it will be very terrible for her, but if her husband is taken from her too it will be far, far worse. It would kill her. Who will there be to comfort her if you are gone? And I sadly fear that it is a hopeless quest that you are so anxious to go on, my son, a hopeless quest."

All this has taken far longer in the telling than in actual fact. The house was an old one and built entirely of wood and it had taken but a few moments for the flames to seek out almost every corner of it. It was doomed—that was plain from the start-and everything in it must surely be doomed as well. The crowd stood round, gazing at the blaze, awe-stricken, helpless. None could face that raging furnace. It would have been suicide if anybody had attempted to do so.

On the very outskirts of the curious natives stood Peter. The one thing to which he had never been able to accustom himself, in spite of the human blood in his veins, since he had been brought to Dualla three years before was fire. It terrified him. There is no beast of the forest that does not share that common dread and Peter for the first five-and-twenty years or so of his life had, after all, been little if any better than a beast of the forest. For some little time after the house had caught fire he had kept at a distance, but by degrees curiosity and, more particularly, his love for Mary Passinger's little boy had induced him to come nearer and nearer until at last he was on the outskirts of the crowd.

It was not until then that he saw, by the light of the flames, the grief-stricken face of the mother, and a wave of thought engulfed him. He thought of the gentle touch of her hand on his shoulder, he thought of how she had hung her own crucifix round his neck; he thought of the kindly, welcoming smile with which she never failed to greet him; and his mind was made up. Somehow he must save Jackie, he told himself. Somehow he must make his way into that upper chamber and snatch the child from the jaws of death. Only for a moment he hesitated; then he made a dash for it, fearful lest his nerve might fail him at the critical moment.

Right and left he scattered the astonished on-lookers, knocking them over like ninepins in his haste to get through them. Close past Mary Passinger he ran, so close that he laid his hand for a second on her bowed shoulders as he passed, then with a mighty spring he caught the lower limb of a tree, pulled himself up on it and disappeared amongst the foliage.

But not for long. In a few moments he could be seen clambering along a stout branch that reached out towards the house. As he neared the end of it it began to bend perilously until at last he got to a spot beyond which he simply dared not go; and still he was a long way from the upper windows. The crowd watched him spellbound; even Mary was forced to raise her tear-filled eyes and follow his every movement. Could he get there?

For a long moment he stood upright on the straining branch, then bent his knees and the next second sprang for the sill, while a gasp went up from the onlookers. Full twenty feet he sprang, bringing down a shower of twigs and leaves as he crashed through them, and they saw the fingers of one hand catch the sill. For a long moment, that seemed an eternity to Mary, he hung and she thought he had failed; but with superhuman strength he pulled himself up until he could get a grip with the other hand, and a moment later he had disappeared into the room, heedless of the flames which belched from the window.

There was another eternity of waiting before he appeared again, this time with a bundle in his arms. John Passinger ran below the window and Peter, leaning perilously far out, dropped his bundle. Little Jackie Passinger fell unhurt into his father's arms, still half asleep. Blue eyes opened for a fleeting moment as he was passed to his mother, weeping for joy now, but he only murmured "Mummy" and then "Peter" before they were closed in sleep again, the fearless, innocent sleep of childhood.

And Peter? While he still leaned out of the window to see that the child was safe there was a crash and he disappeared. For a second his fingers were seen making a futile grab at the sill, then a dull, rumbling thud and a shower of sparks which shot high up into the heavens told that the floor had fallen, carrying Peter with it, and a moan of horror went up from the watching crowd.

But Peter was not dead yet. A moment later, through the greedy flames which shot from the verandah window, there crawled painfully a scarcely recognisable figure. All its hair was singed away and on its now bare neck there gleamed dully a little golden crucifix. Willing hands lifted Peter and carried him to a distance from the house, where they laid him down, and soon Mary came hurrying up with her husband and child and her father.

"Jackie?" whispered the smoke-grimed, half roasted creature between scorched lips.

"He is here. You saved him, Peter. He is quite well."

"Don't wake him. He must not see me like this," Peter groaned.

Mary knelt down at his side, half raised him and leaned his back against her knee. Then she laid her hand on his shoulder as she had done twice before.

"God bless you," said Peter. And so he died.

Two days later he was buried and there was hardly a soul, man, woman or child, who did not attend the funeral. And when they had all gone away, except the Passingers and a few others who had been the chief mourners, the last, sad tribute of respect was paid. John stood alone at the foot of the grave, held Peter's own club high above his head in his left hand for a long moment, then let it fall to the ground, the salute that is given only to the heroic dead.

THE END

RAMBLE HOUSE's

HARRY STEPHEN KEELER WEBWORK MYSTERIES

(RH) indicates the title is available ONLY in the RAMBLE HOUSE edition

The Ace of Spades Murder
The Affair of the Bottled Deuce (RH)
The Amazing Web
The Barking Clock
Behind That Mask
The Book with the Orange Leaves
The Bottle with the Green Wax Seal
The Box from Japan
The Case of the Canny Killer
The Case of the Crazy Corpse (RH)
The Case of the Flying Hands (RH)
The Case of the Ivory Arrow
The Case of the Jeweled Ragpicker
The Case of the Lavender Gripsack
The Case of the Mysterious Moll
The Case of the 16 Beans
The Case of the Transparent Nude (RH)
The Case of the Transposed Legs
The Case of the Two-Headed Idiot (RH)
The Case of the Two Strange Ladies
The Circus Stealers (RH)
Cleopatra's Tears
A Copy of Beowulf (RH)
The Crimson Cube (RH)
The Face of the Man From Saturn
Find the Clock
The Five Silver Buddhas
The 4th King
The Gallows Waits, My Lord! (RH)
The Green Jade Hand
Finger! Finger!
Hangman's Nights (RH)
I, Chameleon (RH)
I Killed Lincoln at 10:13! (RH)
The Iron Ring
The Man Who Changed His Skin (RH)
The Man with the Crimson Box
The Man with the Magic Eardrums
The Man with the Wooden Spectacles
The Marceau Case
The Matilda Hunter Murder
The Monocled Monster

The Murder of London Lew
The Murdered Mathematician
The Mysterious Card (RH)
The Mysterious Ivory Ball of Wong Shing Li (RH)
The Mystery of the Fiddling Cracksman
The Peacock Fan
The Photo of Lady X (RH)
The Portrait of Jirjohn Cobb
Report on Vanessa Hewstone (RH)
Riddle of the Travelling Skull
Riddle of the Wooden Parrakeet (RH)
The Scarlet Mummy (RH)
The Search for X-Y-Z
The Sharkskin Book
Sing Sing Nights
The Six From Nowhere (RH)
The Skull of the Waltzing Clown
The Spectacles of Mr. Cagliostro
Stand By—London Calling!
The Steeltown Strangler
The Stolen Gravestone (RH)
Strange Journey (RH)
The Strange Will
The Straw Hat Murders (RH)
The Street of 1000 Eyes (RH)
Thieves' Nights
Three Novellos (RH)
The Tiger Snake
The Trap (RH)
Vagabond Nights (Defrauded Yeggman)
Vagabond Nights 2 (10 Hours)
The Vanishing Gold Truck
The Voice of the Seven Sparrows
The Washington Square Enigma
When Thief Meets Thief
The White Circle (RH)
The Wonderful Scheme of Mr. Christopher Thorne
X. Jones—of Scotland Yard
Y. Cheung, Business Detective

Keeler Related Works

A To Izzard: A Harry Stephen Keeler Companion by Fender Tucker — Articles and stories about Harry, by Harry, and in his style. Included is a compleat bibliography.

Wild About Harry: Reviews of Keeler Novels — Edited by Richard Polt & Fender Tucker — 22 reviews of works by Harry Stephen Keeler from *Keeler News*. A perfect introduction to the author.

The Keeler Keyhole Collection: Annotated newsletter rants from Harry Stephen Keeler, edited by Francis M. Nevins. Over 400 pages of incredibly personal Keeleriana.

Fakealoo — Pastiches of the style of Harry Stephen Keeler by selected demented members of the HSK Society. Updated every year with the new winner.

RAMBLE HOUSE's OTHER LOONS

The End of It All and Other Stories — Ed Gorman's latest short story collection

Four Dancing Tuatara Press Books — *Beast or Man?* By Sean M'Guire; *The Whistling Ancestors* by Richard E. Goddard; *The Shadow on the House* and *Sorceror's Chessmen* by Mark Hansom. With introductions by John Pelan.

The Dumpling — Political murder from 1907 by Coulson Kernahan

Victims & Villains — Intriguing Sherlockiana from Derham Groves

Evidence in Blue — 1938 mystery by E. Charles Vivian

The Case of the Little Green Men — Mack Reynolds wrote this love song to sci-fi fans back in 1951 and it's now back in print.

Hell Fire — A new hard-boiled novel by Jack Moskovitz about an arsonist, an arson cop and a Nazi hooker. It isn't pretty.

Researching American-Made Toy Soldiers — A 276-page collection of a lifetime of articles by toy soldier expert Richard O'Brien

Strands of the Web: Short Stories of Harry Stephen Keeler — Edited and Introduced by Fred Cleaver

The Sam McCain Novels — Ed Gorman's terrific series includes *The Day the Music Died*, *Wake Up Little Susie* and *Will You Still Love Me Tomorrow?*

A Shot Rang Out — Three decades of reviews from Jon Breen

Mysterious Martin, the Master of Murder — Two versions of a strange 1912 novel by Tod Robbins about a man who writes books that can kill.

Dago Red — 22 tales of dark suspense by Bill Pronzini

The Night Remembers — A 1991 Jack Walsh mystery from Ed Gorman

Rough Cut & New, Improved Murder — Ed Gorman's first two novels

Hollywood Dreams — A novel of the Depression by Richard O'Brien

Seven Gelett Burgess Novels — *The Master of Mysteries, The White Cat, Two O'Clock Courage, Ladies in Boxes, Find the Woman, The Heart Line, The Picaroons*

The Organ Reader — A huge compilation of just about everything published in the 1971-1972 radical bay-area newspaper, *THE ORGAN*.

A Clear Path to Cross — Sharon Knowles short mystery stories by Ed Lynskey

Old Times' Sake — Short stories by James Reasoner from Mike Shayne Magazine

Freaks and Fantasies — Eerie tales by Tod Robbins, collaborator of Tod Browning on the film FREAKS.

Six Jim Harmon Double Novels — *Vixen Hollow/Celluloid Scandal, The Man Who Made Maniacs/Silent Siren, Ape Rape/Wanton Witch, Sex Burns Like Fire/Twist Session, Sudden Lust/Passion Strip, Sin Unlimited/Harlot Master, Twilight Girls/Sex Institution*. Written in the early 60s.

Marblehead: A Novel of H.P. Lovecraft — A long-lost masterpiece from Richard A. Lupoff. Published for the first time!

The Compleat Ova Hamlet — Parodies of SF authors by Richard A. Lupoff – A brand new edition with more stories and more illustrations by Trina Robbins.

The Secret Adventures of Sherlock Holmes — Three Sherlockian pastiches by the Brooklyn author/publisher, Gary Lovisi.

The Universal Holmes — Richard A. Lupoff's 2007 collection of five Holmesian pastiches and a recipe for giant rat stew.

Four Joel Townsley Rogers Novels — By the author of *The Red Right Hand: Once In a Red Moon, Lady With the Dice, The Stopped Clock, Never Leave My Bed*

Two Joel Townsley Rogers Story Collections — Night of Horror and Killing Time

Twenty Norman Berrow Novels — *The Bishop's Sword, Ghost House, Don't Go Out After Dark, Claws of the Cougar, The Smokers of Hashish, The Secret Dancer, Don't Jump Mr. Boland!, The Footprints of Satan, Fingers for Ransom, The Three Tiers of Fantasy, The Spaniard's Thumb, The Eleventh Plague, Words Have Wings, One Thrilling Night, The Lady's in Danger, It Howls at Night, The Terror in the Fog, Oil Under the Window, Murder in the Melody, The Singing Room*

The N. R. De Mexico Novels — Robert Bragg presents *Marijuana Girl, Madman on a Drum, Private Chauffeur* in one volume.

Four Chelsea Quinn Yarbro Novels featuring Charlie Moon — *Ogilvie, Tallant and Moon, Music When the Sweet Voice Dies, Poisonous Fruit* and *Dead Mice*

Five Walter S. Masterman Mysteries — *The Green Toad, The Flying Beast, The Yellow Mistletoe, The Wrong Verdict* and *The Perjured Alibi*. Fantastic impossible plots.

Two Hake Talbot Novels — *Rim of the Pit, The Hangman's Handyman*. Classic locked room mysteries.

Two Alexander Laing Novels — *The Motives of Nicholas Holtz* and *Dr. Scarlett*, stories of medical mayhem and intrigue from the 30s.

The Werewolf vs the Vampire Woman — Hard to believe ultraviolence by either Arthur M. Scarm or Arthur M. Scram.

Black Hogan Strikes Again — Australia's Peter Renwick pens a tale of the outback.

Don Diablo: Book of a Lost Film — Two-volume treatment of a western by Paul Landres, with diagrams. Intro by Francis M. Nevins.

The Charlie Chaplin Murder Mystery — Movie hijinks by Wes D. Gehring

The Koky Comics — A collection of all of the 1978-1981 Sunday and daily comic strips by Richard O'Brien and Mort Gerberg, in two volumes.

Suzy — Another collection of comic strips from Richard O'Brien and Bob Vojtko

Dime Novels: Ramble House's 10-Cent Books — *Knife in the Dark* by Robert Leslie Bellem, *Hot Lead* and *Song of Death* by Ed Earl Repp, *A Hashish House in New York* by H.H. Kane, and five more.

Blood in a Snap — The *Finnegan's Wake* of the 21st century, by Jim Weiler.

Stakeout on Millennium Drive — Award-winning Indianapolis Noir — Ian Woollen.

Dope Tales #1 — Two dope-riddled classics; *Dope Runners* by Gerald Grantham and *Death Takes the Joystick* by Phillip Condé.

Dope Tales #2 — Two more narco-classics; *The Invisible Hand* by Rex Dark and *The Smokers of Hashish* by Norman Berrow.

Dope Tales #3 — Two enchanting novels of opium by the master, Sax Rohmer. *Dope* and *The Yellow Claw*.

Tenebrae — Ernest G. Henham's 1898 horror tale brought back.

The Singular Problem of the Stygian House-Boat — Two classic tales by John Kendrick Bangs about the denizens of Hades.

Tiresias — Psychotic modern horror novel by Jonathan M. Sweet.

The One After Snelling — Kickass modern noir from Richard O'Brien.

The Sign of the Scorpion — 1935 Edmund Snell tale of oriental evil.

The House of the Vampire — 1907 poetic thriller by George S. Viereck.

An Angel in the Street — Modern hardboiled noir by Peter Genovese.

The Devil's Mistress — Scottish gothic tale by J. W. Brodie-Innes.

The Lord of Terror — 1925 mystery with master-criminal, Fantômas.

The Lady of the Terraces — 1925 adventure by E. Charles Vivian.

My Deadly Angel — 1955 Cold War drama by John Chelton.

Prose Bowl — Futuristic satire — Bill Pronzini & Barry N. Malzberg .

Satan's Den Exposed — True crime in Truth or Consequences New Mexico — Award-winning journalism by the *Desert Journal*.

The Amorous Intrigues & Adventures of Aaron Burr — by Anonymous — Hot historical action.

I Stole $16,000,000 — A true story by cracksman Herbert E. Wilson.

The Black Dark Murders — Vintage 50s college murder yarn by Milt Ozaki, writing as Robert O. Saber.

Sex Slave — Potboiler of lust in the days of Cleopatra — Dion Leclerq.

You'll Die Laughing — Bruce Elliott's 1945 novel of murder at a practical joker's English countryside manor.

The Private Journal & Diary of John H. Surratt — The memoirs of the man who conspired to assassinate President Lincoln.

Dead Man Talks Too Much — Hollywood boozer by Weed Dickenson.

Red Light — History of legal prostitution in Shreveport Louisiana by Eric Brock. Includes wonderful photos of the houses and the ladies.

A Snark Selection — Lewis Carroll's *The Hunting of the Snark* with two Snarkian chapters by Harry Stephen Keeler — Illustrated by Gavin L. O'Keefe.

Ripped from the Headlines! — The Jack the Ripper story as told in the newspaper articles in the *New York* and *London Times.*

Geronimo — S. M. Barrett's 1905 autobiography of a noble American.

The White Peril in the Far East — Sidney Lewis Gulick's 1905 indictment of the West and assurance that Japan would never attack the U.S.

The Compleat Calhoon — All of Fender Tucker's works: Includes *Totah Six-Pack, Weed, Women and Song* and *Tales from the Tower,* plus a CD of all of his songs.

Totah Six-Pack — Just Fender Tucker's six tales about Farmington in one sleek volume.

RAMBLE HOUSE
Fender Tucker, Prop.
www.ramblehouse.com   fender@ramblehouse.com
228-826-1783   10329 Sheephead Drive, Vancleave MS 39565

www.ingramcontent.com/pod-product-compliance
Lightning Source LLC
Chambersburg PA
CBHW030324020726
47493CB00004B/1155